# THE BONES IN THE ATTIC

Moving into an upmarket new home in Leeds, rising radio star Matt Harper is shocked to find the skeleton of a small child in his attic. The grisly discovery takes him back to the summer of 1969, when he lived with his aunt only a few streets away, reawakening dim and disturbing images from his childhood.

While Detective Charlie Peace heads up the nominal police investigation into the bones, Matt's unease leads him to revisit the past in an attempt to solve the mystery himself. Tracking down the other members of a gang of local children he'd briefly been part of then, he gradually unearths a shared secret that has laid buried ever since. Everyone remembers little Lily Marsden's meetings with her older 'friend', and the hippy couple's baby she wanted to rescue, but Matt can't help feeling there's something else they're holding back. Were the bones in the attic the result of a tragic accident, or has time concealed a more sinister truth?

# THE BONES IN THE ATTIC

**Robert Barnard**

HarperCollins*Publishers*

This novel is entirely a work of fiction. The names, characters and incidents portrayed in it are the work of the author's imagination. Any resemblance to actual persons, living or dead, events or localities is entirely coincidental.

Collins Crime
An imprint of HarperCollins*Publishers*
77–85 Fulham Palace Road, London W6 8JB

The Collins Crime website address is:
www.**fire**and**water**.com/crime

First published in Great Britain
in 2001 by Collins Crime

1  3  5  7  9  10  8  6  4  2

A catalogue record for this book
is available from the British Library

ISBN 0 00 712135 0

Set in Meridien and Bodoni
Typeset by Rowland Phototypesetting Ltd
Bury St Edmunds, Suffolk

Printed and bound in Great Britain by
Clays Ltd, St Ives plc

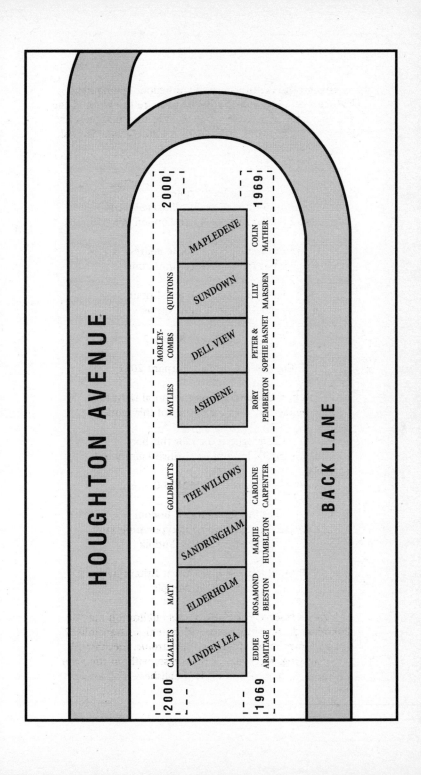

HOUGHTON AVENUE

BACK LANE

**2000**

**1969**

CAZALETS — MATT

GOLDBLATTS

MAYLIES

MORLEY-COMBS

QUINTONS

COLIN MATHER

**1969**

**2000**

LINDEN LEA

ELDERHOLM

SANDRINGHAM

THE WILLOWS

ASHDENE

DELL VIEW

SUNDOWN

MAPLEDENE

EDDIE ARMITAGE

ROSAMOND BEESTON

MARJIE HUMBLETON

CAROLINE CARPENTER

RORY PEMBERTON

PETER & SOPHIE BASNET

LILY MARSDEN

# CHAPTER 1

# Remember You Must Die

'It's a good size for a dining room,' said the builder and decorator, who had said to call him Tony. 'But then, I don't suppose you have family meals any more. No one does.'

'Sunday,' said Matt. 'And any time there's something on offer the children particularly like.'

'How many you got?'

'Three. They're my partner's.'

The man nodded. He was used to all kinds of permutations and variations. In fact, he often reckoned the decline of the stable family had been wonderful for his business.

Matt stood in the centre of the big room, unconscious for the moment of Tony, or of anything else except the house. It struck him that he and the house were at a crucial moment in their existence: the house had nothing of him, or of Aileen, but it did *have* him there, considering, determining its future. And his own.

He loved it. Standing outside in the lane waiting for Tony he had felt his heart contract at the mere sight of the stone. Stone. Solid, thick, permanent stone. Outside

1

he had heard a radio, loud, from next door through an open window. Inside he heard nothing. And here it was, waiting, with its wooden fireplace, its bell-push to summon the long-gone servant, its tentative moves in the direction of Art Deco. Eighty years old, or more. Waiting for what he, Aileen and the children were going to make of it. A strange thought struck him. He wondered if a stone house like this might have kept his marriage together.

Thank God it hadn't.

'What colour were you thinking of?' Tony asked.

'I thought blue – not too strong. The windows aren't that large, and it's a long room, so we need something pleasant and airy.'

'Blue. You're thinking of paint, then?'

'I'll have wallpaper if I find something that I *know* is right – something that grabs me round the throat. Otherwise I'll have paint till I find something. Anyway I like paint: clean colours and clean surfaces.'

Tony nodded, and as they went into the hallway he said:

'I wish I could say I'd seen you play.'

Matt shrugged.

'Why would you? You'd be a Leeds United man. There was no great reason seven or eight years ago to make the effort to see Bradford City play.'

'Seven or eight years ago there was no great reason to go and see Leeds United play. Dullest football in the North was what they served up then.' He thought, and then added: 'Mind you, the new manager's making a world of difference.'

'He's good with the media too,' agreed Matt. 'Does one of the best interviews of anyone in the Premier League.'

2

Tony shot him a quick look, then slapped his thigh.

'Got you! You're on Radio Leeds. Matthew Harper. I was thrown by the "Matt".'

Matt smiled and nodded, used to the delayed reaction.

'That's right. I thought I'd take my full name, especially once they started using me for ordinary newsreading and chat shows.'

'I don't hear it that often, I must admit. I go more for music, me. And I never connected the name with the footballer. But I have seen you now and then on *Look North*.'

Matt noted that the man, who had shown since he had arrived the sort of casual deference usual to a customer, was now positively respectful. Matt knew from experience that anyone involved with the media, on however low a level, received the degree of deference formerly given to members of the professions. He had got beyond the phase of feeling flattered by unearned respect, so he said briskly:

'Let's go upstairs, shall we? . . . I won't be getting the bedrooms done till we're well settled in. I may even try to do some of it myself, maybe get the children to help.' They had gone round the bend in the staircase, and were standing on the landing. Tony poked his head into the bedrooms, bathroom and lavatory.

'Best leave the bathroom to professionals,' he said. 'Too fiddly by half. The bedrooms won't present too many problems. Stick to paint there, if you want my advice: then if the children keep wanting theirs changed it won't come too expensive.'

'Yes, I'd already thought of that. Knowing my lot and their clothes and toys and reading matter and habits they'll want them changed at least once a year.'

3

'By 'eck, they have it made, the young 'uns these days,' said Tony with feeling.

'Yes, I'd love to know who starts each new vogue. What infant genius suddenly decrees it's yellow this year, and Aussie soaps are out, and shoe soles are three inches high, and the whole childish world bows agreement and starts pestering parents.'

'Probably some future Richard Branson,' agreed Tony. 'Anyway you've got four very nice-sized rooms here. That's the advantage of these older houses: you're not squashed in like sardines. When was it built, did you say?'

'About 1920 the estate agent said, or maybe a bit earlier. Did you see the bells downstairs to summon the servants? I suppose the First World War or its aftermath did away with all that.'

'Happen. Anyway, the kids who go into these new estates won't get bedrooms like these – cubbyholes more like. And certainly not one each.'

Matt grimaced.

'Hmm. I was hoping to keep one of the bedrooms for my study. You might not think it to listen to me, but a lot of the things I do on Radio Leeds need preparation. It would be good to have somewhere I can shut myself away in.'

'So, two of the kids sharing a bedroom, and one having a bedroom to him or herself. Sounds like a recipe for non-stop guerrilla warfare to me. And I speak from experience.'

'I was hoping to bribe them by promising them the attic as a games room.'

Tony still looked sceptical.

'Have you looked at it?'

'Just poked my head through the trapdoor.'

'Attics are fine for games rooms if you are thinking of things like Monopoly or Trivial Pursuit – things you can play on the floor. They're pretty useless for snooker tables, or anything you have to stand up for, even supposing you could get a table up there. Want me to have a look?'

'Would you?' Matt took the pole with the hook on the end, clicked open the trapdoor, then pulled down the metal stairs and tugged at the light cord. He led the way up.

'There's proper flooring down, but it's pretty old, and I don't know that I'd trust it.'

He stood on the edge of the trapdoor, but Tony, coming up behind him, strode out on to it.

'Sound as a bell. They used good materials in them days. Hasn't been used much, by the look of it. You can see the problem with a games room, can't you? Put a snooker table in the middle and the kid might be all right potting the balls, but he'd hardly be able to straighten up.'

Matt saw his point.

'It was just an idea. I've never heard our lot express a wish for a snooker table. I might be able to persuade one of them it would be exciting to have one of the bedrooms up here.'

'You might. How old's the eldest?'

'Isabella's fourteen.'

'You might have more luck with a boy. Still, teenagers like to get away from the others. The young ones may think it would be exciting, but when it comes to it they get nervous. You might be able to block a small part of this attic off. In fact, it's practically been done for you.'

Tony pointed back towards the trapdoor. Just beyond

it was a low piece of brick walling, and when Matt's eyes penetrated the gloom, he could see another one beyond it. He hadn't noticed that section when he'd made a quick exploratory viewing before.

'Roof supports,' explained the builder, putting his hand on the rough piece of brick walling. 'They've just continued up with the walls from either side of the landing below.' He looked down across the roughly-constructed brick wall and towards the far wall. 'Hmm. They haven't bothered with flooring here. Plenty enough space in this half, I suppose.' He climbed carefully over, and walked along one of the beams, Matthew following on behind him. 'You could make a real cosy little bedroom in this far bit, if you put a window in the roof.' He and Matt came to a rest by the second brick wall. Matt looked to either side, where the wall was supporting the base of the roof. It and the other one they'd climbed over rose about eighteen inches for the whole breadth of the house.

'You could pull a few bricks out to make a door,' said Tony. 'Wouldn't affect it as a roof support, or cause any other structural problems . . . Hello! What's that?'

There was something against the far side of the wall, on the rough and dusty felting that had been laid over the ceiling below. It was dusty too, but a lighter colour gleamed through, and as their eyes became accustomed to the gloom they thought that whatever it was was assuming a definite shape – a shape they were reluctant to acknowledge.

'It looks like . . . like a skeleton . . . A little skeleton,' said Matt at last. 'It can't be.'

'Got a torch?'

'Sure. Downstairs. The electricity wasn't turned on until yesterday.'

He made his way back along the beams, down the metal ladder, then fetched his powerful torch from the kitchen. By the time he got back to the attic he thought he had got his ideas in order.

'You know, it's got to be some kind of animal,' he said. 'Maybe a squirrel – got in here and couldn't get out.'

He turned the torch on to the little pile.

'Big squirrel,' said Tony, disbelievingly. 'The bones look human to me. Could be a child, quite a young one. But too large for any animal I could imagine finding its own way in here.'

His matter-of-fact tone brought it home to Matt. He gripped one of the beams in the ceiling, and turned away from the sight. The pathos of the little tableau had seized his mind. A dead child, brought up here and laid out where no one would find it. Or, worse . . . But here his mind refused to contemplate the more horrible possibility. He walked away, back to the floored area, back to the safety of proper lighting.

'You're right,' he said to Tony, who had followed him. 'It looks like a human skeleton. Playing football you get to know about the human body. So much of you gets bruised or broken that you spend half your time with the doc or the physio, looking at X-rays of one part or other of yourself. It looks like a little body, laid out there and left.'

'Not newly-born, though,' said Tony. 'Not a secret unwanted baby.'

'No, not a baby.'

'What are you going to do?'

Matthew thought. He came up against all sorts of odd eventualities vicariously, through reading the news and interviewing people for Radio Leeds.

7

'Doesn't seem to me I have any choice,' he said. 'If those are human bones the police have to be informed.'

'Use my mobile if you like.'

Matt took it, but then on impulse turned and climbed back down again and then down the stairs to the kitchen. He wanted to put as much space as possible between himself and that horrible memento mori in the darkness above. He dialled 999.

'Hello. I think I need the Leeds police ... Well, I suppose I want to report a suspicious death.'

Twenty minutes later Matt was standing at his back gate, indulging in a rare cigarette. Tony had gone off, saying the police could get in touch with him if that was necessary, and there wasn't much point in going further with the redecoration plans until the police had given the go-ahead. He talked as if he found skeletons in empty houses every other week.

Matt looked at the house, at Elderholm. He had loved these houses as soon as he saw them, and had begun to feel he belonged there even before he moved in. Now he just had to hope this was not going to cause a revulsion. His eyes travelled around his new home. There were two stone terraces in Houghton Avenue, four houses each – solid, roomy houses, sitting square on earth and telling the world they were built to last, as a house should be. He had not met any of the neighbours yet, but he felt that he – that they; him and Aileen and the children – would fit in. Surely the houses weren't going to disappoint him? A figure loomed, standing back from the window, upstairs in the house next door. He was being watched.

On cue something was provided to make watching worthwhile. A police car nosed its way round the lane leading from Houghton Avenue, and on a sign from him drove forward and drew up beside him. A tall black man got out and put out his hand.

'I'm Detective Sergeant Peace.'

'Matthew Harper.'

'The footballer. I thought it might be you when they gave me the details. I've heard you often on Radio Leeds. It's nice to hear about things going on locally that aren't criminal. And is this the house where you made the discovery?'

'That's right. You'd better come in.'

They went through the kitchen into the hall. Charlie looked around him appreciatively.

'Nice and spacious, even if it does need a lot doing to it. You've got children?'

'Not of my own. My partner's. Maybe we'll have another. I love children. That's why –'

Sergeant Peace cut in.

'Yes. It must have been distressing. My wife's just had our first. But let's not jump the gun, shall we? Lead the way.'

Matt started upstairs again, then up the retractable staircase to the attic. Advising care he led the way across the beams, and then took up the torch he had left on the low brick wall. The two men, standing together, looked down at the collection of bones, somehow forlorn in the beam of light. Sergeant Peace suddenly turned away.

'Ugh. Brings it home to you. You think that's a child, don't you?'

'It's all I can think it could be.'

'I'm pretty sure you're right. When you've got a baby to look after you often think how fragile it is, how defenceless, but this . . .'

'Looks as if it's been here a long time,' said Matt, eyeing the layers of encrusted dust.

'Yes. But that may be deceptive.' Sergeant Peace paused, thinking, 'I tell you, I'm used to bodies, but this is way outside my experience. We're going to have to wait for a full forensic report and not jump to any conclusions . . . I feel like getting out of here, don't you?'

'Yes!'

When they were down again in the large old kitchen, complete with Aga stove and a greasy area on the wall behind the hot plates, Sergeant Peace got on to headquarters, reported the finding of what was apparently a child's skeleton, apparently too a long-dead one, and requested a forensic team. When he had told them as much as he knew, he said he'd wait for back-up and signed off. Then he turned back to Matt.

'Now, Mr Harper –'

'Matt.'

'Matt. I'm Charlie. And we're both from London, I can hear, though we've both covered it up.'

'Yes. Bermondsey.'

'I'm Brixton. Come up when you signed for Bradford, did you?'

'No. We moved to Colchester when I was a boy. But I've never wanted to go back.'

'Me neither, though I'm not sure why. I thought London was the bee's knees when I was living there. Sheer ignorance I suppose. Now, are you the owner of this house?'

'That's right. As of last Friday.'

'Who was the seller?'

'Man called Carl Farson. Son of the actual owner, Cuthbert Farson, who's a man of nearly ninety.'

'So the son's got power of attorney has he?'

'That's right.'

'Any idea how long the father lived here, if he did?'

'No idea, but he did live here. I met the son briefly at the estate agent's. He's a man of around sixty himself, and he said he didn't grow up in the house, though he visited his dad here often.'

'I see. Who were the estate agents handling the sale?'

'Sewell and Greeley, in Pudsey.'

'Right. So you were just looking around, were you?'

'Yes, with a decorator, name of Tony Tyler. We were planning what needed doing, and wondering whether the attic could be used as a bedroom or a games room. I'm beginning to think we'd better put any plans like that on hold for a bit.'

'Yes. The kids are bound to find out.'

'And children have very long memories,' said Matthew thoughtfully. 'About some things anyway.'

'They do. Looked to me, at a glance, as if the attic hadn't been much used.'

'That was our impression. Maybe one end, near the trapdoor, had had a few tea chests there, or ordinary luggage, or just this and that. It was less dusty there. But anybody clearing them out wouldn't necessarily go to the far end where there's no flooring, in fact there'd be no reason for them to do that at all. We only went because we were wondering about this bedroom.'

'I'm sure you're right. Now – oh, that looks like the team.' Outside two police cars were drawing up in the lane. 'There's not much you can do here for the moment, Matt. Could I have a home and a work tele-phone number for you?'

'Sure. Home is 2574 945 and at Radio Leeds it's 2445 738.'

'Right. I'll be in contact as soon as I know anything.

11

If I get your partner, she'll know about it, will she?'

'Aileen's away at the moment. I plan to tell the children tonight if circumstances are right.'

'Fine.' Charlie opened the door to the forensic team and directed them up to the attic. He was silent until he was sure they were well out of earshot, then he turned to Matt.

'In confidence, Matt: if we're right that this was a child, but the bones have been up there a long while, this is not likely to be a high-priority investigation.' A grimace passed over Matt's face at the thought of the child's brief life being considered of so little account, its death – its murder, or whatever it turned out to be – passed over so casually. 'I know, I know,' said Peace. 'It's sad, and I know what I'd feel if I'd made the discovery. It's a question of priorities, of the likelihood of getting results, of police resources and budgets. You're into news gathering. You'll know all about the pressures on us. I'd be willing to bet the best we can hope for is putting a name to him or her. OK, I *hope* we can do better than that, but I'd be wrong to make any promises.'

'Right,' said Matt with a sigh. 'I'll be off.'

'Good to have met you,' said Charlie, shaking hands. 'I'll be in touch as soon as I have any concrete information. And of course I'll tell you the moment the forensic people have finished and the house is your own again.'

Matt thanked him, but a flash through his brain asked the question whether the house would ever be his own. He put the thought from him. Of course it would. It would have to be. He slipped out the back door, dodging a further car-load of policemen and women clad in white overalls, and went out the little back gate and towards his car.

'Excuse me.'

Matt turned round and looked down. A small man had come out from the house next door to his, and was standing beside him looking up. He was about five feet four, thin and weedy in appearance, with sparse hair and frown-lines on his forehead. There was a sort of self-importance about him that was neither comic nor impressive.

'Yes?' The moment Matt had said the word it sounded ridiculously cold, and, concealing a degree of reluctance, he held out his hand and said: 'You must be one of my new neighbours. I'm the new owner of Elderholm. I'm Matt Harper.'

'Ah . . . Edward Cazalet. I believe I should have heard of you. The estate agent has mentioned it to someone. You're some kind of footballer.'

Matt, mischievously, decided to take him literally.

'Centre half as a rule. My footballing days are over now. I work for Radio Leeds and *Look North*.'

The man nodded. Those two things had swum within his ken.

'Ah . . . I – I hope there's nothing *wrong*?'

He cast a limp hand in the direction of the police activity, as if he was nourishing the hope they were rehearsing for *The Pirates of Penzance*. Matt felt a strong disinclination to give him a reason for their presence in Elderholm.

'I hope not. That is what the police team is here to find out.'

'My wife and I do *hate* any unpleasantness.'

'No more than I do myself.'

The little man shook his head, as if that were impossible, and to show he had dire forebodings.

'Such a bad way to begin.'

13

'Very true. It was a great shock, finding what I found.'

'Ah. This concerns something that you *found*, or say you found?'

'Something that I found. Not something I could conceivably have brought with me. I am not at liberty to say what it was, of course.'

'N-no, of course not.'

'But it is something that has been in the house for a long time.'

'Oh. Oh dear! Well – I don't know what to say.'

And he retreated back behind his little gate.

Getting into his car and driving away, Matt felt dissatisfaction with the encounter, and with himself. He had always thought of himself as good at reading signs, judging people by their outward appearance and behaviour. This man he could hardly even guess the age of. He looked the sort of person who, even in his cradle, had seemed worried by the human condition, or perhaps the state of the property market. And as a consequence, now, he could have been forty, sixty, or any stage in between. Querulous, pernickety, with an old-fashioned concern about keeping up appearances. He couldn't hide it from himself: he didn't like the man. And Cazalet in his turn had seemed determined from the start not to like him.

Then he shook himself. What did it matter? He was only one of seven sets of neighbours in the old stone houses. And he could well have a pleasanter side to him that did not show through on a first casual encounter.

Still, there was no disguising the fact that this rated very low on the thermometer of warm welcomes.

# CHAPTER 2

# Broadcasting It

Matt didn't tell the children that night. For some reason they were off on a tangent about getting another animal 'as company for Beckham', though since they never even considered the possibility of a second dog, Matt regarded that as a bit of a smokescreen for acquiring something new, interesting and different. As the various possibilities – cat, rabbit, hamster, parrot – were canvassed he kept out of the discussion, rather as he would in an exciting radio talk-in, only expressing himself forcibly when someone proposed a snake. 'It's your mother who'll have the final say,' he said, 'so nothing will be done until she's back. Imagine her coming home and finding a cobra curled up in front of the fire.' It was a topic, though, that he did not feel inclined to shatter by breaking the news of the skeleton. He postponed that without regret until they were in a more receptive mood.

He was scheduled to do the local news bulletins on television during the morning and afternoon of the next day. As he went through from the Woodhouse Lane entrance to his studio he paused to listen to his current *bête noire* talking on the phone in her office.

'Well get your fucking finger out,' she was rasping. 'I told you what I want, Tony. I want that fucking programme broadcast. It's bloody brilliant, and it's going to be shown. What the fucking hell are you, a man or a mouse?'

Liza Pomfret belonged to one of the BBC dynasties. Not one of the visible ones, like the Magnussens or the Michelmores, but traceably a Corporation dynasty. Her grandmother had been one of the high-ups in charge of early evening magazine programmes on television in the early sixties, and her father had been one of John Birt's faceless apparatchiks in the nineties. As part of her grooming process Liza had been shunted up North into local broadcasting after a spell on one of the various holiday programmes. One of the latter had been held up or cancelled because a young reporter investigating an adventure holiday had been decapitated while emerging incautiously from a helicopter. Since she had arrived in Leeds Liza had spent a great deal of her time on the phone pressurizing her old colleagues to get it shown, behaving as if it was a combination of *Hiroshima Mon Amour* and *Apocalypse Now* and its loss would be a cultural tragedy.

'Approach the family *again*,' she was yelling, her face an ugly puce shade. 'Put *more* pressure on them. Tell them it's what Simon would have wanted.'

Oh yeah? thought Matt cynically. And the next thing we know, by a slip in the editing process, Simon's beheading will be on TV for the nation to gawp at, earning itself a 'First on terrestrial television' tag and splashed all over the tabloids.

As he turned to continue his walk to the news studio Vic Talbot his producer padded up behind him.

'Keeping your eye on the opposition?' he asked softly.

'Opposition?'

'The centre forward of the other team.'

'I don't get you.'

'You're playing for the local-chap-makes-good team, and she's playing for the national-high-flyers team. With a bit of luck she'll either shove her foot in her mouth or be swiftly transferred to greater things in the great wen. Leaving you with your foot firmly on the ladder going up.'

Vic said it encouragingly, even admiringly. It was the first time Matt had realized he was regarded as a man with a bright future at BBC North.

Not long after the eleven o'clock news bulletin he was phoned by Sergeant Peace.

'I've got one piece of positive information,' he said, 'and the rest is very interim. The positive part –'

'Is that the bones are human,' said Matt, with a heavy heart. 'You wouldn't bother with anything further if they weren't.'

'True enough. Right, beyond that: presumably a child, around eighteen months or two years old, but they're still cagey on the sex. And been there *quite* a time, though they won't be naming any figure for a while yet.'

'I could have guessed they weren't put there yesterday,' said Matt ungratefully.

'We don't much like guesses in this business,' said Charlie. 'I've been doing a bit of rummaging myself. Elderholm was bought in 1977 by Mr Farson – the elder one, that is – from Hannah Beeston, who was moving to a bungalow in Armley Ridge Road. She died of cancer in 1985.'

'I see. So the date the bones came there is going to be very important.'

'It's likely to be. But it's worth noticing that both the owners were elderly. Mrs Beeston was born with the century – 1900. Farson was born in 1913. It sort of adds to the oddity, doesn't it?'

It certainly seemed to Matt, on thinking it over afterwards, that it did.

He was abstracted for the rest of the morning, and in the twelve o'clock bulletin stumbled on the pronunciation of 'Harewood'. When they went down to the staff canteen for coffee and a sandwich at twelve-fifteen, Vic Talbot said:

'Got something on your mind, Matt? Was that the police who rang you earlier?'

'Yes . . .' He thought for a moment, then said: 'Funny thing happened to me yesterday. Rather nasty too. I went to see the new house in Bramley with the decorator I've got lined up.'

'And?'

'We went up into the attic and found a little skeleton. The police phoned me today to say that it was definitely human.'

Vic was unusually slow taking it in.

'A child's, you mean?'

'Yes. Just laid out, covered with dust, in a place where no one would see it unless they were really inspecting the place. It was sort of touching as well as eerie.'

Vic Talbot thought.

'So someone, at some time, has had a dead child on his or her hands – maybe he's killed it – and he's just put the body up there and left it.'

'Something like that,' said Matt slowly. 'Unless . . . but I don't want to think of other possibilities.'

'But Matt – that's a *marvellous* story!' came a voice

18

from behind the table. 'And one of our people involved!'

Matt raised his head, looked first at Vic, then turned to confront Liza Pomfret with the sort of expression he might have put on for a circling vulture. 'Our people' indeed! Liza was as much one of 'us' as a fox in a chicken run.

'No go, Liza. Not for the moment.'

'Yes! This moment! Someone else might get on to it. They're pretty sure to if you're not making a secret of it. I've got a vacant slot in my programme this afternoon.'

'Play a Spice Girls record. Anything but me.'

'Matt, I know you're not a newsperson by training –'

Matthew breathed a 'Thank God' and said: 'There will be no media coverage of this by us or by anyone else until I've told the children. That is not negotiable.'

'When are you telling them?'

'Tonight, if the circumstances are right.'

'There you are, then,' said Liza, putting her inadequately-skirted leg on one of the chairs at their table and reassuming an air of good nature. 'Let's do the interview now: you can tell the story quite simply, and I'll put it in tomorrow's show if you give me the go-ahead. Don't you want to find out who this poor kid was? You're not going to do that without publicity I'd be willing to bet.'

She nearly ruined her case by using the word 'kid'. Matt distrusted educated people who did that – people like both the main political leaders in the country. They would never use it except to sound like men of the people. But her final remarks went home. They were surely not going to get anywhere without publicity.

'Look, Liza, I'm busy at the moment. When I've got a spare minute I'll get in touch with the police, see what

19

their reaction is. If Sergeant Peace gives it the OK I'll ring you – say about half past three.'

Liza Pomfret removed her leg from the chair, put her hands splayed downwards on the table, and fixed Matt with her world-hardened teenager eyes.

'Matt, I want it done *now*, while it's *hot*.'

'Sorry, Liza, I'm busy,' said Matt getting up. He fixed her with his equally determined eyes. 'No way are you going to talk to me about it before three o'clock.'

Liza's chat show on Radio Leeds ran from two to three. She got his point immediately, turned, and marched out of the canteen. Matt turned to his producer.

'Defeat of the infant commissar,' he said. He was rather liking the idea of a war of attrition between him and Liza.

When he rang Charlie Peace soon after three, Charlie took a few moments to think it over, then said:

'On the whole I think it's a good idea. This isn't any ordinary case. We're going to need all the assistance from the public we can get. If we take it that it was twenty, thirty years ago the body got there, then most or all of the people living in those houses then will be scattered around West Yorkshire now, or very likely out of the area entirely. People don't stay put the way they used to. This could be a way of getting in touch with them.'

Very reluctantly Matthew rang Liza Pomfret and told her he'd be along to record an interview at quarter to four. Then he turned to Vic Talbot.

'If she tries to get any part of the interview on to one of the TV or radio news programmes tonight, send her away with a flea in her ear. If you stand firm, I'll do an interview for the *Look North* programme tomorrow.

If you cave in, that's the end of the subject as far as I'm concerned.'

When he took himself along to the Liza Pomfret Talk-In studio at a quarter to four, she was very cool and businesslike, and said she'd just ask a wide-open question and let him tell the story in his own way. Wanna bet? Matt said to himself. He sat down while she fiddled and made Führer-like gestures to the technician on the other side of the glass panel.

'I've got Matt Harper here,' Liza began, in her bright, hard voice. 'Most of our listeners, and viewers too, will know him from our sports and news broadcasts. You played football for – where was it?'

'Bradford City. For seven years.'

'Right. Now Matt, you had an experience yesterday that was way outside your football experience, didn't you? More *Jane Eyre* than . . .' But here she stopped. The idea of the attic had triggered *Jane Eyre*, but the football field didn't trigger the name of any work of fiction. 'Well, just tell the listeners, will you, Matt?'

Matt shifted in his chair, still not entirely comfortable with what he was doing.

'Of course,' he began. 'Yesterday I went to look over a house I'd just bought in Bramley – going over it with the decorator to see what needed to be done before we moved in. Eventually we went up to the attic to see what potential it had to be used, maybe as a games room, and while we were up there, in a far, dark corner, we found, neatly laid out and hidden by a low wall, a small skeleton.'

'But Matt! How absolutely thrilling! I've never heard anything so *spooky*!'

'It *is* a dead child we're talking about, Liza.'

'Yes, but I mean! . . .'

21

She faded into silence. Matt felt a bit sanctimonious, reminding himself of a non-conformist cleric he had once interviewed on the subject of Sunday shopping. But the whole rebuke had hit home and the fact that her reaction was a delayed one was attributable either to her insensitivity or to stupidity, Matt was not greatly concerned which.

'The skeleton was not just a collection of bones, but a complete one and laid out – as if a dead child had been put there. It was very dusty, like everything else, and we certainly got the impression that it had been there a long time, not just put there in the last few weeks while the house had been empty.'

He had kept his voice even and unemotional, and Liza's reaction was now distinctly more subdued too.

'So what did you do?'

'I don't think there's much option in matters like this. You have to call the police. They've been to the house, sealed it off, and I've just had it confirmed that what we found is the skeleton of a child, maybe eighteen months or two year's old.'

'And how long do they think the skeleton has been there?'

'I think it will be a while before they are willing to give an opinion on that. It's a complicated matter.'

'Of course. I see. So what do you want to say to our listeners?'

Matt considered a moment before replying.

'The houses are stone houses, fronting on to Houghton Avenue, in Bramley, with a dirt lane leading round to the back doors. The house is called Elderholm. The police would be interested to hear about any disappearance of a child, boy or girl, twenty, thirty years ago – in fact, I'd say anything over ten years. Particularly any disappearance that for one reason or another didn't get reported to the police.'

'Could you suggest some reason for that?'

'Perhaps a surprise move away from the district, with nothing being heard of the child later? Maybe a family of travellers? But I agree it's not easy to account for the disappearance of a child this young that doesn't get reported to *someone*.'

'Well, Matt,' said Liza, having regained something of her chirpy radio tone, 'you really have frozen our blood today. If anyone out there thinks they may know something that's relevant, however small, they can call the police, or why not call us –'

But Matt had pulled out his earphones and left the studio.

On thinking it over he wondered if he had been wise, recording the appeal so early on. If he could have put a more definite date for the death of the child he could have pinpointed the people who were living in the Houghton Avenue houses at the time. As it was, the catchment period was too wide.

Then he remembered Charlie Peace's remark about people not staying put in the same houses the way they once did. True enough. But twenty or thirty years ago they did, so that, whenever the child was put there, many of the same people would have been around for quite a while before and after. Except of course for the children, who would have grown up and mostly set up home elsewhere.

Having recorded the piece for Liza he had reduced his options, and he had no choice but to tell the children before it went out on air and people started talking about it. If Aileen were there she could probably have told him how they would take it, but he himself could only guess. That night he cooked supermarket pizza with lots of favourite toppings added. It was a way of ensuring that all the children would eat together. He let them go at their favourite food for a fair while, and it was when they were picking at the remains of the crusty edges that he broached the subject.

'I've got something I want to tell you all,' he said. They all looked at him, including Beckham, who was waiting by the table for leftovers and gazed at him through the fronds of his Old English Sheepdog mop. 'I don't think we want to make a big deal of it, because it's something that happened a long time ago.'

'*What* happened a long time ago?' asked Isabella, thinking rightly he was putting the cart before the horse.

'The death of a child,' said Matt simply.

'It's the new house, isn't it?' asked Lewis. Matt nodded. They thought for some time, then two spoke at once.

'How old was the child?' asked Stephen, who was seven.

'Most houses would have had deaths in them, wouldn't they?' asked Isabella.

'The child was about two or under,' said Matt. 'And yes, most old houses would have had deaths in them, including the deaths of children. A lot of children died in the past, when doctors didn't know as much as they do today.'

'So why is this special?' asked Lewis.

'It's special because yesterday, when I was at Elderholm with the man who's going to do the place up, we found the child's skeleton in the attic.'

'Oooh!' The children shivered exaggeratedly. Matt waited to let it sink in.

24

'Had it just died there all alone?' asked Isabella. 'Got shut in or something, and nobody knew it was there?'

'We don't think so. We think it was probably taken there, laid out there, when it was already dead.'

'Why didn't they bury it?' asked Lewis, aged eleven. 'Everybody gets buried or cre– cre . . . don't they?'

'It's because it was murdered, isn't it?' asked Isabella. She was the brightest, as well as the most sensible, of the brood.

'It's possible,' said Matt, unwilling to go down the hopeless slope of trying to deceive her. Even Aileen couldn't tell Isabella what to think. 'But we shouldn't jump to conclusions. There may be some other reason we haven't even thought about.'

'We don't *have* to go up into the attic, do we?' asked Stephen, which also struck Matt as sensible.

'No, of course we don't. We can just put boxes and cases and things up there, and shut them away.'

'Still, you'd sort of look up and think, wouldn't you?' said Lewis. Matt could have hit him.

'Can we go round?' asked Isabella. Matt regretfully shook his head.

'No, we can't. I wish we could. You could have seen that there's nothing to be afraid of. But the police have sealed the place off till they're finished with their work.'

'Who's afraid, anyway?' said Lewis, offended. 'I just meant it was sort of . . . yucky.' An idea occurred to Matt.

'We can't go into the house, but we could take Beckham for his evening walk there.'

'First tiddle-tour in Bramley,' said Lewis. 'Yes!'

Beckham was notoriously unreliable at night if he didn't get a properly-accompanied evening walk. By now it was eight, and the late April sky was darkening.

They piled into the car, Beckham taking his place between the two boys in the back seat, looking intelligently round him. It was a journey of three miles or so, and Matt noticed that the subject of the dead child was not mentioned the whole way. Were they avoiding it, or did it not mean so much to them as he had imagined it would?

Matt drew up on his parking space on the other side of the lane, and Beckham jumped out, barking. He had been there before, but just into the house and not often enough to dull the novelty. They put him on the long lead, because they would have been at a loss to look for him if he went off exploring as he liked to do. They all went over to the gate of Elderholm, which was wreathed in police tape, and looked over it to the back door, properly sealed up.

'Do they do that every time there's a murder?' asked Isabella.

'I don't know. Whenever there's an unexplained death, I suppose, or something involving a mystery. When that happens the Forensic people need to go over the house carefully to get clues.'

He kept his tone matter-of-fact, and the children nodded.

'Who are Forensic people?' asked Lewis.

'People with a scientific training in solving crimes,' answered Matt, thinking that was near enough.

'Thank you for telling us like this,' said Stephen, and put his hand into Matt's.

And that seemed to be it. Isabella soon turned away, and they all began to walk. Matt drew up the rear, wondering if this really was all, or if they were still mulling over the death, and they would quite soon come to a decision about it and the house. They went along the lane, then turned down towards the road. Beckham was in an ecstasy of sniffing and leg-raising, the two things intimately connected. Once down into Houghton Avenue proper the messages came thicker and faster, and he was visibly committing every odour to memory when suddenly he froze. After a second or two he turned his head cautiously back. All four of them turned too.

Caught in the light of a street lamp, crossing from one of the gardens to the lawns of the church opposite, they saw a long skinny creature with a bushy tail. It was part reddish-grey, part dirty cream, and it looked towards them with alert, calculating eyes, without a trace of fear.

'Is it a dog?' whispered Stephen.

'No, it's a fox,' said Matt. 'What they call an urban fox.'

'What's that?'

'One that lives in a town instead of the country. They scavenge from dustbins, live on anything they can get.'

Beckham was transfixed. Something told him to run at it, but prudence held him back. The fox, having sized them up, thought for a minute, then proceeded, brisk but unhurried, on its way, hopping through the church gates and disappearing from sight.

The children seemed to have been holding their breath for minutes.

'That was *wonderful*!' said Isabella.

'I wish Mummy could have seen it,' said Stephen.

'She will,' said Matthew heartily. 'There's probably a family of them.'

Beckham now charged forward, hectically sniffing at the places the fox had been, whining operatically and implying that he would have chased it if only they had let him off. The magic moment was over. But Matt had a feeling that, whatever doubts there might have been about the new house in the children's mind, they had now been wiped away.

# CHAPTER 3

# Learning Curve

Over the next few days Matt felt his body churning with a growing and nagging impatience. Ridiculous, when the bones had been there years, decades, but still . . . He phoned Charlie Peace the day after the Radio Leeds appeal, and he said there'd been three or four people ringing in and volunteering information, and that they would be followed up. He sounded very official, as if someone was listening in. He was hardly more forthcoming on the question of the little skeleton.

'That takes time. Bones in themselves are near impossible to date. It could be a question of what's been discovered in the vicinity. But I have got a piece of good news.'

'That makes a change.'

'The boffins are moving out of your house as we speak. You can get your man in and start the decorating at once.'

That was a relief. Matt rang Tony Tyler's mobile number straight away, and said he'd add a couple of hundred to the agreed price if they could start within the next day or two. They arranged to meet in Houghton Avenue when Matt's shift on Radio Leeds ended at twelve o'clock, or as soon after that as Tony could manage.

When he drew up and parked by the hut that served the house as a garage Tony was nowhere to be seen, but he saw at once that the police tape was gone from the back door of Elderholm. At last he could go inside again. It was time for instant decisions about colours and floor coverings.

'Excuse me.'

His hand had been on the latch of the back gate, and the voice came from behind him. A woman – fair rather than blonde, and perhaps in her late forties – had come up, smiling expansively, with perhaps a slight nervous consciousness that she was intruding. She was smartly dressed for gardening – no contradiction in terms, because Matt could guess that her gardening consisted of a snip here, a strict tying back there, with the heavy work being done by a hired help or by her husband.

'Yes?' He smiled, though: he didn't want to be on bad terms with all his neighbours.

'I think you must be Matthew Harper.'

'That's right.'

'I heard you on the radio yesterday. I was just trying to find some nice music and heard the name Houghton Avenue. Such a fascinating story about the bones. Rather horrible and terrifying too, of course! But happening here!'

Matt rather thought the stuff about the bones had come well before there had been any mention of Houghton Avenue. The lady was clearly of the type that wouldn't admit to listening to anything less than Radios Three or Four.

'It was certainly a rather unpleasant surprise to come across them,' he said.

30

'It *must* have been! I'm Delphine Maylie – Del to my friends. I can *just* hear that like me you're from the South.'

Except that I'm cockney, and you're stockbroker Sussex, thought Matt.

'That's right. Bermondsey. But I left when I was eleven.'

'I *bet* you wouldn't go back, would you?'

'Well no, not willingly.'

'People down there have such a strange view of the North, don't they? They think it's all blackened stone and belching chimneys, but it's *lovely*!'

Something in Delphine aroused a spirit of contrariness in Matt.

'There are plenty around who wouldn't mind seeing a few belching chimneys, I'd guess.'

'Oh, come *on*.' she said, protestingly, with a winsome smile. 'There's hardly any unemployment in Leeds, and all the jobs now are much cleaner and more hygienic than the old ones. When you consider the asbestosis and the phthisis and all that sort of thing that people got from the old jobs . . . But now, tell me about the bones.'

'There's really nothing to tell beyond what I said on the radio. The police got a few calls after the programme, and they're following them up, but they're pretty cagey about details. You probably know more about who used to live around here than they do.'

'Not really,' said Delphine, her eyes showing her sense that he had failed in his duty of gorging her curiosity. 'We've only been here five years. Mr Farson was one of the old-timers. He'd been here about twenty years I think. But the families who'd been here almost since the houses were built have all gone now, and had even when Garrett and I arrived.'

31

'I suppose that's not surprising,' said Matt. 'I believe the houses are nearly ninety years old. I suppose you don't know where any of the old-time people are now?'

Delphine frowned.

'Now you mention it, I have heard talk about someone who grew up here – I don't remember which house. She's living down in Lansdowne Rise – which is *rather* going down in the world, in spite of its name. Now what was the family? . . . But I don't think that would help, because I'm pretty sure she married. I expect Mr or Mrs Cazalet could help you.'

He gave her a loaded glance, which she returned in good measure.

'I'm not sure they would want to,' Matt said. 'He gave me the impression that he blamed me for finding the skeleton at all.'

She raised her eyebrows, then leaned forward and tapped her forehead.

'Not the neighbours one would have chosen for you. But you'd think they'd want the poor little thing to have a decent burial, wouldn't you.'

'You would,' said Matt, mentally taking the decision to pay for it himself if necessary.

'Here's your decorator,' said Delphine, as Tony's van drew up. 'I *do* hope things go smoothly. Good luck with your enquiries. And I do hope you and your partner will come for drinks with Garrett and me as soon as you're settled in.'

Her eyebrows were raised a fraction, as if inviting him to confide in her why his partner had not so far put in an appearance. Matt did not feel impelled to tell her that Aileen was currently nursing the father of her children through leukaemia in his native South Africa. Still less did he want to confide that the man was still legally her husband. He was not yet sure that he wanted to get on terms of personal confidence with his neighbours. But he registered, as he went to greet Tony, that Delphine knew who his decorator was, and knew he had a partner – and also that the word came naturally to her sort of circle. He thought she was someone he could do business with, but beyond that? He didn't so far feel called upon to make her a bosom buddy.

For the next half hour he and Tony were totally businesslike. He had picked out a suitable floor-covering for the kitchen, and a paper that reached out and grabbed him for the dining room. Now he chose paint for the kitchen, sitting room, hallway and landing. The last area would cause most disruption if it were not done before they moved in. But otherwise he did not see why he shouldn't organize the removers to bring most of the furniture from the Pudsey flat the day after work was finished.

'Then we can make decisions about the other rooms in our own time,' he said to Tony, 'so the children can have their say. Either we can have them done one by one, or else I can take the children away for a week and have several done at once.'

'You're wanting to get the children settled in as soon as possible I suppose,' commented Tony.

'Well, yes, I am. Get them settled in before their mother comes back. I brought them round the other night, and we all saw an urban fox, and somehow – there's no rhyme nor reason to it . . .'

'I know, I know. I've got children. And you want to strike while the iron is hot and they're in love with the place. I think you're wise.'

'That is exactly it. I'm afraid it might wear off. I'm probably hoping for the impossible but it would suit

33

me fine if they never mentioned the bones in the attic again.'

'Not much chance of that, with appeals for information on the radio, and the police conducting an investigation.'

'Not very much of an investigation,' commented Matt. 'They're doing about as much as if it were a long-ago teenager's bad mistake.'

'Which it wasn't?'

'Of course not. Like we said at the time, it was too big.' Matt shook his head in frustration. 'But the police high-ups seem to be allotting it zilch in terms of time or money.'

But they *were* doing something. Five days later, when Matt had been given a date by Tony for organizing the move, Charlie came by appointment to the studios of BBC Leeds. Matt had been intending to take him to the canteen when he suddenly had a mental picture of Liza Pomfret taking the next table to theirs and straining her ears for what she could make out of their conversation. He changed his mind immediately. They went out into the spring sunshine and down to the Merrion Centre pub, where they found a dim corner devoid of shoppers devouring shepherd's pie or lasagne, and settled down over two pints to discuss developments.

'First of all,' said Charlie, 'something I didn't know before, because this isn't the sort of case that comes up every day: it's not possible to "date" bones in themselves – say when they were alive, roughly when the person died. Bits of flesh might be another matter, but there were none.'

'I see. So no joy on the date?'

'Well, not initially. Come back to that. The scientists are leaning in the direction of a little girl for the victim.

34

Obviously we'll be interested in the houses and their inhabitants, particularly the children. By the way, on the question of date we made a bit of an assumption early on, based on the dust and the area around the bones – frankly it was more of a guess than anything. We thought the bones were over twenty years old. Going on that, we found that the last houseowner who'd been there more than twenty years was your Mr Farson, who moved there in 1977. Now aged eighty-seven, and living in a nursing home in Rodley – inter-mittently compos mentis, but about as unreliable as you'd expect. We've spoken to the son, who as you told me has never lived there. Visited his dad frequently, but had no call to go up into the attic, not surprisingly, though he'd been up to move a few tea chests out before he put the place on the market. It was all a great surprise to him, of course.'

'What happened to the other families in the vicinity?'

Charlie shrugged.

'We haven't found out a great deal about them yet. There's only one person still around in Bramley, and her name's Lily Fitch.'

'Is this someone who lives in Lansdowne Rise?' Matt asked. Charlie Peace raised his eyebrows.

'Been doing some detection on your own, have you?'

'Just talking to one of the neighbours about who among the old timers is still around.'

'And did she say Lily Fitch was the only one still in the area?'

'Yes, though she didn't know the name, only where she lived, which apparently in her eyes is a social drop.'

Charlie nodded.

'She's the only one we've come up with.'

'No, wait a minute,' said Matt, remembering the

conversation. 'She – Delphine, no less – didn't say she was the only one still in the area. She said she was the only one she knew about. She's new around here – only been here five years.'

'Right. And who's the longest resident at present?'

'The Cazalets next door, apparently. We had a little encounter on the day I found the skeleton. Mr Cazalet didn't think police added to the tone of the neighbourhood. He blamed me. My having been a footballer was another black mark in his eyes. He probably foresaw Gazza-style drunken binges.'

'Sounds like a nice type of neighbour. Our neighbours in Headingley have all been incredibly welcoming. They seem to think having a black man living next door adds tone to the neighbourhood. It gets rather wearing. Anyway, we went to talk to this Lily Fitch, and she couldn't tell us much. Came up with one name, Eddie Armitage, living in Halifax. We followed it up, and it turns out he's dead.'

'And that's as far as it's gone?'

''Fraid so. We need names, and we haven't got any. But back to the little kid. Like I said, there was no way the death could be dated from the bones, and insects and rodents had left nothing of the flesh.' Matt involuntarily shuddered. 'Yes, it's not a nice thought, is it?' Charlie agreed. 'The flies and mice feeding, while downstairs Mrs Beeston or Mr Farson were getting on with ordinary living. Did they know, or did they not know? Anyway, no remains of flesh or organs, but there were some scraps of material under the body – tiny scraps, which you wouldn't have noticed even if you'd disturbed the body and looked underneath. Probably no one but a forensic team would have picked them up.'

Matt had immediately pricked up his ears.

'What kind of material?'

'Cotton and wool, a few fragments of each.'

'So the little mite was clothed when she was put there?'

'Unless she was laid out on a sort of bed – maybe a sheet and a blanket, or smaller things. The forensic people thought that was probably the case at first.'

'But?'

'But then they made an analysis of the cotton. It was a type that was imported widely for a time thirty years or so ago, from Bangladesh as it now is.'

'East Pakistan it was then, wasn't it?'

'I think so. Before my time. It's a cheap sort of cotton, of the kind you might make children's clothes with – not designer label stuff by a long chalk, but the sort of underclothes you might find sold in street markets or car boot sales, if they had them then.'

Matt digested this.

'So, this is some poor kid, of poor parents?'

'Most likely.'

'Who never reported her missing. That's what I can't grasp.'

Charlie shook his head in agreement.

'No. It's baffling. Neither thing ties in with the sort of location she was found in. Houghton Avenue, and those stone houses, were and are eminently respectable. The people there wouldn't clothe their children off market stalls, and they would be on to the police the moment they went missing. If for no other reason than that the neighbours would be outraged if they didn't. If it was as long ago as we think, the codes of respectability would be very much operative in a street like that.'

Matt was taking his time to think this through.

'So what do we have? Maybe a swim-suit or a pair of pants on the body?'

'That sort of thing, they thought. And maybe a jersey, or a shawl, or perhaps a blanket to lie on, like we said.'

'So presumably it was a summer crime, when the tot was running around without much on. A hot summer?'

'Could be.'

'Children grow out of their clothes quickly.'

'That's right.'

'And there would be a quick turnover of goods in any street-market sort of enterprise.'

'Your mind's working along the same lines as ours,' confessed Charlie, as if he didn't quite like a member of the public successfully playing at being detective. 'It would be at the time this cotton was being imported in the form of cheap clothes. They wouldn't sit around in a warehouse for years and years. So any summer in the late sixties or early seventies.'

'When was the hot one?'

'The hottest was the summer of sixty-nine.'

'The summer of sixty-nine,' repeated Matt softly, his face rapt in thought.

Charlie shot him a quick glance, but it was some seconds before he took in the implications of what he saw.

'You've been here before, haven't you? You knew those houses in the past.'

Matt shook himself.

'Yes. The summer of sixty-nine. I've been meaning to tell you before.'

'Tell me now.'

# CHAPTER 4

# The Summer of Sixty-Nine

It all seemed very strange to the little boy of seven. Not the house: his own home back in Bermondsey was not so very different, though this one was rather bigger – a late-Victorian terrace house with two bedrooms on the first floor and two more in the attic. He and his brothers and sisters would have killed for so much space. Usually this one just housed his Auntie Hettie. But it was the open spaces around the house that fascinated him: the fields gone to scrub, the little gill as his aunt called it, with the stream beside it, leading up the hill towards the main road, and Armley. He had the ambition to go beyond that; he knew there was a Catholic church and school and even an orphanage (the mere name fascinated him, and he thought it would be something like *Oliver!* which his parents had taken him to see at Christmas). Those buildings were beyond the hilltop which he had so far only seen from below, and he would go and see them soon. Definitely.

'Eat up, Young Matt,' his Auntie Hettie would say, as he sat at breakfast. 'There's a squirrel out there as wants to have a word with you.'

She knew he was fascinated by the wildlife, how it

could exist in the midst of a big city. She called him Young Matt to distinguish him from his father, who was also Matt. But whereas his father had been christened by an evangelically-inclined mother after the author of the first gospel, Young Matt had been named after Matt Busby, the Manchester United football manager. Aunt Hettie did not really need to distinguish between them in this way because his father hadn't come North with him. He was back in London with Young Matt's mother, who had had a hysterectomy, with ensuing complications.

Aunt Hettie had married a soldier soon after the end of the war, and had come North with him to his native Leeds. He was now living with another woman in Pudsey, and if Matt ever mentioned his name Aunt Hettie said 'Good riddance to bad rubbish,' and seemed to mean it. She made a living, a poor one even by Matt's family's standards, cleaning and pulling pints at The Unicorn at lunchtime. Matt was left to his own devices as often as not, but he was used to that in Bermondsey. He had been trained in the ways of the streets by his older brother and sisters, then left with the freedom which that training gave him. It stood him in good stead in Bramley.

Aunt Hettie washed up after breakfast, then dusted and hoovered until it was time for her to go to work, which was about ten to eleven. After that Matt was free till after three. There were sandwiches in greaseproof paper on the draining board, and if he felt hungry he took them with him. If he didn't feel hungry, he often didn't eat them till just before his aunt came home. He had no watch, and sometimes let himself into the house in Grenville Street to look at the clock on the mantelpiece in the front room. At other times he went and peered in at the butcher's shop down towards Amen Corner, where a clock with bold black hands was fixed to the wall facing the window. When she came back his aunt sometimes asked him where he'd been and what he'd done, but less so as the days stretched into a week, and then into two. She treated him more like a lodger than a young nephew. That rather suited Young Matt. On the whole he was happy.

'I miss you, Mummy,' he said, on the memorable occasion when Aunt Hettie took him down to the phone box on Raynville Road and rang by arrangement the number she had been given for the hospital. He said the same to his elder brother and sisters, who were there too, and he meant it when he said it. It sounded more pathetic than his state warranted, though, because on the whole he was managing very nicely without them.

He heard the shouting, that Wednesday afternoon, when he got to the top of the gill. He had toiled upwards in the middle-of-the-day heat, following the well-trodden path by the side of the stream, and this time he made it all the way for the first time.

'Kick it!'

'It's a foul!'

'*Goal*!'

The shouts acted as a magnet whose pull was irresistible. Certainly it was not in the seven-year-old to resist it. They brought back memories of innumerable games in the street at home (and, incidentally, of the odd broken window and spanking). He walked into Houghton Avenue, then forward as the shouts directed him past the church, turning off eventually to a rough field, with, beyond to his right, a playground and a low building which he decided had to be the Catholic Primary School. If he had turned around he would have seen

41

the two terraces of stone houses which dominated the bottom end of Houghton Avenue.

But he didn't turn around. He stood there, his eye following the ball, unconsciously estimating the skills of the ten boys and girls playing five-a-side, the play ranging from one end to the other of the improvised pitch, with blazers and pullovers marking out the goals at either end. He watched, his body still, his eyes glittering. There was never any doubt what he would do if the ball came his way. When it did, the result of a duff kick from one of the older boys, he ran forward, got the ball at the tips of his heavy shoes, then began dribbling it down towards the far goal, swerving to avoid challenges, ducking and diving, weaving in and out, until finally, without needing to take aim, he shot it fair and square between the pullover and the navy jacket, nice and low to avoid dispute.

He turned round, and saw that the game had halted, and they were all looking at him.

'That was bloody brilliant,' said one of the big boys.

'He's light on his feet,' said a girl.

'He's better than that,' said the boy, and repeated: 'He's bloody brilliant.'

'They say I'm good at school,' said Matt, trying to say it modestly. 'Even me bruvver says I'm good.'

He brought this out with a conviction that said 'that's proof positive', and the others seemed to accept it.

'I'm Peter,' said the big boy, and pointing to the girl: 'And this is Marjie.' He added regretfully: 'We can't count that goal, you know.'

'O' course you can't,' said Matt. 'I just couldn't help meself.'

'I've got to go to dancing class,' said Marjie the girl who had spoken. 'He can have my place.'

So he played on – played with eleven-year-olds, twelve-year-olds and older. It was like an initiation into the world of near-grown-ups, the world that his elder brother and sisters usually kept him away from. He scored two more goals, both of them good ones. It was amazing. By the end they were treating him as one of them, forgetting his age and his size (it was not till three or four years later that Matt was to grow from 'a bit of a runt', as his family called him, to a normal height for his age). He counted it from then on as one of the happiest days of his life.

'Coming for a Coke or something?' asked Peter, when they wound up the game, gesturing towards the stone houses.

'Could you tell me the time, please?' Matt asked.

'It's a quarter to three.'

'No. I'd better go. Me auntie'll be back from work soon.'

'Want a game tomorrow?' asked Peter. 'We'll probably play again.'

'Yes *please*!' said Matt, and raising his small fist he ran off back to the gill and down towards Grenville Street.

When he had finished telling Charlie all this, or at least a flattened, less moonstruck version of it, there was a moment's silence as they finished their beers, and while Charlie tried to get his mind around all that he'd been told.

'And this was the summer of 1969?' he asked

'Yes, the summer of sixty-nine.'

'Nothing to link it to the bones in the attic?'

'No. It was just a start, though . . . My memories are so vague . . .' Matt sat up straight and looked at Charlie

Peace, his face both puzzled and troubled. 'I remember when I was called home I was relieved to go, as if I had escaped from something. And I remember for weeks afterwards I was *wondering*.'

'Wondering what?'

'Wondering if . . . I don't know . . . if anything had happened. If what I was uneasy about had actually happened.'

Charlie cogitated on this.

'How did you come to buy Elderholm?'

Matt had been expecting this question.

'When I played for Bradford City I always lived in the Bradford area. But even so I remember coming to see where my Auntie Hettie had lived – she died in the early 80s – and walking up the gill to look at the stone terraces of houses, and the field where I'd played football. When I moved in with Aileen in Pudsey I was nearer, and I'd sometimes drive off the Stanningley Road on my way to work at Radio Leeds and have a look at them.'

'And then you saw the estate agent's sign?'

'No, actually I saw a property ad in the Thursday edition of the *West Yorkshire Chronicle*. I knew at once I had to have it. We were looking for a bigger place, and suddenly it felt as if we had just been waiting for this one.'

'But why? I don't see why?'

'Because . . . because the memory of that football game is one of the highspots of my life. Something I cherish and look back on, and laugh, feel happier, feel proud about. The time when I was recognized, when people – OK, kids, but older kids – outside my own family and friends saw that I had talent. Daft I know, but –'

'So that outweighed the uneasiness about what came after?'

'No . . . not exactly . . . It's as if that added to the attraction too. Trying to remember what it was that worried me – that nagged away and had me wondering for weeks after I got home. And recently wondering if it was connected with *this*.'

'And nothing has come back to you?'

'Nothing concrete. Vague memories. I'll get on to you the moment a concrete one comes to me, if it does.'

'Good. I must go,' said Charlie, collecting his things, becoming instantly more of a policeman.

'Me too,' said Matt, standing up too. 'I've got a couple more bulletins to do, then I'm off for drinks with a new neighbour tonight. Delphine – call me Del – Maylie, the one I told you about. Condescending, interfering type of body, but that could be useful. Actually, I'm wondering if she has something for me.'

'If she does, pass it straight on to me.'

Matt nodded, but he didn't sense any great urgency in Charlie's tone to match his words. The priority allotted to the case was if anything getting lower rather than higher. He finished his stint at Radio Leeds, then drove back to Pudsey, stood over the children while they did the little homework they'd been given, than packed them into the Volvo and took them over to Elderholm. He gave them four pounds each to get their chosen takeaway from the joints at the top of Houghton Avenue, where takeaways had replaced shops that sold the necessities of life – or had takeaways become one of the necessities? Then Matt straightened his tie and strolled along to the Maylies at Ashdene, the first house in the other terrace.

It was Delphine who opened the door.

'Oh *hello*! You found us! So good of you to come. It's a pity your partner's not back, but that means we can do it again when she is, can't we? This is Garrett, by the way.'

'I'm the gardener,' said Garrett, lurking in the dimmer part of the hallway and having generally the appearance of a human dishcloth. 'She lets me off in the house with just a bit of washing-up now and again.'

'Don't mind him – I don't,' said Delphine. Then lowering her voice, she said. 'Now come through. I've got a couple to meet you. I realize the Cazalets might have been more useful, but I couldn't endure the thought of them asking if we had Ribena and sitting there saying they did think there were standards that should be kept up and what did we think about the problem of dog dirt. Now come along . . . This is Matt Harper the footballer, and the man you've heard on Radio Leeds. This is Jacob Goldblatt, and this is Hester. From The Willows.'

Jacob looked comfortable and intelligent, with balding grey hair and a neat round paunch. His wife struck Matt as more intense, and perhaps brighter and more observant. It seemed to go with her lean but well-defined long face. Matt sat down, allowed Delphine to get him a vodka and tonic and let the conversation swirl around football and his transition to the media world, and whether local radio was doing a good job. It was when the talk seemed in danger of getting on to Leeds United's prospects in the Premier League that Matt asked the Goldblatts:

'Have you been here long?'

Mrs Goldblatt looked relieved that the trivialities were over. She liked to make use of her observancy skills and insight.

'Twelve years. That makes us not quite the oldest inhabitants, but not too far off. We know about your interest in the houses, by the way, and the reasons for it, though we didn't hear you on Radio Leeds or *Look North*. We knew Mr Farson, of course, who used to own Elderholm.'

'But not much more than just to speak to,' said her husband.

'What was he like?'

'Perfectly nice to pass the time of day with,' said Hester. 'Being a widower he didn't entertain or anything like that. Mostly we talked over the garden hedge. The only time I set foot in the house, and that was just in the kitchen, was when I'd taken delivery of a parcel for him. The kitchen looked as if it hadn't been changed since the houses were built, and I did wonder whether an elderly chap like him wouldn't be better off with some modern cooker rather than an Aga. But of course, you'll know what the kitchen looked like.'

'The modern cooker has just been installed,' said Matt smiling. 'I cook but I don't slave if I can help it. Did you notice Mr Farson becoming senile?'

They cast looks at each other.

'Well . . . not at first,' said Jacob. 'Just little things like saying something a second time a minute or two after he'd said it the first time – the usual sort of things. He seemed to be losing his grasp, but quite gradually. Then – when was it? – one day last year it must have been, Hester saw him in the middle of the day gardening in his pyjamas.'

'I didn't know what to do,' said Hester, looking at Matt with genuine compassion in her face. 'If I'd gone out and said anything he would have been so embarrassed and ashamed. On the other hand he could have

47

walked up to the shops like that, which would have been even worse. Luckily we had his son's telephone number – old Mr Farson had given it to us when he went to stay for a few days with his daughter in Milton Keynes. So I rang the son up and he was round like a shot. He came to see us later to thank us, and said he'd been noticing the signs for some time. That was really the beginning of the end for poor old Mr Farson. They say he's hardly capable of any sort of conversation now.'

'I heard he was a bit better than that,' said Matt. 'I suppose it's a question of which day you catch him on.'

'Comes to all of us,' said Jacob Goldblatt.

'It does not!' said Delphine brightly. 'We've all got to live in the hope that we can keep that particular – wolf from the door. Tell him about the woman, Hester.'

The long, concerned face paused for a moment in thought.

'Well, I didn't tell anyone at the time, apart from Jacob. It was a while ago now – five, six, seven years, I couldn't really say.'

'Seven or even longer,' said her husband.

'Probably you're right. It usually *is* longer than one thinks, at our age. Anyway, it was nothing more than an incident, really. I was at my back door putting milk bottles out, and I saw this – this *figure* go past down the back lane. There must have been something about her, perhaps about the way she moved, almost floated, but anyway I stood there for a moment, and the footsteps stopped outside Elderholm. We're in the one two down from you, Mr Harper, by the way: The Willows. So I was curious, frankly, and went down to my gate and looked along. She was outside what is now *your* house, looking over the gate, up at the house. This was another situation where I didn't quite know what to do. One

48

doesn't want to seem like a busybody, does one?'

'Doesn't usually bother you,' said her husband.

'Ignore him. I wondered for a moment if it was Mr Farson's daughter, whom I'd never seen: but I'd heard she was crippled. And if it was her, why was she looking up at the house? Eventually I just called out "Can I help you?"'

'What happened?' asked Matt. Hester looked troubled.

'She turned and came towards me. I realized at once she was mad, or disturbed, or whatever euphemism one cares to use. She actually answered my question, though she was reluctant, hesitant. She said "I don't think so. There's nothing anyone can do. It's still there. I can sense it's still there." This was beginning to get uncomfortably like an Elizabethan play – poor Ophelia or someone like that, going mad in white satin. But I did ask her what was still there, and she looked at me wildly and said "You shouldn't know. Best you don't. Nobody should know. But I *feel* it's there. Poor little thing." And then she just hurried off down the lane and then round the corner and out of sight. I went into the house, and saw her hurrying up Houghton Avenue towards the main road and the buses.'

'And you never saw her again?'

'No. I won't say I never gave it another thought, because you do, don't you? As with Mr Farson and his senility, it's a reminder of how fragile one's grip on things is.'

'What was she like?'

'Oh dear. It's a long time ago. Thirty to thirty-five, I'd say. The face wasn't particularly lined, but the hair was going grey – fairish hair going grey. I attributed that to the ... madness. Quite tall for a woman ...

49

willowy. I did wonder whether it could be the daughter of Mrs Beeston, the owner before Cuthbert Farson. I knew she'd had a daughter who went to Australia. The woman didn't speak with an Australian accent, but then she wouldn't necessarily, would she? Then I thought she'd have to be a lot older. Before long I forgot about it, and just remembered it when Delphine told us about the . . . about your discovery.'

She looked at Matt, as if challenging him to make sense of it all. It was a challenge he felt he'd taken up already.

That afternoon Charlie managed to leave the Police Headquarters at Millgarth at five o'clock for once. When he told Matt that the case of the bones in the Elderholm attic was likely to get low priority because of the pressure of more recent and serious crimes, he was telling no more than a half truth. Crime was rather below its usual high level in Leeds that late Spring, whether because the minor villains had taken off for the Continent to join in the cheap booze and fags racket and the major villains had flown to Spain to confer with their fellows in exile on the Costa del Crime Charlie couldn't guess, but he relished the prospect of a lazy evening at home. The fact that the little bones were being treated in the usual way the police had of treating cases there was no serious prospect of finding a solution to niggled away at the back of his mind though.

'There we are, young Carola,' he crooned, taking his baby daughter out of the little tub he had bathed her in and enveloping her immediately in a towel three times her size.

Carola gurgled with pleasure. She did a lot of gurgling.

'You're better at it than I am,' said Felicity, without jealousy, watching them over her computer. 'I wonder if it's true that fathers go a bit bonkers over a daughter, and mothers a bit bonkers over a son.'

'I've known mothers desperate to have a daughter,' said Charlie, intent on what he was doing, drying gently the tender flesh. 'In human relationships the only possible generalization is that there is no possible generalization.'

'Still, it'd be a good thesis topic,' said Felicity. '"Fathers and daughters in Victorian fiction".'

'I thought you were giving up on English Lit. to write the great novel,' protested Charlie.

'I am. I have, apart from my two classes. But there's plenty of students hungry for a good thesis topic. They could use *Dombey and Son*. And *Wives and Daughters*.'

'Doesn't sound as if either of those is about fathers and daughters.'

'Oh but they are, though. The firm of Dombey and Son "turns out to be a daughter after all" one of the characters says. Then there's *Mary Barton*. I wonder why none of the Brontës was interested in father and daughter relationships. In fact, none of their characters has any parents at all for long.'

'I've got a case at the moment of parents who didn't have their daughter for long,' shouted Charlie from across the hall, as he lowered Carola into her cot. 'She was murdered thirty years ago and nobody seems to have given a toss. At least, nobody reported it.'

Felicity's face twisted in distress.

'How horrible. How come you know about it now?'

Charlie came over and stood in the doorway, half his mind still on his daughter, and whether she would go straight off to sleep. When he was satisfied with the sound of her breathing he came in and told Felicity the story from the beginning. It was rare for Charlie to bring his work home, but this seemed a matter a mother might help on.

'What chance of finding out what happened?' she asked, when he came to a stop.

'Practically none, I guess.'

'So resources are not being lavished on it?' Felicity knew all about the stern exigencies of police priorities.

'A dribble of interest for a week or two more is the most we can expect,' said Charlie.

'What about this footballer? He's obviously interested.'

'Oh yes. I realized he was interested from the beginning. Now I know why. Yes, he definitely wants to know what happened.'

'And that's not because he's a media person now?'

'Absolutely not,' insisted Charlie. 'He's interested because he was around at about the time, and because, though he was very young he was getting vibes from the set-up in those stone houses that disturbed him. I guess that as time passes more will come back to him, particularly if he finds out anything. One thing may trigger off memories of more things – that's a pretty frequent pattern in crime investigations.'

'And couldn't you feed him things that you've got hold of?'

Charlie shot her a glance. She knew him through and through by now.

'Not systematically. On the other hand, there are ways of dropping bits of information casually into a conversation.'

'That's what you intended to do anyway, wasn't it? That's why you brought the case up now.'

52

Charlie spoke slowly and carefully.

'Having a daughter of my own, who I love to bits, makes me care a lot about a kid who apparently was killed, hidden away, and then forgotten. Having gone through the hideous agony of a formal church wedding for this beautiful little girl –'

'You loved it.'

'– not to mention three days in Morecombe for a honeymoon because you wanted to use it in this damn novel I'm not allowed to see –'

'That I admit was beyond the call of duty.'

'– I just feel that this is a little girl I've gone through a lot of suffering for. And there's this little bundle of bones shut away in an attic that apparently nobody cared for at all. It's about time someone did.'

'So you're using me as some sort of sounding board –'

'I am using you as a moral touchstone. Having a father whose only morality is rampant egotism you are especially sensitive on moral issues.'

'You always see my father off, no problem. Don't gloat. So you're using me to give you the moral backbone to bend police rules?'

'Something like that.'

'Go for it. You're just wanting me to confirm what you intend to do anyway. So do it.'

# CHAPTER 5

# Black-Out

The move came about ten days later. He could have roped in some friends, hired a van, and gone in for some macho heaving and pushing, but he decided against it. Being the wage-earner and full-time carer surely excused him from that sort of posturing. It wasn't as though he couldn't afford professionals. He gave the children responsibility for their own possessions, allotting them a tea chest each, and that kept them occupied on the Friday night and on the Saturday of the move. The removal men turned out to be the usual crazy gang, but luckily there was only one interested in football, and he was happy enough with ten minutes' chat at the beginning and the end of the operation. By five o'clock they were camped in Elderholm and beginning the shift-around of their furniture and their possessions. By Sunday evening the house was beginning to feel like a home.

Three nights later Matt had a dream which was not quite a dream. It came to him, like most dreams we remember, just before waking. It involved no action, no people, not even any faces. It was in fact nothing but a voice. It was a child's voice, one his mind must have conjured up from thirty years ago. The voice was just breaking, the voice of a boy edging into adulthood. It was shouting, with the flavour of a jeer strong in it.

> *'Lily Marsden, Lily Marsden,*
> *Face like a bath bun.'*

A silly, childish rhyme. With the name Lily in it. But Matt knew his mind was increasingly taking him back to the summer of sixty-nine.

They were all on the front lawn of Ashdene, kicking a ball around aimlessly, after they'd all enjoyed a game on the playing fields of the Catholic school.

> *'Lily Marsden, Lily Marsden,*
> *You're not a very fast 'un.'*

It was one of the younger boys, not Peter who had praised his footballing skills the day before.

'The name is Elizabeth,' said the girl. 'Nobody calls me Lily. It's a horrible name.'

The words were unwise.

'Horrible name, horrible girl,' muttered Peter, who began dribbling the ball down towards the laburnum at the end of the garden near the road.

Young Matt looked anxiously at Lily. He had not particularly noticed her in the football game the day before, but he had in the one that had just been wound up – in which she had not played very well. Matt couldn't think of anything worse than being told you couldn't play football well, but on reflection he was not sure the rhyme had had anything to do with football. Lily's face was pudgy, with a small mouth and bright eyes that seemed to look through you, when they looked straight at you. That wasn't often, however, and only for the quick, sharp glance of someone who was weighing you up before looking away again. Otherwise she looked at the ground, or at the tree-tops, and gave the impression of thinking her own thoughts.

'Come on,' said Rory, a boy of about eleven, whose house Ashdene was. 'Let's go and raid the fridge, see what we can find.'

A house with a fridge was something new for Matt. He knew of shops with refrigerators, but not houses. He trooped behind them through the front door with a pleasurable sense of anticipation. The inside of Ashdene struck him at first as not very different from his own home in Bermondsey, but then he realized that all the rooms were much bigger. The kitchen especially. That was where they all congregated, perching on the table or on the kitchen chairs, watching while Rory opened the fridge and took out big bottles of Coke. The next phase was even more interesting. Rory opened up a special little box in the top of the fridge and drew out a good-sized carton of ice-cream. He put it in the middle of the table and fetched them all a spoon each from a drawer in the kitchen cabinet. To the young Matt it was as good as being given the freedom of the kitchens at Buckingham Palace. He tucked in, driving his spoon deep in, and slowly eating the strawberry concoction. Heaven! He always liked relishing luxury. He had learnt young to space out his pleasures and little treats. All his life he was to eat his vegetables first, before the delights of going on to the meat or fish.

He was not the only one to be impressed.

'Your parents must be very rich,' said a girl called Sophie, about Rory's own age. 'Having a fridge. And whenever we come here there's ice-cream in the freezer-box. And they don't care if we eat it all up.'

Rory shrugged. He had an early sense of his grandeur, though in other respects he seemed to lack confidence.

'No, they don't care. They just say "Have you had friends in, then?"'

'Do you get lots of pocket-money?' asked Matt. That was a bone of contention at home in the East End, and the supply had become very erratic since he came to lodge with Auntie Hettie.

'Not bad,' said Rory, preserving the mystery by not being too specific.

'Parents just don't know the cost of things,' said Peter.

'Ours don't anyway,' agreed Sophie feelingly.

So Sophie was Peter's sister, was she? In Matt's drowsy memories she was blonde, curly-haired, and very forward – or perhaps determined was a better word. She knew what she wanted. He remembered this because it contrasted so completely with Rory Pemberton, who seemed to have no idea what he wanted, beyond showing off about his parents' money.

'There's other ways of getting money than holding out your hands for more pocket-money,' said Marjie. Matt pricked up his ears at this, but Marjie didn't volunteer any further information, and Matt was puzzled because she seemed to be looking at Lily Marsden. Lily, however, was not returning her gaze, but was digging deep into the ice-cream as if her spoon was a pick-axe.

'Here, greedy, you're taking more than your share!' said a boy called Colin. He looked at Rory.

'There's more in the freezer,' Rory said. He went into the scullery and, opening up another box-like structure, took out a second carton.

It was the first time Matt ever saw a freezer.

*     *     *

That morning the grown-up Matt was on the twelve to seven shift at Radio Leeds, and taking some of the hourly TV bulletins. The children were still at their old schools in Pudsey, and when they had been packed off up to the Stanningley Road and the Seventy-Two bus, Matt bundled Beckham into the Volvo and drove off to give him a treat: an hour-long walk in Herrick Park.

While Beckham ran here and there in ecstasy, meeting up with old friends and cautiously making sniffy contact with stranger-dogs, Matt followed on, occasionally calling him if trouble seemed to be brewing, but mostly leaving him to his own devices. That meant his own mind was free too, and as he walked he went over in his mind the memories that the name Lily had triggered.

Peter and Marjie had been his friends from the first day. He had liked them, in his childish way, because they acknowledged so enthusiastically his footballing skills. Now he warned himself that the liking was based on ridiculous grounds. They had then both been in their early teens, Peter with deep brown floppy hair, Marjie with fair hair tied behind in a rough sort of pony-tail. He felt he could put faces to them – faces *then*, of course. Who could say what their faces were like *now*?

Rory he ought to have been pals with, being closer to his own age, but he knew he hadn't been. Was it *because* his parents had had money – more money, apparently, than most of the parents in the terraces of stone houses, therefore much, much more than his own parents back in London? Probably that was it. And anyway, age seemed to have little to do with it: he was so far outside their age range – seven to their eleven to fourteen – that he had just attached himself as a sort of mascot to whoever he liked most.

Lily Marsden's face he remembered quite clearly. Not at all a pleasant face: withdrawn, inward-looking, mean perhaps. Was she the Lily Fitch who now lived in Lansdowne Rise? If so, and in spite of all her efforts, she had become Lily, not Elizabeth. Colin he could just about put a size and a shape to: around twelve, he would guess.

There must have been more. Two teams of five-a-side meant there must have been more. Were the ones he remembered some kind of nucleus of the group, or was his memory a sort of random affair at the moment, which might swell out and clarify later on? Lily Fitch had apparently mentioned an Eddie Armitage, who was dead. That could be a red herring: he could have been part of the group at some stage of its existence other than the summer of sixty-nine. In any case, at the moment the name rang no bells of any kind.

He realized suddenly that there was *something* in his memories of that second day that rang warning bells – something that could have led up to the feelings of unease or foreboding that he was later to take home with him when his mother was recovered. Going through those memories he realized it was the mention of money, of there being other ways of getting it than demanding more pocket-money. He had known footballers who had found interesting ways of making money, often involving Asian betting syndicates. He sensed behind Marjie's loaded remark an allusion to a figure, a person, someone in the shadows, yet connected to, or presumably known to, the group.

That afternoon Isabella rang him at Radio Leeds. There was a film on they all wanted to go and see, and they could easily get their homework done before they had to take the bus into town. Matt gave them permission to take the money from the stock in the scullery cupboard, which they knew about and were to use in emergencies. Then he leaned over and took down the Leeds telephone directory. Fitch, L. was at number 8, Lansdowne Rise.

His television duties were finished by seven o'clock. It was twenty past when he cruised slowly down Lansdowne Rise, looking for number 8. The little street, on the border of Bramley and Kirkstall, was a mixture of turn-of-the-century houses very like the one his Auntie Hettie had lived in two streets down, and between-the-wars ones that had been fitted in between them. It was the latter sort that Lily Fitch inhabited – lower and more cramped-looking than the earlier ones. Smaller families meant more cramped houses. He got out and locked the car: he intended staying a while. Then he slipped through the little gate and rang the doorbell.

The woman who answered the door was not holding a glass, but that looked to Matt to be her natural stance. The impression was enhanced by a whiff of juniper berries that a draught from the hallway wafted out on to the evening air. She had switched on no light, so Matt could not get a look at her face.

'Yes?'

'Mrs Lily Fitch?'

'If you like.'

'Ah . . . My name is Matthew Harper, and I'm –'

'Wait a minute.' She switched on the outside light, though the sun had not yet gone down. She peered at him. 'I've just been watching you on the television.'

'That's right. I'm the sports correspondent and general dogsbody for Radio Leeds and *Look North*.'

'Well I never! What can you want with me?'

60

There was no coyness in her words, though maybe a desperate hope.

'I'm wondering if your maiden name was Marsden.'

An indefinable look – was it caution? – wafted over her face.

'Ye-e-es.'

'I think we may have known each other many years ago.'

'Oh?'

'I wonder if I could come in. There's something I'd very much like to talk to you about.'

There was a definite moment of hesitation – no reason why there shouldn't be, with a strange man asking admittance, even one who in a sense had just been in her living space by the wonder of television. The hesitation, though, was momentary and was succeeded by a decision. She stood aside and let him in. Matt thought it probably was the status generated by his television appearances, combined with his suggestion that they had known each other. They went through to an over-full and shabby living room.

'Like a drink?'

Matt was about to refuse when it struck him that accepting one might start the forming of bonds between them.

'That would be nice.'

'Gin? Or I've got lager.'

'Lager's fine.'

While she fetched a can and a glass, pulled the tab open and poured, Matt looked surreptitiously at her face. Very puffy and blotched red, but the same small, unattractive mouth, now with a strong expression of discontent and disappointment.

'You say we've known each other in the past,' Lily

Fitch said, sitting down, her glass of gin on one arm of her chair, clutched but not sipped at.

'I think so. A long time ago, when I was a little lad.'

'Oh? When was that?'

'The summer of sixty-nine.'

This time the expression of wariness that came into her face was palpable.

'Would that be the matter the police were here rabbiting on about?'

'Yes,' admitted Matt. 'I've just moved into Elderholm, one of the stone houses on Houghton Avenue, and I found the skeleton of a small girl in the attic there.'

'Nasty for you.' She looked at her glass as if she needed a deep draught but didn't feel she ought. 'And was it there that we knew each other?'

'Yes. I was staying with my Aunt Hettie, a couple of streets away from here. I was seven, and I came up and played football with all you children from Houghton Avenue.'

She thought for a bit. Was she trying to remember, or trying to decide what to say?

'Don't remember you. Kids came and went.'

'Of course. Naturally. I think you let me join in because I was very good at football for my age. Otherwise you'd have told me to scram. I later became a professional.'

'Nice.' She gave the impression that she would have liked to cast an appraising and sexual eye over him, but was holding herself back. 'I don't see yet what this has to do with me.'

'We think the child, or its body, may have been put in the attic about that time: the summer of sixty-nine.'

The face briefly screwed up, as if she didn't like that phrase.

'I still don't see what it has to do with me.'

'No, of course not. We were just children, weren't we? But all the old house-owners have died or moved away. You're the only one we know about still in the area – but the children will mostly be alive, won't they, even if many of the parents will have died or gone into homes.'

Uncertainty about what to say was obvious in her long pause.

'The only one I can remember, Eddie Armitage, died I think. I remember reading about it in the *West Yorkshire Chronicle*.'

'Yes, you mentioned him to the police, and they've established that. He died a few years ago in the Halifax area. Isn't there anyone else you can remember?'

'No – I'd have told the police if there were.'

'Surely you'd remember the other children in the other houses, the ones you played with?'

'Who says I played with them?' Her voice momentarily became strident with the strain of maintaining the lie. 'I don't think I did much, except maybe in the school holidays. Mostly I went around with others from my school. I was at Armley High, but a lot of the kids in those houses went to the Catholic schools.'

'I see.'

Perhaps she sensed a degree of scepticism in him, because she said: 'Wait a minute. There was a family called Best, or Beest –'

'Beeston?'

'That's it. There was a daughter, a few years older than me, and she married an Iti waiter and went to Australia.'

'She'd have left quite a bit before 1969, wouldn't she?'

'Maybe. I'm no earthly good with dates.'

'When were you born?'

'1956.'

'So you'd be about thirteen when I knew you?'

'If you did. That's right.'

'Which house was it you lived in?'

'Sundown. Just next to the one where you turn as you come round the lane.'

'I see. Were you an only child?'

'Yeah. And my parents were killed in a pile-up on the M1 when I was eighteen. I suppose that's why I married that no-hoper Mickey Fitch. Can't think of any other reason. I thought I needed someone to protect me.'

'The marriage didn't last?'

'Last?' She laughed harshly. 'It lasted a bloody sight longer than it should have done. There's a kid, some-where. It was ten years before I got up the courage to chuck him out – Mickey I mean. Christ, life's a bitch. A fully-fledged, paid-up bitch. Here, have another lager.'

But Matt stood up. He wasn't going to get anything more out of her now.

'My lot will be back from the cinema soon. Their mother's away. I'd better get home and get them some-thing to eat. Look, here's my card. I'm sure there are things lurking around in the back of your memory. I'd like to have another chat if anything, however small, does surface. Just give me a call, at home or at Radio Leeds, and I'll be round.'

But, driving home, he felt pretty sure that, however much she might want to, she would not be calling him. Her behaviour was all of a piece, and it had nothing to do with her memory. For the police's benefit she had come up with one name, knowing the man was dead.

64

Faced with his incredulity that her memory could be as poor as it seemed to be, she had produced another name, knowing the woman was in Australia, and had gone there long before the events of sixty-nine.

On the other hand, if she knew nothing about the events, this lady who had married an Italian, she must have known a lot about the families who lived around her as she was growing up. And she would have no reason to conceal her knowledge.

Because that was what Lily Fitch had been doing, Matt was quite sure. The near-total loss of memory about the children who lived around her told him that. Whether she rang or not, he felt sure he would be speaking to her again, or hearing about her and her activities.

# CHAPTER 6

# One Who Got Away

The next morning, on the way to Radio Leeds, Matt stopped by at Millgarth, the West Yorkshire Police head-quarters, and spoke to Charlie Peace in the open area near the door, watching fascinated as a duty constable fended off the verbal assaults of a general public which seemed to think the police were responsible for pot-holed roads, lost cats and dim street lighting. When he had told Charlie of the incidents from his childhood he had remembered, and the dim pickings from the Goldblatts and Lily Fitch, Matt said:

'I think I might try and get in touch with Mrs Beeston's daughter.'

Charlie nodded.

'Rosamund Scimone. Yes. Difficult for us to justify spending time on her, since she was in Australia at the time, but she might spill the beans on background stuff if you approached her in the right way.'

'Could you spell the surname?'

'S.C.I.M.O.N.E.'

'How did you get it?'

'We looked up Mrs Beeston's funeral notice in the *West Yorkshire Chronicle*.'

Matt pondered, ignoring signs of impatience in Charlie, who was on the way to a job.

'I've been thinking about this daughter. Lily Fitch said she was "a few years older" than her, but it must have been quite a few. Her mother was born in 1900, so at the least she was born in the early forties – during the war, in fact.'

'Babies did get born in the war,' Charlie pointed out. 'All I know about it I got from the television, but if the husband was older than her, which husbands usually were then, he'd most likely be doing Civil Defence or ARP work, not be away fighting Rommel in the dessert.'

'That's true.'

'There were several brothers and sisters named before her in the funeral notice. Probably she was an after-thought, conceived in a comforting cuddle while Jerry was overhead trying to pulverize Armley.'

'Did the report say anything about where this Rosamund lived?'

'Oh yes – Tasmania. That's the island at the bottom, isn't it?'

'Yes . . . And Lily Fitch said her husband was a waiter. I just wonder whether they mightn't have gone there, set up a restaurant, and stayed there. I suppose Hobart would be the first place to try.'

'Sounds like sense. Wherever they are, with a name like Scimone you're in with a chance,' Charlie pointed out. He looked at his watch, raised his hand and was gone.

When Matt rang 153, though the operator said there were no Scimone R's in Tasmania, she said there were two Scimone L's in Hobart.

'That'll be the husband,' said Matt, 'and probably a child. Could I have both?'

He waited until the children were well in bed and asleep before he made the call. It seemed odd to be ringing somewhere where it was already next morning.

'Hobart 746981,' said a woman's voice, strongly Australian.

'Is that Mrs Scimone?' Matt asked tentatively.

There was a moment's silence.

'Well, not exactly. I am married, but I kept my maiden name, so I prefer Ms Scimone. I mean, who'd want to be called Stopes, especially a Catholic. Who's calling please?'

'My name's Matt Harper. I'm wanting to talk to the Rosamund Scimone who grew up in Houghton Avenue, Bramley, in Leeds.'

'Oh, it's mother you want.' Matt thought he should have known that from the moment he heard the voice. Charlie would have realized the voice wasn't old enough for the mother, but Matt was new to the detection game. 'Is it anything to do with Dad's death?'

'No, it's not. I'm sorry to hear he's died.'

'Just a coupl'a months ago. Mum's still devastated. Keeps the restaurant going all right, but it's like she's on autopilot. They'd been married thirty-five years.'

'I wondered if they'd opened a restaurant.'

'First Italian restaurant in the whole of Tazzie. Before they came ''spaghetti'' meant a tin of spaghetti in tomato sauce on toast. Mother learnt all the tricks of the trade at Uncle Aldo's restaurant in Melbourne, then they came here and opened La Terrazza. Beaut little place. Dave and I are wondering whether to go in with her. It's a good earner, no mistake, and it would mean it would carry on after Mum decides to chuck in the sponge.'

'Are you an only child?'

'Oh no. I've got a brother, Carlo – Charley he calls himself. He lives in Sydney and is into computers. He'd eat his meals off the screen if he could. If we don't take it over it'll be sold. What did you want to talk to Mum about?'

'Well, it's sort of about her childhood, and –'

'That's all right, then. It'll take her mind off Dad. She needs that at the moment. Any little thing just sets her off. So keep to the early days and you'll be right. Got her number?'

Matt checked that he'd got the right number, and then rang.

'Hobart 767323.'

The voice was quite English, with a dash of Yorkshire still. It was not so much old as tired.

'Mrs Scimone? I've just been talking to your daughter.'

'To Leona? Yes, there's a lot of confusion.'

'It was you I wanted to talk to. You see, I've just bought Elderholm, in Bramley –'

'Oh really! The old home! Does that mean Mr Farson is dead?'

'He's in a nursing home. The son has powers of attorney, and he sold it to me.'

There was silence. You could hear her thinking of the changes time made in families.

'I never knew him well. Even people I did know well I've lost touch with. Australia's a lovely place to be, but the distances mean that old ties become frail. Thirty years ago you didn't ring home at the drop of a hat.'

'I suppose not. I hadn't thought of that.'

'Even Mum, I wrote to her, rather than rang her. She came out when Leona was born, and I went back when she moved out of Elderholm, to help with the arrangements. Then it was just for the funeral. Useless that – I should have gone when the cancer was diagnosed. But Leo and I were – well, we were just everything to each other.' Her voice cracked. Danger sign, thought Matt. 'Our lives, our restaurant, all the things we did together . . . everything else became like a dream. Including all our lives before we met, Leo's in Parma, mine in Leeds. I had a good childhood, though my Dad died when I was little, but somehow it's hardly even a part of me now. It's me before I became what I am. Does that make sense?'

'I think so. It's not really about your childhood I wanted to talk to you about, Mrs Scimone. It's the families in the other houses.'

'Oh? The two terraces?' There was silence as she thought about this. 'I suppose I remember most of them, though I haven't thought of them for years. Some of the families were still living there when I went back in seventy-six.'

'It's the children I'm particularly interested in. Could you tell me about the ones you remember?'

There was a brief pause, which brought Matt's heart to his throat.

'I suppose so . . . I'll not ask why you want to know, but I can't see as it would do any harm. I left when I was twenty-three, that was in 1966, and there were quite a lot of young children around then. Let's see, just at random: well, there were Peter and Sophie Basnett – lovely children.'

'They were brother and sister, weren't they?'

'Oh yes. Their father was something in local government – the Finance Department, I think. They lived in Dell View. They were still there when I went back, but Peter seemed changed. But then, you do change

70

between ten and twenty, don't you? Adolescence doesn't come and go without leaving traces.'

'What sort of change did you notice?'

'He'd been such an open, confident, happy child. He was more thoughtful, almost morose.'

'And Sophie?'

'Quite a little madam. She'd have been seventeen or eighteen by the time I went back. Boys, boys, boys, and getting the means of having a good time. A real little go-getter and good-time girl. I felt quite sorry for the Basnetts.'

'Anyone else?'

Again there was a pause before her reply. She had to wrench her mind from her dead husband.

'There were the Pembertons in Ashdene. I wasn't very fond of them. They were on the way up, and made no bones about it. Everyone in the other houses was a sort of stepping stone, or they were discarded if they couldn't be of any use. There was a boy, let me see . . . Rory. I suspect he was an accident. I always felt a bit sorry for him, though the children who lived around were too young to see it. He sort of bought his way into things. Had no family life to speak of, though he tried to hide it . . . and then there was Marjorie Humbleton.'

'That would be Marjie, I suppose?'

'That's right. Such a pity. They always shorten names here in Australia, and it's usually Marge, which is worse . . . We *never* use margarine in the kitchen at La Terrazza – that was the first thing I was taught . . . But Marjorie was a lovely girl – always cheerful, and enterprising, and into things.'

'Was she still around when you went back in seventy-six?'

71

'No. Either Peter or one of her parents told me she'd got a job in London. The Humbletons were still there in Sandringham, next door to Mum, and they missed her, I remember that. But she was a youngest child like I was, and they did have several other children in the area, and grandchildren.'

There was a pause, as she thought. Matt thought it best not to interrupt her.

'Ah yes: a girl called Elizabeth, or Lily. The parents, the Marsdens, died in a horrible motorway pile-up. Not a little girl I liked. Rather cunning, sorry for herself, doing things in a sort of underhand way. Parents weren't generally liked either. She was married to a garage worker by the time I went back. That was unusual and commented on: respectable girls didn't get married at eighteen in those days.'

A longer silence told Matt that it was becoming more difficult for her. Matt knew he had been unable to con-jure up the whole gang of children he had played with, and perhaps it was the more personality-lacking ones that she too was having difficulty with.

'I've heard talk of a boy called Eddie Armitage,' he said at last.

'You're right,' she agreed, but hesitantly. 'Eddie. A quiet boy. Lived next door in Linden Lea. Parents ran a fish shop. Do you know, that's all I can remember of him.'

'And Colin something?'

'Doesn't ring a bell. Remember, his family could have moved there after I left to be married. I probably wouldn't have had anything to do with him when I went back in that case ... There's someone else ... Another girl ... Some name like Caroline ... A bit fey, if you know what I mean, and a worrier. Lived in The

Willows ... I did *see* her when I went back, and I remember being concerned for her.'

'Concerned?'

'As if she was losing her grip on reality. But I didn't know her well, and so . . .'

'Can I ask just one more question?'

'Yes, you can.'

'You mentioned your mother coming to visit you in Australia. When was that?'

'That's easy. That was when Leona was born. The winter of sixty-nine. And now it's time for *you* to answer some.'

So Matt had to come clean to Rosamund Scimone – about the finding of the bones, about his own brief involvement with the children in Houghton Avenue back in the summer of sixty-nine, and about the little that had emerged since. Mrs Scimone was obviously knocked for six. If it took a lot to take her mind off her dead husband, murder – the murder of a small child – certainly did it.

'It's just – just incredible. Mum, living there all those years, and up in the attic –'

'We don't absolutely *know* the bones were there in your mother's time.'

'You seem pretty much to have decided. I went up there, you know, when I went back in seventy-six. I got down the four or five tea chests that were there, to pack things for the move.'

'Was that all there was up there?'

'A few games and jigsaws that I gave to the Catholic orphanage across the road.'

'That's gone now. It's a cheap private estate of doll's houses. So you were only in the main part of the attic – the bit with the proper flooring?'

73

'Yes. There was nothing to go into the other bit for – or so I thought.'

'Going back to your mother's trip to Australia. Could you tell me exactly when that was?'

'That's easy, Leona was on time, end of July. Mum had been here about a fortnight I guess. She came on the *Canberra*, so she must have left England the second or third week of June. She stayed four months – poor Mum, she missed out on a summer that year. If it had been Sydney or Brizzie she'd have had a winter better than any good English summer, but not in Tazzie. Anyway, she left in November, by one of the old *Strath* boats – the *Stratheden* I think. They took forever. She had Christmas on the boat, and got back home on New Year's Eve.'

'That was a long time away.'

'Yes. Well, it was hardly worth making the trip unless you stayed a while.'

In the silence that followed Matt had the impression that she was holding back on him. He decided to jump in.

'Was someone house-sitting, or making sure everything was all right?'

'I was trying to work out whether to tell you . . . I suppose I have to now. The house was empty, but Marjorie Humbleton was looking after it. Mum trusted Marjorie. I would have too.'

'And what was she supposed to do?'

'Just check it hadn't been broken into, then go in the evenings and put lights on – different ones each night. I don't suppose it would have fooled anyone who really kept a watch on the house, but Mum was worried about burglars and squatters, so she paid Marjorie a pound a week or something to do that.

Marjorie's family wasn't terribly well off, so she was glad of it.'

'I see.'

'I can hear from your voice you think Marjorie did it, put it up there. I'm sure it wasn't in her. I knew her well –'

'Till she was about ten.'

'– Well, yes. But still . . . she was a lovely child. It just wasn't in her to do something like that.'

'People do terrible things in terrible situations. Going by some of the things that happen these days, and if it had been much younger I'd wonder if she hadn't killed her own newborn child.'

'Oh!' wailed Rosamund Scimone. 'But Marjorie wouldn't!'

'Anyway, it *wasn't* newborn, and I'm not accusing Marjorie.'

'You sounded as if you were.'

'No, I'm not. Children are human. Just to take one possibility: if she was looking after the house for six months, she must now and then have given the key to someone else, when she couldn't do the switching on and off of the lights herself. I'm not jumping to the conclusion that because she had the key she dumped the child's body herself. In fact, I'm not even making the most obvious and easy assumption.'

'What's that?'

'That it was while your mother was in Australia that the body got into the attic.'

The next morning, while the children were getting for themselves all the healthy things they ate for breakfast and washing them down with fizzy drinks Matt went out into the back lane, hoping everyone in the two terraces was similarly occupied with breakfasts, and walked along from the point where the lane turned on its way to Houghton Avenue. Then he walked slowly back and noted down in his memory the names of the houses in order. Those in the farther terrace ran: Maple-dene; Sundown; Dell View and Ashdene, the first and last being end houses with only one shared wall. His own terrace ran: The Willows; Sandringham; Elderholm and Linden Lea. Once back inside he made a list of them, and put it with all the notes he had made during and after the conversations he had had in the last couple of weeks. He took the bundle of papers with him when, having got the children off on the way to their buses, he drove off to his early shift on Radio Leeds and *Look North*.

In the intervals between bulletins he first drew a rough diagram of the houses. Then, after getting his notes into some kind of order, he went through them chronologically, entering the names of the children and their families as he had learnt them. Then finally he entered the names of the families currently occupying the houses, though there he had to leave several blanks. He wondered whether he had been a bad neighbour, or whether they had.

Early afternoon he rang Charlie.

'I've got something I'd like to show you, if you're not busy.'

'I'm busy until four, then I'm definitely off. It's our first wedding anniversary. Why don't you come round for a drink?'

'Oh, you'll want to be alone. I wouldn't want to intrude.'

'You won't be. Come and see the daughter and heir. We've got a baby-sitter coming at seven-thirty, then we're going for a meal to La Rascasse. Are you free before then?'

'At five-fifteen.'

'That's fine. The address is 13 Wellington Terrace, Headingley. See you there.'

So by six o'clock Matt had found the Peaces' flat, made the acquaintance of Felicity and Carola, played silly games with Carola and her rattle, and then settled down with a whisky and water, but a very small one because he was conscious he was drinking with a police officer. He and Charlie sat on either side of a coffee table, papers spread out in front of them. Felicity was in and out of the sitting room, getting ready for the evening, but she kept close tabs on what was being said.

Matt began by telling Charlie about his conversation with Rosamund Scimone. Then he turned to the papers. 'I've made a little map of the houses. With the names of the children who were there in 1969 – I know next to nothing about their parents, but I suppose I'm going to have to find out. Let's start down my own end with Linden Lea. This is the house currently owned by the Cazalets.'

'The ones you're not keen on?'

'That's it. Creepy type. Mrs has not yet shown. Thirty years ago it housed Eddie Armitage. He's a boy Mrs Scimone has no memories of apart from the name. I have no memories of him at all. Not much information on the parents except that they owned a fish shop.'

'Bit of a blank so far,' commented Charlie.

'Right. Next, Elderholm. Centre of our interest. No children resident but its owner Mrs Beeston was away in Australia throughout the second half of 1969, to be with her daughter Rosamund who was having her first baby.'

'Ah!'

'Then next door is Sandringham – owned by the Humbletons. Daughter Marjorie or Marjie, who I remember well. Lovely girl, I thought, as a not particularly worldly-wise seven-year-old. Still Rosamund Scimone agrees, and so did her mother. Marjorie had the key to Elderholm all the time Mrs Beeston was away.'

'Really? Why?'

'Switch on lights at night, to deceive potential burglars and squatters, and generally keep an eye on the place.'

'Makes sense, I suppose. This gets more interesting.'

'Last house in this terrace, The Willows, currently owned by the Goldblatts. Then home to a girl called Caroline, surname uncertain. Mrs Scimone thought she had a failing grip on reality. Mrs Goldblatt encountered what she described as a mad woman, who seemed to have a particular interest in Elderholm.'

'Not in her own home?'

'No. Interesting. Next terrace: Ashdene, currently owned by the Maylies. Then owned by the Pembertons. House seems to attract the socially ambitious. Rory Pemberton is said by Mrs Scimone to have been generally neglected by money-conscious parents.'

'That's the boy you told me about yesterday?'

'Right. I told you about Peter and Sophie Basnett too. They lived in the next house, Dell View. I have happy memories of him. In the ten years Mrs Scimone was away he seems to have become morose, and Sophie a teenage sex-kitten.'

'Pretty natural progressions, both.'

'Cynic. Next Sundown, with Lily Fitch whom we both know. Neither she nor her family generally liked. Then the last house, Mapledene. I've got nothing on that. Possibly the home of Colin, the only child I've got a name for but no location. Or possibly a childless house. There do seem to have been an awful lot of houses with children in them at the time.'

'Maybe not surprising,' said Felicity, doing up buttons on her dress at the door to the sitting room. 'Those houses are quite expensive now, Charlie tells me, but at that time they may have seemed a bit dated and tatty – just the thing for a young family who wanted something other than your standard semi.'

'Quite apart from the fact that the birthrate's much lower today,' said Charlie.

'Could be, I suppose,' said Matt. 'But anyway there's got to be some children from elsewhere.'

'Why?'

'We used to play five-a-side. We've only got eight so far.'

'Fair enough,' said Charlie. He had got up and was changing his shirt for a natty purple-check one. 'You know, I'm surprised about one thing.'

'What's that?'

'All those children, all that publicity, and yet so far not a single communication from any of them.'

But that was about to change.

# CHAPTER 7

# A Voice from the Past

The next morning Matt bumped into Liza Pomfret in the corridor of Radio Leeds. Well, not so much bumped into as sidled past, trying to bury his head in the notes he had made for his usual morning slot of 'why doesn't the Council do something?' and 'why do these so-called refugees have to come *here*?' – the usual morning mix of the genuinely bemused or confused and the congenital whinger.

'Oh, Matt,' said that corncrake voice that managed to sound so different when it went on air. 'What gives in the baby-bones saga?'

Matt flinched, and didn't bother to hide it.

'The baby-bones saga? You have sweet ways of describing things, Liza. Actually not much.'

'You haven't given up on it, have you? We should be thinking of a follow-up.'

'We can't think of a follow-up unless we have something to follow up with,' said Matt, 'and so far beyond a firming-up of the date we've got very little.'

'The date's been firmed?' pounced Liza. 'When to?'

Matt kicked himself.

'Well, around 1969, but that's very provis –'

'Oh no, that's marvellous! That gives us something much more solid to go on.'

'The people who used to live in those houses have been so much dispersed,' said Matt, cunningly as he thought, 'that I think it would probably be more useful to go national now.'

'Super idea!' said Liza, with terrible enthusiasm. 'We'll film an interview, and I'll get on to the *Crimewatch* people and get a slot there. I've got a friend on the programme.'

Whatever TV programme came up Liza invariably claimed to have a friend on it. She had no notion of making her lies likely ones.

'Maybe, Liza, maybe,' Matt cast a hurried glance at his watch. 'Look, I've got to go. I'm on in two minutes.'

'Oh Matt – on *your* programme they can just play a record.' Another of Liza's amiable characteristics was that she never let the fact that she was after a favour from you get in the way of getting in a good kick on the shins if the opportunity arose. Matt comforted himself with the idea that this would prevent her getting very far up the greasy pole, but he didn't entirely convince himself. Still, if he was being considered for greater things, it would be sweeter still if it was at the expense of the brutally dismissive Liza Pomfret.

He was far from happy later in the day when, preparing to stand in for a two-twenty news summary on BBC Two he heard his name on the Liza Pomfret show.

'I don't know if you remember the item we had on a week or two back – the gruesome discovery of a child's bones in a house in Bramley. Chills the cockles of your hearts, doesn't it? That was a house bought by Matt Harper, the former Bradford City footballer, now our own Matthew Harper, newsman and sports reporter.

81

Well, I was talking to him earlier today, and he tells me that the date the poor little thing died is now put at around 1969. Well, we're going to go national on this, but here's a chance for all you older listeners to get in first. Have you any memories of those old stone houses in Houghton Avenue, Bramley that could be of use to the police or of interest to us? Get in touch –'

Matt shut the studio door on her voice. She made it sound as if they were running some kind of competition to get on air, like *Who Wants to be a Millionaire*? He began to think how, should the need arise, he could go about getting further publicity for the case without involving Liza Pomfret.

But Liza had her uses, though he would never in a million years admit it. Among his mail at the studio next morning he found a letter without a signature. It just ended 'with best wishes', and he didn't think that was due to an oversight. Such letters were not unknown. He had had amorous propositions like that – suggesting times and places for them to meet but not vouchsafing names. He sometimes got letters objecting to items he had read in the course of duty on news bulletins, and sometimes – particularly if they were from racists or religious nutters – they jibbed at giving him their names. He generally just considered them as sick and as often as not simply put them in the waste-paper basket unread.

He looked at the envelope. Neither expensive nor cheap – standard chain-newsagent stuff, addressed by computer. He unfolded the letter again. It too eschewed handwriting or typewriter. Computers, someone had learnt, were difficult to trace back to their user. Or perhaps the writer was just computer-bound, like so many.

*Dear Mr Harper,*

*I heard today on Radio Leeds an item about a child's skeleton in a house in Houghton Avenue. I am not now a resident of Leeds, or of the North, but by chance I caught part of an earlier item on the same subject. Having just heard the second item I thought I should write to you because this time I heard your name. Or perhaps this time I just registered it, as I hadn't done before – registered who you are, I mean. Because it's been a long time, hasn't it?*

*I thought I should write because it occurred to me that you might be worried. You are the little whipper-snapper who came and played football with us that summer of sixty-nine, aren't you? I'm afraid I don't follow football at all closely these days, otherwise I might have identified you earlier. Football was always a pos-sibility as a career for you, wasn't it? I can still call you to mind on that field. You were so good – out of our league entirely.*

*Since I heard the item today I have sat here wonder-ing what to do, wondering whether you are worried that you might have had a part in what happened that year. You were so young – seven, wasn't it? – that your memo-ries must be rather few and scattered, and you may think you did something, even without knowing it, that contributed to what happened then. I'm writing to you to tell you that was not the case. You were too young to understand and anyway you were told nothing. You left to go home the day before it all happened. Your con-science can be clear, and you can get on with your life. I hope it is a happy one.*

*With best wishes.*

83

Matt sat, looking at the two sheets of paper in front of him. Then he read it through again. Something in the letter was ringing a bell. A memory was struggling deep down in his subconscious to surface, to make itself felt. It was only in fact at the end of his shift, as he came out into the sun and was making towards his car, that it came forward and took hold of him.

He had to steady himself with a hand on the roof of his Volvo. Then, after a minute or two, he got into the car and drove off, possessed by memories.

There was no possibility of playing football that day. The rain was so constant and so penetrating that anything outdoors was out of the question. They were sitting on the floor playing Totopoly, and the older ones had been teaching Matt the rules. He considered it a rotten game. They were in Peter and Sophie's house, and Marjie was there as well. Peter's mother had just put her head round the door and said that she had to go up to the little row of shops on the Stanningley Road.

'You stay in the dry,' she said. 'Matt will get wet enough when he has to go home.'

So she knew him, had accepted him as part of the group.

'You didn't think much of that game, did you, Matt?' said Marjie, who had been watching him.

'Not much,' said Matt, who had childish honesty. 'Even Chinese Chequers is better than *that*. Anyway, I like to *do* things.'

'Do things?'

'I mean, not just sit.'

'Well, why don't you start training to be a footballer?' suggested Peter. That interested Matt. He had thought you just *became* a footballer, because you were good at

84

it. 'We could start with some limbering-up exercises.'

There was lots of room in Dell View's big living room. You could never have done exercises in any of the rooms in Matt's home in Bermondsey. They did limbering-up exercises, with Peter telling him that this was to loosen up the upper body, this was to strengthen the thighs and calf muscles. Matt went along dutifully, but was conscious of feeling ungrateful.

'We do this sort of thing at *school*,' he said at last.

He was conscious of Peter casting his mind around for some routines that he wouldn't yet have done at school. Probably both of them were relieved when they heard the back door bell. Marjie went to open it, and brought back the boy called Colin, and another boy of about his age. Concentrating, the grown-up Matt could not put a name to him yet, but he could put a face. He was one of the footballers, but not a boy who put himself forward.

'We've been watching,' announced Colin.

'Careful,' said Peter, in a low voice. 'Remember we've got Jack-the-lad here.'

'She went there,' said Colin.

'Who?' Marjie asked, her voice scarcely rising to the level of a whisper. Colin mouthed his reply.

'Lily.'

They thought they were being very clever, but Matt understood. He wasn't just a pair of nimble legs.

'What do they *do*?' asked Sophie out loud. There was a pause. Peter, behind him, mimed the taking off of clothes, starting to pull his open-necked shirt sexily off his shoulder. He thought Matt couldn't see him, but he saw in the long hall mirror. The little boy looked at Sophie. The girl's eyes were avid with interest. But when she spoke her tones were scornful.

85

'Fancy someone paying for *that*,' she said.

'I don't think she earns much,' said Marjie, still whispering.

'I should think not,' said Sophie. '*Lily*!'

'She looked pleased an' all 'appy-like as she went up towards the 'ouse,' said the other boy.

'That's Lily, Harry,' said Peter with a sigh. 'You don't know her like we do. She's pleased with *herself*.'

'You'd have to be,' said Sophie, 'to think it's worth getting paid, to show off *that*.'

'Watch it,' said Peter. 'Remember young whippersnapper.'

That was the word that had done it. Not just the word, but other similar ones that seemed to sum up the relationship: Jack-the-lad, Georgie Best, the young hopeful, and so on. Matt ought to have hated it, found it condescending, but he hadn't. He'd seen the jokey names as protective – felt there was someone looking after him in this strange environment of older children who were – now he could define it, then he could only feel it – out of his class. Not just older, but better off. He felt now that Peter was trying to act towards that solitary little boy he had then been as a substitute father. Even now he felt a glow of gratitude.

Perhaps some remnants of that feeling of responsibility had lodged in the grown man's brain, and that was why he had used the word in his letter. Because Matt felt sure it was Peter Basnett's letter: it wasn't just the word 'whippersnapper', it was the whole mind-set. Matt took up the letter again, and read it through, slowly and carefully.

That sentence at the end about his being too young to understand and being told nothing of what was going on smacked to him of wishful thinking – of convincing himself after the event of what he wanted to believe. Yes, he had been too young to understand in the wider sense of the word, but no, he had not been too young to know that something was going on, and that it was something to feel uneasy about. It was true he had never been told anything, but still things were said in his presence that, in spite of Peter's best efforts, he could, even at that age of seven, piece together and half understand. He felt sure he had known even then what they thought Lily had shown to the man she had gone to visit, who she had been paid by. He was a boy with two elder sisters.

There was something else puzzling in the letter. Peter said he didn't live in Leeds or in the North. Yet he had heard both the original interview and Liza Pomfret's update of the day before. Rather odd. Was he on an extended visit to Leeds? Or was he lying? No – wait: he said he had 'caught' an earlier item on the same subject. That could have been Liza Pomfret's interview on Radio Leeds, but it could equally be the piece he did on *Look North*. That had a much larger catchment area, extending down to Derbyshire, Nottinghamshire and Lincolnshire. If he lived so far South, it would justify him saying that he no longer lived in the North.

One other thing was useful about the letter. The memories it provoked had brought the boy Colin into focus: pushy, opinionated, pretty pleased with himself. The other boy in the partnership, Harry, had been the junior one, and Colin made pretty sure he stayed that way.

When he got home and had heard the children's competing accounts of their awful days at school (which sat very ill with their determination not to change schools if it could be avoided) he reached down the Leeds telephone directory and the old Bradford one he had had when he lived in that area. There was a handful of Basnetts in Leeds, but no P. Basnett. There was an L. P. Basnett in Horsforth, and he dialled the number and asked for Peter Basnett.

'No Peter Basnett here,' he was told. 'I'm Laura Phyllis.'

When he tried the only P. Basnett in Bradford he found that it was Philip, and the voice was much too young. Radio Leeds could be heard in Halifax and all sorts of other towns in the immediate area, but somehow he did not feel he was going to get anywhere that way. It was too easy. Peter would not have told a lie he could so easily be caught out in.

Except that . . . Matt tried to put into words the thought at the back of his head. If he wanted to write to someone to reassure him that he had played no part in a terrible event without revealing his own identity, he would have kept it very brief and matter-of-fact: I fear you may be worried . . . I can assure you you had gone home before it happened . . . You can put your mind at rest. Nothing more was required.

Yet this letter went beyond that, well beyond. It almost seemed as if the writer would like to resume a relationship, one of which he had happy memories – as Matt himself certainly had of his relationship with Peter.

He would even go further. He felt that, fighting a rearguard action against the eighty per cent of himself that wanted to remain anonymous and unknown, wanted to have heard the last of the matter of the dead child, there was twenty per cent that wanted to be found, wanted to see how the young Matt had grown up, wanted – even – to have the matter of the child out in the open at last.

Could it be that he had used that word 'whippersnapper' deliberately to set him on to his track? Was Peter waiting somewhere in West Yorkshire, half hoping and half fearing that he, Matt, would get a lead on him. A lonely person, perhaps? An unfulfilled one? Feelings of guilt contending with instincts of self-preservation?

The next morning, at breakfast time, and on his way to another job, Tony Tyler dropped round to see if he had made any decisions about decorating the bedrooms.

'I'm not going to pick anything for the main bedroom until Aileen is here to OK it,' said Matt. 'More than my life is worth. As to the other bedrooms, the children have been humming and hahing.' He turned to them, sitting over their Cornflakes and Frosties: 'The one who makes a *firm* decision and sticks to it will be the one who gets their bedroom done first.'

Isabella, Stephen and Lewis sat, spoons poised, thinking for a moment. Then they downed tools and ran upstairs, talking and arguing. Matt looked at Tony and grinned.

'I haven't made any decision about whether I try to do some of it myself, or with their help, such as it will be. But it's beginning to look as if I shall be too busy. There is one thing I've been wanting to talk to you about, though. This kitchen ceiling –' he looked heavenwards '– it looks to me as if it could do with another coat.' Tony Tyler, also looking up, grimaced.

'I think you're right. We thought we might get away with two, but it looks as if we were wrong. To tell you the truth we were covering years of grime – decades, probably.'

'Yes, he doesn't seem to have been house-proud. I

think he was a widower by the time he moved here.'

'I could get someone to you tomorrow morning.'

'Fine.'

'I'll send Harry. He says he knows you already.'

'Oh? Harry who?'

'Harry Sugden.'

'Don't register the name.'

'Harry says he used to play football with you when you were a lad.'

Matt was conscious of Tony's eyes on him.

'Yes,' he admitted. 'I never told you I'd been in these parts before.'

# CHAPTER 8

# Team-mate

Harry Sugden was already on the job when Matt slipped home from work the next day. Matt dallied behind the back gate and looked at the overalled figure standing on a metal stepladder, methodically coating the ceiling with a further layer of paint. A good, systematic worker, he decided. Whether that meant anything more – that he would be a reliable witness to events that had happened thirty years ago – Matt reserved judgment.

He opened the gate and went forward. He thought he saw Harry register his approach by a flicker of the eyelids. Matt opened the door and went up to him, his hand outstretched.

'Hello, I'm Matt Harper. I gather I don't really need to introduce myself.'

Harry leant down and took his hand. He was a man in his forties, his fair hair starting to recede, but with an uncomplicated smile and a feeling of honesty about him.

'Well, I'd not say I'd ha' recognized you if I'd passed you in the street,' he admitted, 'though I might ha' done if I'd stood beside you at the bar. Any road, who doesn't change between seven and thirty-seven.'

'I have, anyway. Ready for a cuppa? Tea or coffee?'

'Tea please.'

Harry came down his ladder and set paintpot and brushes out on the newspaper laid over the floor.

'By 'eck, it's been a long time,' he said. 'But now I look at you properly I can see the little lad still there in the face.'

'I'm surprised you remember me at all,' said Matt, busying himself with the teapot and milk bottle.

'You were that good,' said Harry simply '– a reet little Georgie Best, and we all said the same. And back then you weren't much bigger than the football you were kicking. It were a pleasure to see you score goals, even if they were for t'other side.'

'I'm afraid I never quite lived up to that early promise.'

'Don't say that. You were playing in t'Second Division, as it wor then – I don't call that not living up to promise. I'd've been proud to ha' played wi' you if you'd only been playing i' the Fourth!'

'Well, I'm not saying it isn't nice to be remembered,' Matt said, always more proud of his promise than his achievements. 'After all, I suppose I was only here for three or four weeks.'

'Happen it wor about that. We tried to make a little Northerner of you, because half the time we couldn't understand your cockney. You've lost all that, lad. Is it working for the BBC as done that to you?'

'No, I lost it, most of it, when we moved to Essex. My father got a good job in an engineering works in Colchester ... Funny thing, but I can't even imitate cockney particularly well now.'

'Well, you could 'a acted in *EastEnders* then, if it'd been goin'. It were "barf" for "bath" and "bruvver" for "brother" back then. You stood out, I can tell you, and you wouldn't 'ave if you'd talked like you do now . . . Mind you, we both stood out. We were outsiders like.'

'Oh? I'm guessing you weren't from round here.'

'I weren't,' said Harry cheerfully. 'I were from down the 'ill, like you. I were at a loose end because me best mate were away in a caravan in Brid, and the kids here were always one or two short of players for their five-a-side games. You probably didn't realize it, but I wasn't part of the group. I were with it, but not of it, if you take my meaning.'

'No, I don't think I did realize that at the time. I was very young, and I probably missed a lot. That's what I'm afraid of, when I try to think back to that time. What I do remember about you is your going around with someone called Colin.'

'Oh aye? Well Colin were a bit of an outsider an' all. He used to come in the summer to stay wi' his grandparents. His mum and dad were teachers, an' they liked to use their long holidays to travel round Europe. They wanted a bit o' time wi'out kids, which I reckon you can understand.'

'Teachers were they? I remember him as a bit bossy, a bit of a know-all, so that figures. We had teachers' sons at my Colchester school, and they were often like that. Who were his grandparents?'

'The people at the far end house.' Harry nodded in the direction of the curve in the lane. 'I think their name was Mather? Colin were always there a month or more i' the summer.'

'What I remember about you two was you both keeping an eye on a girl called Lily,' said Matt. Harry put down his mug of tea on the stepladder, frowning.

93

'I don't mind that. I remember Lily – Lily Marsden she were then. But she were older than me and Colin. Why would we be keeping an eye on her?'

'Sorry, I'm not making myself clear. I don't mean minding her. I was trying to find a polite way of saying watching her, spying on her.'

Harry Sugden grinned.

'Well, that Lily Marsden were always up to summat, an' you know what lads are like at that age – smutty as hell.'

That tied in with the hints from the other children about what Lily was getting up to.

'It was something like that was it? Or you two thought it was. My memory is that she was calling on someone, going to see some man and getting paid for whatever she did.'

'By 'eck, you've got a memory. Tell you the truth, I do mind it now, but not a lot more than you've said.' He took up his tea again and drank thirstily. 'She were goin' somewhere and gettin' money for doin' summat. O' course it could have been anything: running errands for someone who was disabled, or old, or . . .'

'But you and Colin didn't think so.'

'None o' them did, none o' the kids around here. It were – I dunno – it were her way, the way she talked about it, the sly, secretive way she referred to it. Ee, she were a funny lass. There was no pinning her down. She – well, she *knew* things us kids could only guess at.'

'Sex?'

Harry scratched his chest. Matt clearly hadn't hit the nail squarely on the head, but Harry was at a loss to explain the essence of Lily's strangeness.

'That I suppose. But – I don't know as I can put my finger on it. I were never that clever wi' words – it were more psychological than physical, if you catch my meaning. No doubt there were that as well, in some shape or form, but what pleased her specially was that she were being *told* about things – things most children in them days would know nowt about, whatever they might pick up today. She were on equal footing with an adult.'

Matt thought for a moment.

'Who was this person she was going to?'

'Search me.'

'You and Colin knew she was visiting someone, but not who?'

'I think that's right. You're callin' on memories I hardly knew I 'ad, so I may be messin' you about entirely. But I think we found out the house she was visiting, an' we kept watch on it, but I don't think we ever knew who it were.'

'Where was the house?'

'It were down in our part o' Bramley – where your auntie lived and where I lived. *Down* in every sense o' the word from these houses. It were one o' the streets off from the Raynville Road – you know them. We lived in Lansdowne Avenue.'

'My auntie lived in Grenville Street, and Lily Fitch as she is now lives in Lansdowne Rise.'

'Does she now? Then there's Grenville Grove, Leighton Terrace an' several more little streets as go off from Raynville Road. Could be any o' those. It weren't Lansdowne Avenue – that were our own street, an' I'd'a known who she were visiting if it were close to our 'ouse. Anyway, we lost interest because squatters moved into a 'ouse in one o' those streets and we got more interested in them, otherwise I bet we could'ave found out. 'Ave you spoken to Lily?'

'I have. She's saying nothing.'

'She wouldn't if she had anything to do wi' this baby business.' He shot a quick look at Matt. 'It *is* that we're talkin' about, isn't it?'

'It is.'

'Aye. Tony told me.'

Matt felt a bit shamefaced about his secrecy.

'I didn't tell him till yesterday that I'd known these houses when I was a boy. Made me sound like the poor little kid who looks up at a big house and dreams of owning it. This was a big house to me in those days.'

'To me an' all.'

'You don't remember anything more about those days that could be useful?'

'Not a thing.' He thought before saying carefully: 'It doesn't seem likely, does it, that them children were involved. I mean, apart from Lily they were pretty nice kids.'

'Maybe you're right. But Lily Fitch is hiding something, I'm sure of that.'

'That were always her way ... Mind you, I'd 'ave to say I probably wouldn't 'ave known if there were anything up. Soon as me mate came back from Brid I'd've been off wi' him, and not playing up here. I knew me place.'

'You can't remember when that was?'

'Give us a break! After all these years? But I think you were still around.'

'And you never played up here with them in later years?'

'Not as I recall. I'd played on and off in earlier years, but not later ... Some o' them were gettin' a bit old for playing – "leiking" as we used to call it down the 'ill. They were coming up to an age when they'd be

96

more interested in the other sex. I must 'ave met some o' them around, living pretty close like I did, but I don't think I 'ad anything more to do wi' them as a group.'

'So you wouldn't know where any of them went to in later life, where they landed up?'

Harry Sugden shook his head slowly.

'Not most of them, but just the one I do. Though I don't know about "landed up", because this were – oh, must be eight or ten year ago now. I were on me own then, trying to run me own business. It didn't work out – I 'ad to keep the costs so low to compete that I never made a living wage. This one I'm talkin' about drove as 'ard a bargain as anyone. If he had the money to buy a house on the Otley Road – close to Lawnswood Cemetery, do you know the ones I mean? – you'd ha' thought he could've paid a decent screw to 'ave it decorated. But no –'

'Who is this you're talking about?'

'Pemberton was the surname. I can't call to mind the Christian name but it were something unusual.'

'Rory.' Matt reached for the telephone directory, but shook his head. 'No Pemberton R. here.'

'Probably ex-directory. Most people wi' money are. They're allus being hounded by telephone salesmen.'

'You don't recall the house number?'

'No, but it were one of those posh jobs they built just before the war, wi' flat roofs and curved bays out front. I only have to drive by to find the number.'

'Would you do that?' Matt paused, wondering whether to offer petrol money.

'Don't think of it,' said Harry, and Matt registered his sharpness. 'I'm only too glad to 'elp.'

'Did you and Rory say anything about the old times?'

'He wasn't interested. Like as not he thought I were

using the fact that I used to play five-a-side wi' 'im as a way of screwing a bit more out o' him, but it would ha' needed more than that I can tell you. Only time he reacted wa' when I mentioned Lily Marsden.'

'Oh?'

'I see her now an' then, shoppin' in Armley, or at the Owlcotes Centre. She's the only one I ever do see, an' she doesn't recognize me. Any road, it seemed natural to mention that I knew she was still in the area. But it didn't seem to be welcome to 'im.'

'Not welcome?'

'He got broody like. Then he said: "Damned woman. It all started wi' 'er." I said "What did?" but he just turned and went out of the house and banged the door.'

Harry Sugden was as good as his word. He rang Matt in the early evening to tell him that the house he had redecorated was number 48. Matt decided there was no time like the present.

'I thought we might take Beckham to Golden Acre Park for his evening walk,' he said to the children.

'Why should we go there?' asked Lewis.

'What's there?' said Stephen.

'Birds. And moles. But mostly lots of unusual birds.' There was a flicker of interest. 'Anyway I've got something to do out there. You can all take Beckham around the lake. But don't let him tangle with a goose.'

'Could he kill one?' asked Isabella.

'No, he'd come off worse. Everyone comes off worse who tangles with a goose. So keep him on a long lead.'

The children had been disappointed in their hopes of a nightly sighting of the urban fox. He or she had been seen just the once since they moved in, and since that was by Stephen alone, the other two were sceptical of his claim. Matt thought it a good idea to take them to a place where there was a more reliable source of wildlife observation, though the birds of Golden Acre were almost unnatural – so stuffed with bread by visitors that they were a terrible warning against welfare dependency.

The birds were an immediate hit. The children didn't worry about, or even notice, their weight problems but were so stunned and enchanted by the number and variety to observe that for a time they were speechless. Beckham, after an initial flurry of excitement, decided he was horribly outnumbered and outsmarted. He had already developed a cynicism about the squirrels around the Houghton Avenue houses, due to their numbers, and their thoroughly unfair advantage of being able to climb trees. He put on a blasé air and trotted behind the children, sniffing the ground and ignoring the beasts of the air.

'Stick to the main path,' shouted Matt. 'Otherwise we'll never find each other.' And he went back to the car and retraced his route to the part of the Otley Road closest to the Ring Road. He parked round the corner from number 48 and walked back to it. It had a gate and a small neat front garden. It was indeed a thirties house – spacious, clean-lined and attractive. He rang the doorbell and waited.

'Yes?' The door had opened without a sound from inside. The hall was thickly carpeted and the blonde who opened the door was so heavily made-up as to be a health-hazard to asthmatics. She was in her late thirties, smartly dressed, and looking as if she regarded staying in as just as much a challenge to her desirability as going out.

'I'm looking for Mr Pemberton –'

'Rory?' The woman was genuinely surprised. 'Good heavens, he hasn't lived here for ages.'

'I'm sorry – I'm obviously very out-of-date,' said Matt, casually friendly. 'Did he leave a forwarding address when he moved?'

'Oh, I know where he lives. I didn't buy this from him or anything, it was part of the share-out. I'm his wife – ex, anyway.'

'I see. I need to talk to him – I knew him as a child. Does he still live in Leeds?'

'Near Bingley. *Very* nice place for him and his current, if they're still together. One thing I'll say about Rory, he always does well for himself. He really understands money.' There had been a footstep behind her, and a saturnine young man's head appeared behind her shoulder. 'Wouldn't you agree, darling?'

'A prat who money clings to,' said the young man. 'Why are we talking about Rory?'

'It's this man who wants to talk to him.'

'Best of luck. You'll find five minutes will exhaust your interest. Why don't you give him the address, Nita? Rory's never asked us to make a secret of it.'

'I suppose not,' said Nita Pemberton, if that was what she called herself now. 'Well, it's 27 Chalcott Rise, just off the Saltaire to Bingley Road – the A650. A *very* nice neighbourhood.'

'Well, if Rory's got nice neighbours, they've struck unlucky,' said the young man, disappearing into the bowels of the house.

Nita raised her eyebrows in a look of complicity at Matt that said she had not chosen her current companion for his brain.

'I didn't say he had nice neighbours,' she said with a sigh, 'only that it's a nice neighbourhood. Quite a different matter.' Matt nodded, thinking of the Cazalets. 'Knowing Rory he'll hardly know they're there, and they'll hardly know he's there. All they'll know of him will be the click of bottles being put in the bin, and the sound of whatever gas-guzzling car he's currently driving.'

'Well, thank you for the address,' said Matt. 'I'll pay him a call when I can.'

'Make it when he's sober,' said the woman. 'Otherwise he'll meander on about babies and God knows what. You won't get any sense out of him.'

But when Matt had piled the children into the car, and was listening to their excited chatter – their determination to bring their mother there, their speculation as to whether she would let them keep a bird, species undecided – he wondered whether the best thing to do was to visit Rory Pemberton when he was likely to be half-seas over.

# CHAPTER 9

# The Social Round

The more Matt thought about it, the better he liked the idea of catching Rory Pemberton when he was drunk. Drunkenness, as he knew from his footballing days, could take many forms, from quarrelsomeness to unreasoning happiness, from surliness to unquenchable (and usually very tedious) garrulousness. It sounded from Rory's ex-wife as if his took the form of a maudlin raking-over of his past. In any case, if it didn't work out he could try him again when he was sober. He might not even remember that they'd had a previous conversation. Did he get drunk in pubs and winebars, Matt wondered? Or was he a solid, determined home-by-himself drinker? Either way, Matt fixed on the following Friday to conduct the experiment.

The next morning an aerogramme from Aileen made it clear she would not be getting back in the immediate future.

'Pity,' said Matt to the children at breakfast. 'I was hoping to hold a little drinks party here so she could meet the locals.'

'You haven't met several of them yourself,' Isabella pointed out. 'We've met more of them than you have.

Why don't you hold a party anyway, and I'll do the catering.'

'Do you mean you'll buy in some nibbles?' asked Matt.

'No I don't. I mean I shall provide some delicious and unusual canapés and scrumptious biscuity snacks, all free except for the cost of the ingredients.'

Isabella had emerged from her wanting to be a vet phase and gone into a great cook (or possibly smart caterer) phase. These were phases not of the moon but of the television schedules, and she could next be expected to go through an interior decorator phase, or possibly a costume designer for glossy televisualizations of the classic novels phase. Catch her while she can be useful, Matt thought.

'You're on,' he said. 'What about Thursday evening, six till eight?'

'If you're going to have people in, I'm going to Jack Quinton's,' announced Stephen.

'Who's Jack Quinton?' Matt asked.

'He's my friend round here,' Stephen said, pleased to have one, while the others had failed to find anyone of their own ages. Matt was not worried about this. Isabella and Lewis would find friends, or else just keep up with the ones they had at school in Pudsey. They were naturally gregarious children – unlike, he suspected, Rory Pemberton, and perhaps Eddie Armitage. But perhaps he shouldn't compare children of today with children of that earlier age. Perhaps childhood had changed in those thirty years.

Before driving to work Matt popped along to Delphine Maylie in Ashdene, who looked rather put-out to be caught in her early-morning deshabille (and she did indeed look rather like a peeling wall). However

103

she co-operated enthusiastically in putting together a list of everyone who lived in the eight houses of the two terraces. Delphine predicted who would jump at the invitation and who would fail to turn up, and in the event she proved one hundred per cent accurate. Matt printed out at work some fairly informal invitations and Lewis went along delivering them after school.

The price Matt had to pay to Isabella was a visit to Leeds Market, where he cringed in the background as she demanded to taste all sorts of meats and cheeses at the speciality stalls, and a trip to Sainsbury's at Greengates that included a quick dart into Homebase to buy the most exotic house plant they had, which was clearly of the dead-within-a-fortnight variety but pretty and brilliant while it lasted. Matt had to admit on Thursday, when at last Isabella allowed him to sample them, that the nibbles were indeed tasty and adventurous, and beautifully set out. He had thought of economizing on the drinks, but eventually bought rather good wines, and plenty of gin, sherry and vodka. I am trying to butter them up, after all, he said to himself. Certainly when people started arriving they were appreciative, and they mingled well since they nearly all knew one another. He had added to the guest-list Charlie and Felicity, and Carl Farson who had sold him the house, on the pretext of letting him have a look at what had been done to it. Farson was friendly on the phone, but said he would only be able to pop in briefly. Matt was interested to note when the Peaces arrived that everyone seemed to know who Charlie was.

He was on less certain ground in relation to many of his guests. Several of them realized this, and made haste to identify themselves.

'Jason Morley-Coombs,' said a young man with gleaming slicked-over hair and smooth unguent-massaged face making Matt think he must be a sucker for all those television advertisements that confused masculinity with delicious smells. 'Hello!' the man said, holding out a soft hand as he breezed in from the hall-way. 'We haven't met. I live in Dell View. And this is the lady-friend.'

'Hello,' said the lady-friend, giving the impression that anything beyond that would be regarded as an intellectual challenge.

'I'm Matthew Harper,' Matt said, shaking her hand and waiting for her to give herself a name. She shook the hand and smiled. Giving herself a name was pre-sumably unduly assertive.

'You used to be in football they say,' said Jason, accepting a glass of wine from Isabella. 'Wise career move. Lots of money there, eh, old chap?'

Matt screwed up his face.

'At the very top,' he said. 'A big difference between the top and the not-quite-top. And a big difference between then and now. Ten, twelve years ago, when I was – well, not in my prime, but –'

'Point taken, old chap,' interrupted Jason. 'But you must have hung up your boots pretty young. I've been hearing your voice on the old car radio for a fair while now. Why cut off the flow of golden guineas?'

'I was out of the game through injury too often,' said Matt. 'The story of present-day British sport. More like a bumper episode of *Casualty* than *Chariots of Fire*.'

'Still –'

'It's the only body I've got,' insisted Matt. 'I got out while it was still in reasonable functioning order. What do you do?'

'Solicitor, I'm afraid. Frightfully dull, and none of the prestige it used to have. I've just joined the family firm in Armley. Dad put me on to these houses – thought they were a good buy. He knows Armley and Bramley like the back of his hand. He's acted for people in every square yard of them.'

'Really?' said Matt, a twinge of interest pricking him for the first time in the conversation. 'Anything notable around here?'

'Oh Lord, I wasn't really listening when he told me, old chap. Dad tends to go on and on about the old days. A car accident case – a pile-up on the M1. Case doesn't seem to have got very far, but knowing Dad he screwed some money out of someone. And an industrial accident one – Dad was a pioneer in that sort of case, so he's much in demand these days. Seems to have got the family the means to buy one of these houses.'

'Really?'

'But that was a while after the time you're interested in,' said Jason. He shot Matt a look. 'I do listen to the radio, like I said, in intervals of bending the odd ear to my clients' woes. If I had anything of interest on your dead baby case I'd have told you – and if I get anything of interest in future I'll bring it straight to you. Rely on me, old chap.'

Matt thanked him and moved away, thinking he'd been 'old-chapped' enough. The father might just be worth getting reminiscences out of, though. He saw Charlie and Felicity talking to Delphine and Garrett Maylie, with Delphine looking enthusiastically multi-racial, and he decided to leave them to it. Anything of interest would be passed on. He looked around the big dining room and, reluctantly, decided to bite the bullet. Pausing only to refill his glass, he wandered over to where the Cazalets were talking to a couple who earlier had introduced themselves as the Quintons. He, Matt had gathered, was in property. The conversation seemed to be about environmental matters, but that was deceptive: it was really about property values.

'The *moment* you take out the original windows,' Mr Cazalet was hissing, 'it's not just your house that loses value, it's everyone's around you too.'

'It's a loophole in the law,' said Mr Quinton darkly. 'The Council has no power to stop it.'

'Not that they're any use when they do have powers,' said Cazalet. 'Look at some of the garages that have been put up overnight with not a word said. This is a conservation area! It's supposed to be only stone or artificial stone. Diabolical!'

They parted to let Matt join them. Mrs Cazalet was a watery-eyed scrap of endemic disapproval, looking down at her glass of orange juice as if meditating darkly on what artificial additives it contained. The Quintons were slightly more interesting – assertive, inquisitive and energetic.

'I think our Stephen knows your son Jack,' said Matt.

'That's right – he's been round several times. I gather he's – he's your partner's son – is that right?'

'Quite right,' said Matt

'It's awfully nice of you to invite us all,' said Mrs Quinton. 'Such a good idea. I'm sorry your partner couldn't be here.'

'I don't know when she'll be back. It seemed a pity to wait.'

'Is she doing something in connection with her work?' her husband asked, clearly drilled in inquisitorial techniques. Matt looked round to see where Isabella was.

'No, it's family. Private.'

He wasn't inclined to share the pros and cons of Aileen's decision to go and nurse her husband Tom with a social stranger. Nor, for that matter, the problems of 'being in a relationship' with a Catholic.

'Of course, of course. You seem to get on well with the children. Are all the children your partner's?'

'That's right. My marriage produced no children. In fact,' he said, in a burst of confidence-giving that he could not account for, 'my marriage was so long ago I often forget I've been married.'

'Really?' said Mrs Quinton. 'How sad!' Which meant: tell us more.

'Is it sad? I don't know. I was twenty-two at the time, and she was a rather unlikely upper-crust type I met when I was playing with Aston Villa, mostly with the Reserve team. She did a piece on the club for one of the colour supplements.'

'How long did it last?'

'About six months. She walked out saying it wasn't what she wanted. The way she said it made it sound as if she was returning something to Harrods.'

'Still, footballers have very exciting private lives, don't they?'

'Do you mean sex lives? I'm not sure I'd want to comment on that. For some footballers sex is confined to the cricket season.'

Mrs Cazalet was looking at the carpet now, as if it might be strewn with used condoms. She was probably wondering what an exciting sex life did for property values.

'But now you're in radio and television,' said Quinton heartily. 'Quite a change. Do you enjoy it?'

'Yes I do,' said Matt, unable to keep a note of surprise

out of his voice. 'A lot of it's routine, but there's a lot of interesting stuff comes up too, and of course I'm still mad about football.'

'I'm a Radio Four person myself,' said Cazalet, as if someone had asked him his religion. 'Do you just read what's on the – what do they call it? – the prompter?'

'No. Apart from news bulletins I write my own stuff, or make it up off the cuff when I'm doing a talk-in.'

'We've heard about your item on the Liza Pomfret show,' said Mrs Quinton. 'If only we'd lived here a bit longer we might have been of help.'

'It would have had to be a lot longer, I think. We're working on the theory that it happened over thirty years ago.'

'Before our time,' said Mrs Cazalet, as if to dismiss the subject.

'Yes,' muttered her husband. 'We knew Mr Farson, of course –'

'Though he kept himself to himself,' resumed his wife. 'As we do.'

'Quite. But we never knew the lady he bought the house from. So really we're no use to you at all.'

'You didn't know the Basnetts in Dell View?'

'No. Never heard the name.'

'Or the Armitages in your own house?'

'Oh no. It wasn't them we bought it off. I seem to remember there were Armitages at our church about that time though.'

'Which church is that?'

'The Methodist Church in Town Street.'

'They didn't have a boy called Eddie, did they?'

'They had a boy. Quiet type. But the boy stopped coming, and I think the parents moved away.'

'You did know them, though?'

109

'Just to greet, on Sunday morning. The congregation isn't large, you see, and wasn't then. We knew everyone, but just by sight.'

The Quintons had moved away, and Matt felt no compunction about doing the same, leaving the Cazalets keeping themselves to themselves, as they so obviously preferred. He was turning round to see if anyone he hadn't spoken to had arrived when he felt his arm touched, and he was then led away by the Goldblatts. They took him over to the other side of the room, where Isabella, if anything too hospitable, plied them with unwanted refills.

'Lovely eats,' said Mr Goldblatt, in a party voice. 'Someone has imagination.'

'And what an . . . interesting plant,' his wife said. But Isabella had lunged away at the sight of an empty glass, so she took her tone down to a more normal level and said: 'We heard you talking about the Armitages. And there was something – just a little scrap – that we have dredged up, that we were intending to tell you.'

'Don't get your hopes up,' said her husband.

'No, don't. I suppose the Cazalets didn't know about this – they're not the sort that gossip reaches –'

'Keep themselves to themselves,' said Matt with a grin.

'Yes. Isn't it incredible that so many of the English regard that as a virtue? Anyway, this is just some snippet that we remembered and thought might be of use. It came quite casually from Mr Farson's son.'

'Oh? Actually he said he'd just drop in tonight, but I haven't seen him.'

'Well, it was when he came to see us after he'd persuaded his father to go into a home. We got talking about the fact that people are living a lot longer these

110

days, but that this means more and more spend their last years as victims of Alzheimers or one of those conditions.'

'True,' said Matt in heartfelt tones. 'May I die at seventy.'

'When you're a bit older you'll probably add five to that,' said Mr Goldblatt.

'And another five when you're older still,' said his wife. 'Anyway, he said: "We're all just coming to accept it in the old. Sad but common. And mental illness isn't the disgrace it once was. The people next door in Linden Lea when my father moved here had a son who'd had a mental breakdown. They moved away and eventually left the area entirely because they couldn't stand the talk." I'm quoting from memory, of course. That would be the Armitages, wouldn't it?'

'It could be. I haven't got the chronology altogether straight yet. This is all news to me. I suppose they must have moved away at about the time Farson bought the house, or a bit later. The boy, Eddie, would still have been quite young then – perhaps still a teenager. But teenagers do have breakdowns. And eventually he committed suicide . . .'

'It's all beginning to sound like a sad little story,' said Mr Goldblatt.

'It is. Oh, there's the bell –'

But Isabella, he saw, was marching to the front door, and his way was stopped by Jason Morley-Coombs, his bimbo-who-dared-not-speak-her-name in tow, both of them looking as if they'd taken advantage of every refill Isabella had proffered in their direction. Jason's walk had developed a slight stumble, and as he waylaid Matt his speech had a definite slur.

'I shay, I've jusht thought of shomething, old chap.'

111

'Excellent,' said Matt.

'I do know shomeone – well, barely know him, jusht to nod to – shomeone who ushed to live in these houses.'

'Really?'

'Name of Rory Pemberton. My Dad ushed to be his solicitor, before he made the big time. Still ushesh him now and then on local mattersh. One of the original whizz-kid yuppiesh in the City, got the drink habit along with the eighteen-hour working day. Came back up here with hish loot, and still cleansh up nichly on anything going, know what I mean? Wish I had hish eye for a sure-fire quick profit. Now Rory Pemberton –'

'I know of Pemberton,' said Matt, trying to avoid a long session of learning what he already knew. 'Used to live in Ashdene.'

'Did he? Only know he ushed to live here somewhere – Dad told me, of coursh. Well, I bet I could get hish addresh for you.'

'It's 27 Chalcott Rise, just off the A650, this side of Bingley.'

'Oh I shay old chap, you *have* been the great detective, haven't you? And they tell me that our dark-skinned friend over there is your tame policeman –'

'If you'll excuse me,' Matt said, and made his escape towards the front door, where Isabella was just bringing through someone he recognised from their brief encounter at the estate agent's as Carl Farson. He was pushing sixty, his hair silvering nicely, with an air of authority about him. Matt dimly remembered being told he was manager of a big supermarket, one of a chain.

'Hello,' said Matt, holding out his hand. 'Good of you to come.'

'A pleasure. This house seems to have become quite famous locally in the last couple of weeks. It's certainly looking sprucer and more lived in.'

'Didn't it seem lived in when your dad was here?'

'Not really. It was as if he was camping out. He had no one to make it into a home for him.'

'Can Isabella get you a drink?'

'I've already ordered a small martini.'

'I expect you know most of the people here.'

'Some of them,' he said, looking cautiously round as if there were some he was happy to meet again, some not.

'Actually your name has already come up tonight,' said Matt.

'Oh?'

'The Goldblatts told me that you'd mentioned the Armitages to them – the son's mental problems.'

'I believe I did. Nice people – the Goldblatts I mean. The Armitages too, actually . . . I imagine this is in connection with the baby business, isn't it?'

'Yes. I suppose the police have been on to you.'

'They have – the chap over there, in fact. And the *West Yorkshire Chronicle* as well. But there really wasn't anything I could tell them. And if the year 1969 is right, that was years before I knew the Armitages.'

'That doesn't mean the dead baby and the mental illness weren't connected.'

That seemed to be a new idea to him.

'No-o-o. Well, it was when Dad moved here that I got to know them slightly. Dad was still working – you worked till you were sixty-five then, none of this early retirement – and I and my sister did most of the organizing for him. The Armitages were next door in Linden Lea, and they kept a key to this place, to let in gas men,

113

electricity men, and so on. I never saw the son: he was in a mental hospital – they told me that in hushed voices.'

Matt nodded. This was something he remembered himself. Mental illness, like babies born out of wedlock, was unmentionable in some households.

'You got the impression they were somehow ashamed of his mental problems?'

'Well, that was the way I accounted for their attitude. Don't get me wrong: I wasn't particularly interested, and didn't think about it much, but they told me at one point they were intending to put their house on the market, and I decided they regarded such things as somehow shameful – perhaps a mark of their own lack of success as parents – and they wanted to move further away, to somewhere where they weren't known.'

'They didn't give any other reason?'

'Well, they said their son hated these houses. It didn't seem very likely, a lad of eighteen or so . . .' He pulled himself up. 'But I suppose, knowing what we now know –'

'It could just be the truth.'

Carl Farson nodded his head in agreement. Soon after that he slipped away from the party.

Talking to Charlie and Felicity when all the other guests had farewelled and slipped into the evening, Matt said:

'I'd like to know all you've got on Eddie Armitage. Dates of his suicide, details of the inquest, any relative living at the time – just anything at all.'

'Charlie will get them for you,' Felicity assured him. Charlie raised a humorous eyebrow.

'You can take the word of my chief superintendent,' he said.

# CHAPTER 10

# Half Seas Over

Matt did his usual thing and left his car some way away from Rory Pemberton's desirable residence. Thinking it over, and remembering that this was the second time in a few days that he had done that, he would have justified it by saying that his Volvo was old, a machine for transporting children and dog, and that if the residents of the two habitations in question had looked out of their windows they would have decided in advance that its driver was not worth talking to. He was conscious of being in the sort of area where people might do just that.

The houses on Chalcott Rise (which did actually rise) had been built, judging by appearances, for the at least comfortably well-heeled. Like the Otley Road house they were thirties-spacious, with similar gently-curved bows and fresh-painted white plaster. Presumably it was a style Pemberton felt at home in – more airy, more cosmopolitan, than the grimmer air of the stone terraces in Houghton Avenue. The garden, when he got to number 27, was custom-gardened – everything cut back neatly, everything in place, with wood-chippings to keep down the weeds. Already, before he got to the gate, he could hear loud orchestral music through an

115

open downstairs window. He was no expert, but he thought it was the 'Ride of the Valkyries'.

'Turn down that fucking music for chrissake!'

It was a female voice from inside the house – Rory's current discontented bimbo presumably. By the time Matt got to the front door the music had changed to something he dimly remembered to be the music for a big film about space. Presumably this was a CD of classic hits from the silver screen, or in other words loud music you'll just about recognize. It hadn't been turned down.

He rang the bell. The music continued blaring. Nobody came to the door. He rang again, keeping his thumb on the button for five seconds or so. The music thundered on, but this time he heard the voice again, yelling over the din:

'Are you going to fucking answer that? It won't be for me.'

Seconds later footsteps could be heard down the hall, and a chain being taken off the door.

'Yes?'

The man who opened the door was forty-ish, plump to the point of fatness, with red, puffy cheeks and bleary eyes. He had in his hand a tumbler full of brown, nearly dark brown liquid, and he smelled like a distillery.

'Hello. Mr Pemberton?' The pouchy cheeks wobbled as the man nodded. 'My name is Matthew Harper. We knew each other as children.' This was met with a blank stare. 'There's a small matter I'd like to have a chat about, if you could spare the time.' The small matter being a dead baby, Matt thought.

The man's eyes blinked wetly. Matt thought it was touch and go whether he said 'Get lost' or invited him in. After a few seconds he stood uncertainly aside and said thickly: 'Come in.'

He led the way down the tall-piled carpet of the hallway, then into a large, plumply-furnished room, where the music was still scaling the hemisphere from an ostentatious unit on the far wall. Rory went straight over to the drinks cupboard, looked at his own glass and seemed rather puzzled that it didn't need a refill, then remembered he had a guest.

'Want a drink?'

'Thank you. I'd like a beer.'

'Plenty of Scotch.'

'Better not, I'm driving.'

'Fucking police! . . . Er, what was it?'

'Beer please.'

Thought, for Rory Pemberton, was a matter of intense and visible concentration. When it was over he pulled at a door, selected a can, then poured it uncertainly into a glass. As he did so the door behind Matt swung open, a hard-faced young woman marched in and over to the stereo unit, turned off the music, then marched out again. Rory at first seemed uncertain what had happened, then inclined to protest, then registered it was too late. He shrugged, and gestured Matt towards the glass. Probably he thought it would be better for the carpet if Matt went over and got it, and Matt agreed.

By now Rory seemed uncertain as to why he was there, or if there was any reason why he had invited him in.

'Like I said,' Matt began as if they were in the middle of a conversation, 'we used to know each other.' Not surprisingly there was no recognition. Rory just blinked, which he did a lot. 'I used to come and play five-a-side football one summer with you children in Houghton Avenue.'

Rory thought heavily.

117

'Used to enjoy football,' he eventually said thickly. 'Used to play it every school holiday. We never took to cricket.'

'That's right. It was the summer holiday when I came up and played five-a-side. The summer of 1969.'

He looked for a reaction in Rory's face. At first it was totally blank, then the tiniest suspicion of a frown came into the centre of the forehead. It stayed there for a second or two, then the face went blank again and he raised his glass.

'Cheers,' he said. Matt resumed the burden of the discussion.

'I used to come up the gill from Grenville Street, where I was staying with my auntie. I played with your group over several weeks. There was Peter Basnett – I'm sure you remember him: he was rather my protector, because I was a lot younger than all of you. And there was Marjie Humbleton – she was very kind too. And I remember at least once going into your kitchen and eating you out of house and home, or at least of ice-cream in your freezer.'

He had been afraid he had been chattering on to the human equivalent of a blank wall, but the last reminiscence seemed to arouse a memory or strike a chord in the dull consciousness of the man.

'Little scrap of a thing, with a common accent,' Rory Pemberton said, almost clearly.

'That's right.'

'What was the accent? London?'

'That's right, cockney.'

'What happened to it? You move up-market?'

'We moved, away.'

'You could play. You could play football. You were fast and you were incred . . . incredibly accurate.'

'Thanks.'

'They welcomed you in because you were so good.' His attitude puzzled Matt. This was beginning to sound less like praise than an arraignment, a recital of charges by a prosecuting counsel. 'You just barged in and became a member of the gang, and nobody minded that you spoke like a prole.'

'I was only seven. I suppose I didn't know all the initiation procedures,' said Matt, thinking apology was the best option. Rory considered this heavily, then downed his glass and got up for a refill. In the silence Matt heard luggage bumping against the stair-rail, and then the front door closing. He wondered whether this was one more woman walking out on Rory.

'I'm not surprised you remember the ice-cream,' said Rory, coming back and sitting opposite Matt, speaking with a sort of complacency. 'They all came for our ice-cream.' Then the mood darkened again. 'Fucking better than *their* parents ever bought. Everyone knew it . . . *Fucking spongers.*'

'I expect we were,' said Matt. That seemed to ignite a small spark of anger.

'Listen to him! We! Some little tyke from the Old Kent Road barges in and then it's "we"! Makes me puke. I was never "we". I was cheaper than the ice-cream van, that's all I was.' Inside, Matt was torn between laughing at the maudlin self-pity of the man and admiring the surprising accuracy of his assessment. 'I never had any friends. Still don't. That was Vara walking out on me just now.'

'I expect she'll be back.'

Rory shook his head, apparently not greatly concerned.

'No she won't. She gave me a warning. Said she'd

leave me if I didn't get a grip on things . . . Who *wants*
to get a grip on things, for chrissake?' He looked around
the plush living room – conspicuously, almost distaste-
fully proclaiming a good income. 'Does it *look* as if I
can't make a living? Drinking doesn't stop me knowing
where to put my money, I can tell you. If I was as
hopeless as *she* says I am I'd be in some crappy doss-
house begging for pennies on the street . . . I can do
without her. I can do without anybody. I've never
needed friends.' He looked at Matt fiercely. 'Some
people can do without friends.'

People like Ghengis Khan and Count Dracula,
thought Matt. But Rory Pemberton was not in that class.
He wasn't even in the Andrew Lloyd Webber class. Matt
felt he'd never met anybody more in need of friends.

'Other people resent you if you've got money. They
think you're trying to buy them. I wasn't trying to buy
them! But they never wanted me for myself . . . Even
Lily Marsden never liked me.'

'I know Lily,' said Matt. 'She still lives in Bramley.'

His face showed – or perhaps pretended – that that
was news to him.

'Christ, does she? You'd have thought she'd have got
away from that dump. She always had her eye on the
main chance, did Lily. I admired her for that.'

'But it never brought you together?'

He blinked, and a petulant expression took over his
face.

'I didn't say that. I said she never *liked* me . . . And
anyway she was never willing to *share* . . . She never
introduced me to her friend.'

'Oh? Who was that?'

'I told you, Thickie, she never introduced me. Said
the friend wouldn't be interested. You can imagine how

good that made me feel. That was typical. She kept all the good things to herself. Just *used* people.'

'Yes, I think she's still like that,' said Matt. 'Where did the friend live?'

'Down those streets at the bottom of the gill. Can't have been *much*, living there . . . That's where you came up from, didn't you say?'

'That's right.'

'Well, you've pulled yourself up, haven't you?'

'I suppose I have,' said Matt, rather glad that the aggressiveness he had cultivated in his footballing days had long ago left him. 'Do you remember which of the streets Lily's friend lived in?'

'Oh, for chrissake, it's thirty years ago! Thirty bloody years! . . . Anyway, it's not something anybody'd want to remember.'

'Isn't it? I don't think I'm understanding.'

But Rory Pemberton didn't reply. He smiled down into his remaining whisky, then just got up and went over to the bar, refilling generously.

'Don't have to watch it now I'm on my own,' he said, almost as if talking to himself. Matt was doubtful whether watching it had ever had any effect on his intake. He was doubtful too whether he had any idea who he was talking to, but he was glad when, having weaved across the room and sat down carefully, almost like an old man, in his bloated armchair, he said:

'Lily Marsden.' His voice seemed to come as if from some ancient, distant telephone line.

'What sort of relationship *did* you have with her?' Matt asked. The question seemed to puzzle him, and required cogitation.

'No different from any of the others. Except that we neither of us were liked. It was *them* I wanted to be part

121

of. She never wanted that. She teased them . . . Not *teased* exactly. Not in a nice way. But she knew she wasn't liked, and she . . . dangled things in front of them.'

'Things? What do you mean? She wasn't any better off than the others, was she?'

'Not *things* like that. Not material posh . . . possessions. Why do people always sneer at material . . . *things*, eh? Eh? I've always loved material . . .' His voice faded.

'But what did Lily dangle before the others?'

'What did Lily dangle? Sounds like a dirty joke . . . *Who*?'

'Lily Marsden. Who you used to play with as a child. You said she used to dangle things in front of you all.'

'She did . . . We thought she was terrible. We thought she used to take her clothes off for money. Weren't we naive? It seems like another world. These days all we boys would be having it off with her. These days girls of her age are on the streets of Bradford and Leeds, all organized, and with their own pimps. I've . . .'

But Matt didn't want to hear about his personal delinquencies.

'Do you think she did take her clothes off for money?'

'Don't know. It's what we thought. I expect she wanted us to think that . . . But then she came up with this other thing. And of course we were horrified . . . At first.'

He was going off into a hazed, dazed, drunken mood of reminiscence, but there was about his face, pouched and bloated as it was, the wisp of an expression of horror and fear.

'But only at first?' Matt pressed him. But he wasn't

122

going to be pressed. The expression never left his face, and it was a long time before he spoke again.

'The thing, lying there.'

Matt had to suppress his irritation at the abundance of 'things' in the drunken man's thoughts.

'The thing?'

'*Not* a thing!' he said abruptly, almost angrily. 'The baby. Lying by the balustrade. Almost as if it was asleep.'

'But it wasn't.'

'It was like it was laid out. You couldn't see the wound on the back of its head. Her head. It just had a few scraps of clothing on – it was a hot day. And someone had wrapped it in a shawl, and it lay there like it was on a bed. Like it was just asleep. That's how I remember it.' There was pain on his face as his voice faded into silence.

'And how did it get there?'

Pemberton looked ahead. The expression, as the memory faded, lost its horror, and became merely glazed, as it had come and then faded perhaps a thousand times in his life.

'*How* had it got there?' Matt asked urgently.

The eyes closed, then suddenly the heavy body fell forwards, the drink falling out of his hand and spilling over the chair and carpet. Matt darted forward to retrieve the glass, and realized that the chair had several stains on it, all but the new one dried out. Looking around he realized there were other stains on the beige carpet, as if a puppy was being trained. But it wasn't a puppyish sort of household. Rory Pemberton, clearly, made a habit of drinking himself into insensibility.

Matt stood there, wondering what to do. First he took the glass out to the kitchen, where the detritus of several day's glasses and plates testified to Rory's

123

woman's growing dissatisfaction. Matt sympathized with her obvious determination not to spend her life cleaning up after her man. When he went back into the living room Rory was still slumped forward in his chair. Matt considered moving him to the sofa, but decided his weight would make that more trouble than it was worth. In the end he just straightened him so he slept upright in his chair, then he left the room with the lights still on. Pemberton would wake up as he was used to waking up. The fact that he no longer had a woman would worry him much less than if he no longer had a bottle.

In the hall Matt paused for a moment. Was it worth making a brief search of the rest of the house? A moment's thought told him that it was not. The study, if there was one, would contain details of his latest financial coup, not the doings of a gang of children thirty years ago. The only record of those doings in this house was in the troubled brain of the unlikeable man slumped in his wet chair in the plush living room.

Matt let himself out into the twilight.

The next day he spoke to Charlie. He was at home, having a rare weekend off, and baby noises of pleasure and grievance marked his side of the conversation. At the end of Matt's account of his evening at Bingley, Charlie thought for a moment or two.

'Right. I think I've absorbed all that. Let's get a few things straight. This Pemberton mentioned a baby, and described it lying dead by a balustrade.'

'I don't think the word "dead" was used. He said it lay there as if it was asleep.'

'Right. And you didn't get out of him how it came to be there, or whether he was responsible.'

'No. He keeled over at that point.'

'Right. He sounds like my idea of a nightmare witness. But he did call the baby "she"?'

'Yes, definitely.'

Charlie thought for a moment. Clearly he was uncertain how important the new information was – if, indeed, it was information at all.

'And throughout this conversation the man was drunk.'

'Oh yes, no question.'

'That doesn't help, of course.'

'No, I suppose not.'

'He can say he remembers nothing about it, that he was just talking nonsense. That's what plenty of drunks do. We couldn't pin him down on things said in his cups.'

'I'm afraid you'd have to get there very early in the morning to find him sober, and then he'd be ferociously hung-over.'

'If necessary we could try doing that. He might benefit from a couple of hours in the cells.'

'You think that's possible?'

He could feel Charlie shaking his head in doubt.

'I just don't know. I have to justify every hour I spend on this case. It's getting old and stale.'

'It always was.'

'Ah yes, but three weeks with no great progress makes it doubly so. If there'd been a stink at the time, with relatives who were still around to kick up a fuss, then there might be some slight urgency, or some pretence of it. But a dead baby who nobody even knew was missing? Forget it.'

'It seems a pretty funny attitude for a police force,' said Matt caustically.

'Tell me about it. But there you are. It's pretty sure

to be the baby of some kind of transient population, so we only put up a show of being interested.'

'What exactly would you class as transient population?'

'Oh, travellers, tramps, rough-sleepers, squatters.'

'Ah,' said Matt.

# CHAPTER 11

# Nightpiece

Matt's talk with Charlie was snatched from a busy day with the children. Aileen had insisted that the children keep up their churchgoing while she was away, so Matt liked to give them plenty to occupy their bodies and minds on a Saturday. Saturdays during the soccer season were always taken up for him, but now that it was limping to its close he often got them off: his cricket commentaries were not highly regarded by connoisseurs.

Sundays were a bit of a burden to Matt, sitting through the Catholic Mass, which he thought a decidedly rum affair, so that on Saturdays he organized things that all four of them would enjoy: on this one a long walk for Beckham in The Hollies, with the children playing hide-and-seek in the winding walks, and splashing in the fast-running streams; then a long-promised trip to the Royal Armouries, and then – after the hurried phone-call to Charlie – a supper of shepherd's pie followed by jam sponge and ice-cream out of the freezer. The schedule worked to perfection. All the children, even Isabella, were in bed by half past nine.

Matt was tired too, but his head was buzzing. He poured himself a stiff whisky and soda, and when that was gone was on the point of pouring himself a second one when he thought of Rory Pemberton and put the stopper back in the bottle. He sat back in his favourite easy chair and remembered something that had happened that morning on the way to The Hollies. He had stopped the car at the newsagent's just by Amen Corner and the path to the Kirkstall Power Station. He had put his hand on the door handle to get out and buy his morning paper when something stopped him.

On the grass patch beside the newsagency two children were playing, tots of about five or six, one white, one black. And coming out of the door of the little shop was the woman people now knew as Lily Fitch. She turned in the direction of the children, and as she passed them he saw the hand that was not holding a paper give a quick and vicious clip across the ear to the black child. He waited, watching the disappearing woman and the bawling tot.

'She hit that little boy,' said Isabella indignantly.

'I know,' said Matt. Lily was now well away, and he went to fetch his *Guardian*. When he got back to the car he saw that the incident had aroused memories in Aileen's daughter. Until they got to The Hollies she was very thoughtful.

He slept well that night, at first. But when he woke, not long after four, he soon gave up the idea of going back off. His head was a jumble of new ideas, and of memories. Harry Sugden had mentioned squatters, but then it hadn't rung any bell. For some reason Charlie's mention of them had not only connected up with Harry's, but had also triggered memories.

Only they hadn't called them squatters. They'd called

them hippies. Or occasionally, with heavy childish sat-
ire, flower people. The pair had been as good as street
entertainers for the children in Houghton Avenue.

'Hip-hip-hippy! Here come the hippies!' shouted Rory
Pemberton.

'Here come the dippy hippies!' shouted Sophie
Basnett.

'Here come the pot-smokers, high on cannabis!' said
Colin, whose school-teacher parents had educated him
about drugs.

The children were coming up from the field beside
the Kirkstall Power Station, a large area that could be
used not just for football, but for anything else they
cared to play. They'd all decided to go to Matt's Auntie
Hettie's house, knowing she would be pulling pints at
The Unicorn. Matt had been worried that there would
be nothing much in the pantry, but Marjie had con-
siderately bought a large bottle of Coke at the grocer's,
and a bottle of orange squash as well. Some of the
children drank squash because their parents told them
Coca Cola was bad for them; some of them drank Coca
Cola for the same reason.

'Dope-heads!' shouted Harry Sugden.

'Fucking flower-people,' bawled Lily Marsden, who
swore.

'Pot-smokers,' said Eddie Armitage, under his breath.

They were certainly different. He wore a crotch-
length smock, over baggy oriental-style trousers. Her
dress was down to her calves, in similar thin, almost
diaphanous material of a muddy colour. On good days,
and this was one of them, she really did wear flowers
in her hair. The children called him Dippy and her
Flowery Fay, which was their version of a word Colin's

129

grandparents had used about her when they had passed the couple in the car. 'She's fey,' they had said. She did indeed have a sort of distant, elfin charm, and was nearly-pretty, though in a style that no one would have recognised in the strident sixties.

The hippies were wandering back home from the grocer's (where *to*? wondered the grown-up Matt. *Where* was home?) The children had caught up with them, and chanted at them as they dogged their footsteps, quite unafraid of them. Weren't hippies dedicated to peace and love? Nothing to fear from *them*! Peter and Marjie hung back, and so did Caroline. Eddie Armitage only joined in half-heartedly. Matt had a clear picture of him now, and a fairly clear impression of what he was like. Physically he was short for his age, and slight, and he wore hand-knitted Fair Isle jumpers and short trousers. He gave the impression of being only half-formed. He never quite seemed to know what he should be doing. He wanted to be part of the group, yet something held him back. Just like Rory Pemberton, in fact, but nicer.

The pair were just about to turn off from Raynville Road (turn off *where*? into which street?) when the man they called Dippy seemed to take a sudden resolution and turned to face them. The two knots of children stopped immediately. The adult Matt, remembering, felt a kind of fear, mirroring the child Matt's fear, though he was in the hindmost group with Peter and Marjie. The man's hair was fair, almost white – the adult Matt realized it must have been bleached – and his eyebrows were bleached too, but not the eyelashes. A wispy brown beard was forming on his chin, under a small mouth, and the eyes were a queer colour which Matt had never seen before, and seldom since: a sort of violet, almost as if he'd dyed those too. The adult Matt decided that they were scary, but only because they were the sort of people he as a child had never seen before. He had never come across hippy squatters in Bermondsey. Probably they weren't common even in Leeds. Children, particularly young children, only feel safe with the known.

'Is something troubling you?'

The voice was soft, nerveless. The children swallowed. They had not been expecting to be called upon to speak, answer questions. Only Lily could summon up a reply.

'No,' she said. But she said it aggressively.

'Then why are you following us, and shouting?'

'Because you're hop-heads,' sneered Harry Sugden, his courage returning.

'Do you know what hop-heads are?' asked the young man, still quietly.

'Druggies. Dope-takers.'

'They use opium. Hop is opium. We don't use opium.'

'Bet you smoke cannabis,' shouted Colin.

'Now and again. It's very pleasant, and a lot less harmful than the nicotine most of your dads kill themselves with.'

'My dad doesn't smoke,' said Rory Pemberton, but the others just looked disbelieving.

'So why don't you go about your business, eh? And let us get on with ours?'

He looked at them silently for a moment, then turned back to Flowery Fay. They crossed the road, then went up one of the small roads that branched off from the Raynville Road (*which* one did they go up? Matt still could not work that out). The children stood there, silent, bewildered by their novel experience. Then Lily and Rory started them off trouping behind the two outré figures – well behind this time. They were only at the junction of the two roads when the pair turned into the gate of a house rather larger than the other narrow Victorian two-storey ones. The children could hear a baby crying, and when the front door of the house was opened the cries became louder. Lily looked round, and then began to lead them up the street. She stopped after a few yards, and they all stopped behind her. Flowery Fay had come out through the open door and began to walk up and down the little scrap of front garden, a baby in her arms. It was crying lustily, and the mother was rocking it in her arms and speaking low, crooning comfort to it.

'Come on,' said Peter. 'Let's go up to Matt's auntie's.'

When they arrived none of the other children said anything about the restricted space or the general air of near-poverty, though Lily Marsden looked around her with a twist of her lip and an air of contempt. Marjie opened bottles and found some glasses, but her chattering on to Matt only emphasized the quietness of the rest: they had had an experience that they were having trouble in absorbing. It was in fact Matt who broke the taboo on the subject.

'I was frightened,' he announced.

'You didn't need to be,' said Marjie calmly. 'They're just a bit out of the ordinary, that's all.'

'He was talking nonsense about drugs,' said Colin, the expert. 'If you smoke pot you go on to take other things. My Mum and Dad know all about that.'

'Just smoking pot is bad,' said Caroline (Matt still had difficulty getting Caroline's face in focus). 'Look how they went out and left the little baby all on its own.'

'They've got to do shopping,' said Eddie.

Caroline wasn't having any of it. She loved babies.

'Why couldn't one go shopping and the other stay at home? Or why couldn't they take it with them? Other mothers do.'

'They don't do what other people do,' said Peter.

'They probably don't *shop* anyway,' said Rory. 'They *shoplift*. They don't hold with money, the hippies and the flower-people. That means they bludge off other people.'

'You don't know they shoplifted,' said Peter. 'I expect the shopkeeper kept a pretty close eye on them. If you want to shoplift you do best to look like everyone else.'

Matt absorbed this piece of wisdom, and wondered how he knew.

'She looked like a good mother to me,' said Marjie. 'Rocking the baby and talking to it. A lot of mothers think it's best to leave a baby to cry for a bit, but not her.'

'How can she look after her baby when half the time she'll be stoned out of her mind?' demanded Colin self-righteously. 'And he'll be no better.'

'At least they're both with the baby most of the time,' said Peter. 'Not many children have that.'

'That's because they're living on the dole, and in a house that they've stolen,' said Rory.

'You shouldn't be sticking up for them,' said Sophie to her brother. 'They're scum. Just scum.'

'They shouldn't be allowed to breed,' said Lily Marsden.

Lying in bed, thinking it over, remembering, Matt pinpointed in his mind the oddity of the last remark. Children never talked in terms of people *breeding*. Dogs and cats, yes, but human beings? They 'had babies' or 'had children'. They didn't breed. That was a word that Lily had been taught by someone else. Who could have taught her that? What kind of person? Someone who liked swimming against the tide, who enjoyed toying with outrageous opinions . . .

Matt shifted his position in the bed, and as he did so he heard the stairs creak. One of the children going down for something to eat. Matt never remembered getting hungry in the night, but that was probably due to his playing football all the free hours God sent (they played rugger at his Colchester school, which meant evenings of snatched soccer with whatever group he could find as long as the light lasted, then skimped homework before bed). Children were different now. Perhaps sneaking down for a quick snack was their young bodies' way of compensating for a more meagre breakfast than he'd had in his day. Or perhaps it was the result of a much more passive life-style.

Breeding . . . 'They shouldn't be allowed to breed' . . . Best not to make too much of it. It could be someone's casual remark that had taken root in Lily's mind, not any conscious attempt at indoctrination. Not some neo-Nazi mini-Führer taking her over; just someone whose mindset inclined in that direction. Or in the direction of nineteenth-century eugenicists, all too interested in planning for a finer race in the future. Matt knew that a lot of brains that should have judged better had flirted with that idea.

Or was it just someone bitter? For example bitter at a new generation that seemed to bypass all the hard work, the burdensome responsibilities, the sheer grind of life, that older people had shouldered and taken for granted. His father, when he heard of Matt's wage as a football pro – modest enough by present-day standards

– used to gasp and say, 'Bloody 'ell – you lot don't know you're born.' His dad had been fortunate in his Colchester job, but he knew what grind was.

Matt frowned. He should have heard the stair creak again by now, as which-ever-it-was came up with the purloined goodies. He got up to go to the lavatory, opening the door quietly and pausing on the landing. The light was on in the kitchen, and as he stood there wondering what was going on he thought he heard a sob. He forgot about his need for the loo and tiptoed downstairs, stepping to the side of the third stair down from the turn, which always creaked. On the bottom stair he looked into the lighted kitchen. Isabella was sitting at the little table-top beside the fridge and freezer, a slice of bread and jam half-eaten on a plate in front of her. Her head was in her hands, and she was sobbing into them – a soft but continuous sound that went the more directly to Matt's heart because it was so surprising.

He cleared his throat. Isabella straightened, and turned to him a blotchy, grief-stricken face that shocked him. He put his arm around her shoulders.

'What's up, darling?'

'Nothing.'

'Come on, come on. I'm not an idiot. You don't sit crying your heart out for nothing. What's happened? What's upset you?' Isabella let out a great gulp, and seemed about to burst into sobs again. Was it the bones in the attic and the emerging story of them that had upset her, Matt wondered? He knelt on the floor and took her hands in his. 'Come on – out with it. You can tell me, whatever it is.'

*'When is Mummy coming back?'*

It was the last thing Matt expected. It came upon

135

him as a blow, a criticism, an accusation. He had thought they had all three understood and accepted that.

'You know I can't say, darling. We've been over all that.'

'But what if she never comes back? Then we'll have no father or mother. What will happen to us?'

'She *is* coming back, just as soon as she can. And say something dreadful happened: you'd still have me.'

'But why should you want us? I expect you'd rather be free.'

'I don't feel as if you've got me captured. You know I love having a family.'

'But what if they wouldn't let you keep us? You're not even married to Mummy.' She looked at him wide-eyed. 'We wouldn't go and live with Granny MacIntosh! We'd rather go into a home!'

'There's no question of your going into a home. Your home is here with me – and the squirrels and the fox and the birds. I love you – and you all put up with me pretty well.'

'We love you! But why should you care about us? . . . Well, all right, you do. But we want Mummy too.'

'And you'll have her again soon. She'll be back as soon as your daddy is well.'

'Or he dies.'

'Yes, that's true. It's a very serious illness.'

'What if he does get well and Mummy decides to stop with him?'

'She won't do that. She and I are partners now.'

Isabella looked sceptical.

'She might do. We wouldn't want to go and live in

South Africa. Why did she have to go and nurse him?'

'Because there was no one else. Because your mother has a strong sense of responsibility. Because he's the father of her children – you lot.'

'Because she's a Catholic, and if you're a Catholic you're married for ever.'

'Well –'

'That's what Granny MacIntosh thinks.'

'Granny MacIntosh is –' a vision of Granny MacIntosh, hatchet-faced in confronting her daughter, whom she treated as a scarlet woman, and her lover, whom she treated as a damned soul, came into his mind, but he refrained from calling her what he usually called her to himself, a foul-minded old bigot, and simply said: '– a rather old-fashioned lady.'

'She's worse than that, and you think so too,' said Isabella.

'Well, maybe.'

'The boys don't remember Daddy,' said Isabella after a pause. 'But I do. Please don't ever send us back to him!'

Now he held her very close, her wet face against his chest, and he said: 'I won't, I won't, I won't.'

The next day he went with them to Mass at eleven, leaving a roast in the oven. Mass for Matt never got any less rum, but he noticed that Isabella was unusually serious and thoughtful. When they were back home and he was putting potatoes and carrots into the oven he heard Isabella say to her brothers.

'You don't have to believe all they say in church. The priest has to say a lot of it. I don't suppose he believes it. I'm just going to believe what I can believe.' And as he came into the sitting room she said to him: 'Isn't that right, Matt?'

That was a bit of a poser. He tried to say what Aileen would want him to say.

'I suppose that's true of all religions,' he said carefully. 'Some of it is true, and some of it is – ' he couldn't quite hit on the word he wanted, so he ended with '– fantasy.'

He wasn't sure what Aileen would think about his use of that word. He had already decided to ring her that evening and tell her about Isabella's fears, though he wasn't altogether happy about doing so. He didn't want to blackmail her into coming home, but he did very much want her home, and he did feel she should come. The children were more important than her awful husband. Later that day he rang Phil Bletchley, a colleague at Radio Leeds, at home.

'Phil. Matt here. Is there any chance of you giving me another slot on *Look North* tomorrow or Tuesday? A brief one would do.'

'Maybe,' said Phil. 'Monday's not usually crammed. Is this the business of the dead baby in the attic?'

'That's right. There've been some developments.'

'And you want us to cover them, rather than Liza Pomfret.'

'You reach a lot more people.'

'You can't stand her.'

'Is it that obvious?'

'You feel exactly as the rest of us feel. Broadcasters hating Liza is like clergymen being against sin. If they are any longer. All right, I'll make sure you have a slot tomorrow.'

'And keep quiet about it. I don't want her shrieking at me before the event.'

'You see how she gets what she wants? We're all shit-scared of her.'

138

Matt's instinct was to tell him to speak for himself, but a moment's thought made him close the mouth he had opened to protest.

Ten o'clock was Matt's usual time for ringing Aileen. By that time her husband was always asleep, and Stephen could be kept up late specially to talk to her. That Sunday he was a bit later than usual, because he wanted the children well in bed and asleep before the call took place. He knew she would be up, because she had told him that late at night was the only time she had to herself. She never gave the impression she felt at ease in rural South Africa.

'Are the children up?' Aileen asked, after the preliminaries.

'No – I've got them to bed,' said Matt in a low voice.

'Then why are you speaking like that? Anything wrong?'

'Not on the surface,' said Matt. 'Or perhaps I should say not that I'd noticed. I've been blind, I realize that now. Last night I found Isabella down in the kitchen sobbing her heart out over a slice of bread and jam.'

'Isabella! But she's always so sensible!'

Matt was glad her mother agreed with his judgment.

'She's afraid her mummy's never going to come home, afraid I won't want them, afraid they're going to have to live with Mummy and Daddy in South Africa, afraid they're going to be dumped on Granny MacIntosh in Morningside –'

'Not on your life they're not! Oh God, poor kids. Are they all thinking like that?'

'I've no evidence of it. I suspect these are all thoughts that she's been bottling up.'

'We don't *think*, do we? Don't try to see things as

they might be seeing them. Did you manage to convince her it's nonsense?'

'I quietened her. Aileen –'

'Yes?'

'I think it would help if you got paid help in for Tom and flew back, say for a week or ten days. To reassure them. They'd believe you, where they doubt me. We'd manage the cost somehow. I think they need to see and hear you, touch you.'

Aileen could be felt considering this.

'That's one possibility. But Matt, there's a better one: I think my time here may be nearly up.'

'What? Has there been a turn for the worse?'

'No, the opposite. And – but I don't want to talk about it, not in his house. Would it help if you could start giving them the hope that I'll be home soon?'

'It would, I'm sure. Especially if I could give them a time-scale.'

'That's awkward. Anything can happen, obviously. You could say at the earliest in two or three weeks' time, and anyway not too long after that. That would be better than a quick trip home, wouldn't it?'

'*Much* better. And I can just about hold out that long too.'

'What can you mean?'

'You know exactly what I mean. And Isabella's not the only one who wonders how a Catholic regards her not-even-in-name-ex husband.'

# CHAPTER 12

# The General Public

'Matt, your friend in the Constabulary rang,' called Phil Bletchley as Matt turned up for duty at mid-day on Monday. Matt poked his head round the door.

'Any message?'

'Said to ring him. And can we have a chat about your slot tonight? I wondered whether you'd like to man a phone afterwards to collect any information that comes in.'

'I would, but –' Matt felt greatly tempted, but his experience with Isabella made him wary of seeming to neglect the children. 'The thing is, it could go on for ever. I suppose it wouldn't be possible to have the children in here, would it? They're very interested in the case, naturally. The fact is, one of them's missing her mother, and I've only just realized how upset she is. I wouldn't want to leave them alone till late on.'

'Don't see why they shouldn't come in. Square it with the powers that be.'

'I will, so long as that doesn't mean you-know-who.'

'The teenage bride of Frankenstein? Not yet, thank God, not yet.'

When Matt rang Charlie he was at his most sardonic.

'We've got him in the cells, Matt. I sweated blood to get permission to follow him up – it's been a quiet weekend, thank the Lord. When we went out to Bingley to speak to him he was already well into the hair of the dog, and he got obstreperous, which I wasn't altogether upset about. It means we could bring him in, and at the moment he's cooling his heels in the cells. How *do* you cool your heels?'

'I suppose it's after you've been caught in a chase. When do you expect to talk to him?'

'Hmm – well I'm not hurrying it. You've talked to him drunk, so I'll try him sober. Sober takes time. We've got the best drying-out clinic in the world here – it beats the Betty Ford into a cocked hat.'

'Except that when you let them out they go straight to a pub.'

'Nothing's perfect. Our results may be a little short-term, but they serve our purposes.'

'How long are you going to leave him?'

'How long does it take to sober up after a life-time's soaking? By rights we ought to give him a week at least, but there are rules about these things. I'll give him another three hours or so, then see how it goes.'

'Ask him about a family of squatters living just off the Raynville Road.'

When Matt went along to talk to Phil Bletchley he stressed that he wanted to keep all his options open. Ideally he wanted to twitch all sorts of memories in the viewers, particularly people who had lived around Houghton Avenue and the Raynville Road, and then dredge them in and sort them through.

'The new information – new line of enquiry rather –' he corrected himself '– is about a pair of squatters, hippyish types, who took over a house in the vicinity

142

at the time, the summer of sixty-nine, and had a baby.'

'The baby in question?'

'Maybe,' said Matt, in a way that emphasized his desire for caution. 'But I shan't exclude anyone who just wants to talk about the houses in Houghton Avenue – the people who lived there, and particularly the children. I'd like to know what happened to them later. You have a much larger catchment area than Radio Leeds, so we could easily pick up something about one of them who has moved away, but has stayed in the North.'

'One of the children themselves, maybe?'

Matt thought.

'Somehow I doubt it. I'm getting a feeling of a vow of silence which somehow or other they've maintained. I'm also getting the feeling of some kind of outside influence.'

'What do you mean? Not witchcraft?' said Phil Bletchley feelingly. 'I can't stand another spate of witchcraft stories. Sacrificial babies along with eye of newt and toe of frog.'

'No whisper of that yet. All options are open.'

'But you're talking about a person, are you? Not just the *Zeitgeist*, but someone spurring the children on?'

'Yes. Or cleverly pulling their strings. Finding the way their developing minds work and then applying gentle pressures or dangling subtle inducements.'

'Have you any evidence these children's minds were working in the direction of killing a baby?'

'No.' Matt sighed. 'Not really. I may be talking about one or two of them, not the whole bunch. The only concrete thing I have is a memory of talk about some people who shouldn't be allowed to have babies.'

Phil raised his eyebrows, then leapt in on that.

'A memory? Is there something about this story that you haven't been telling us, Matt?'

'Yes. I knew these children. I was around in the summer of sixty-nine.'

'Up from the smoke?'

'Refugee from EastEnderville. Staying with my Auntie Hettie while my mother recovered from a botched hysterectomy, as I now know.'

'Right. And are you going to let this out tonight?'

'I've thought about that. I don't rule it out for the future, but I think now is too soon. Better to leave it as a police investigation, sparked off by the discovery of the bones. Getting in the personal element at this stage might frighten somebody who'd be better left in a state of comparative serenity.'

'Fair enough. So you are thinking of one of the children in particular, are you?'

'Maybe. I have had an unsigned letter. Or there's that shadowy figure in the background, applying the pressure or pulling the strings. I'd really love to hear about him.'


When Charlie at last had Rory Pemberton brought in from the cells he looked terrible. It was obvious he felt terrible too. He cast his eyes around the spare, bare interview room as if he expected to see a bar there, and couldn't believe a room could be empty of such a convenience.

'I've been to breweries that smelt better,' whispered WPC Younger, who was sitting in with Charlie. Pemberton fixed them with a savage stare.

'I'm getting my lawyer on to you, you know that, don't you? Wrongful detention, that's what this has been. It's been downright persecution.'

144

'Why should we want to persecute you, Mr Pemberton?' asked Charlie sweetly.

'That's what I'm bloody waiting to find out.'

'Fair enough.' Charlie read the mantra into the tape, and then sat facing him, wishing they'd used an air freshener before they called him in. 'I'm questioning you about the death of a baby some thirty odd years ago in the Bramley area.'

'Taken your bloody time to get round to it, haven't you?'

'The bones of the baby were discovered three weeks ago in the attic of Elderholm, one of the houses in Houghton Avenue where you lived thirty years ago.'

'Me and a lot of others.'

'Exactly,' said Charlie equably. 'We have already questioned Lily Fitch, or Marsden as she then was. Now we're questioning you.'

A shade had passed over Rory's face at the mention of Lily's name. He stuck however with aggressiveness as his best bet.

'Well, you're wasting your time. I know bugger all about it, so you're wasting my time as well.'

'But on Friday night you were talking to a visitor to your house, Matt Harper, about a long-ago dead baby.'

This time he was really puzzled, but he was frightened too. His brow creased, and for a long time he said nothing.

'Visitor?'

'Not someone you know, or not someone you know well, at any rate. He called on you the night I believe your partner left the house.'

He stuck out his bottom lip.

'Vara? That cow? Good riddance.'

'You were drunk at the time, and you talked about an incident in the past in which a baby died.'

Pemberton spread out his hands in a gesture of feigned matiness.

'Well, there you are. I was drunk. When I'm drunk all sorts of nonsense goes through my mind. That's all there is to it.'

'I don't think so,' said Charlie, still soft and low-key. 'You're drunk most of the day, but you seem to be able to function as some kind of freelance financial speculator. I feel pretty sure that when you were talking about a dead baby you were remembering the real world, an actual baby that you had seen.'

'Well, search me. You say I'm drunk most of the time. Probably I saw it when I was drunk. Some kind of road accident maybe.'

'You don't drive, do you, sir?'

'No, I do not drive. I'm driven. When I was being driven I could have seen a dead baby in a car accident.'

His voice had become irritable again, as if he was talking to an idiot.

'I'd prefer to connect a dead baby in one of the houses where you used to live with the memory you had on Friday of a dead baby. Then you mentioned a balustrade where the baby lay. The houses in Houghton Avenue have little balustrades in the front, with two or three steps down to the front gardens.'

'So what? Windsor bloody Castle has balustrades. The Palace of bloody Versailles has balustrades.'

'I don't think it was at Windsor or Versailles that you saw a dead baby lying on a balustrade,' said Charlie.

Matt rang home when he knew the children would be back from school and asked if they'd like to come and

146

see him do his slot on the *Look North* programme, and stick around while he manned the phone afterwards to see if there was any feedback. He did not need to ask. The children had always been desperate to see more of the place where he worked. What he was really doing was telling them to throw together something to eat and be at the studios in Woodhouse Lane by six-thirty.

It was an exceptionally newsless Monday, so he got a good position on the programme, around twenty to seven. He was interviewed by Patrick Priest, one of the stalwarts of the local news programmes, and a good friend. With the children watching thirstily from a sofa in a far recess of the studio, he went over the story of the bones in the attic, suggested the likely date of the baby's death, and made clear the area of Leeds that he and the police were interested in. Then he got to the new possibilities.

'We're pretty sure that at that time (1969, remember) there was a little family of squatters – I think the locals called them hippies – living illegally in a house in the area. Man, woman, and baby.'

'*The* baby?' asked Patrick as agreed beforehand.

'Maybe, maybe not. We're making no assumptions. The three were squatting, we think, in a house on one of the small roads leading off from Raynville Road in the summer of 1969.'

'The year the Beatles made *Abbey Road*,' said Patrick.

'The year Man. City won the FA Cup,' amended Matt. It seemed like another era. 'But there must be quite a lot of people out there watching this who remember that year well. For example, we don't think there were that many squatters in Northern towns at that time. They would have stood out, and we think some of you –' he turned with a practised transition

147

to look straight into the camera ' – may remember this family. They dressed in hippy style, so this fact, and the fact that they took over an empty house illegally, would have made them conspicuous, talked about. We want to know who they were, and which house they took over, in which street. That is, one of the streets off the Raynville Road, on the border of Armley and Bramley, in West Leeds. If you have anything to offer us in the way of information, ring the police on 0113 2435353, or ring and talk to me here tonight, on 0113 2445738, in the next two hours.'

'Matt is hoping to hear from you,' concluded Patrick Priest.

Matt raised a hand in thanks to his interviewer, beetled out of the studio gesturing to the children to follow him, and headed for the room which had been assigned to him for the phone-in. The telephone was already ringing. He told the children they had to be dead quiet while he was on the phone, and took it up.

'Is that Matthew Hartwell?'

'Er –'

'Well, I'm ringing about these squatters.' An elderly female voice. Promising. 'I think it's absolutely dizgoosting, I mean they just take over places, don't they, and the police do nowt about it, and they get their electricity and gas free, and there's them living off the fat of the land, and it's all at our expense, isn't it, uz ratepayers, we're the ones who pay in the long run, aren't we? Am I on the air?'

'No.'

'Oh.'

'I've noted your views, Mrs – . Thank you very much.' And he put the phone firmly down.

'Who was it?' demanded the children.

'Someone who thought it was a phone-in on squatters.'

The next one was hardly more promising.

'Matt Harper? It's Len Hainsworth here.'

'Yes, Mr Hainsworth.'

'I wanted to ring and tell you I saw all your home matches when you were with Bradford City, and I thought you were brilliant – the best thing in the team when you were on form. Ee, I remember that goal you scored in the FA Cup second round in eighty-seven –'

'Mr Hainsworth, do you have any information for me –'

'No, lad. I just wanted to have the pleasure of telling you that –'

'Then would you please get off the line?' said Matt, banging down the phone. 'Nutter,' he said to the children. 'Celebrity-hunter.'

'Are you a celeb-rity?' asked Stephen, handling the word with care.

'Minor league celebrity of a local kind. I appear on television, that's why.'

Matt thought that from that point on the only way forward was up, and gently upwards it duly went, with the occasional hiccup. At least fifty per cent of the later calls did deal with squatters. He took down details of squats in Headingley, Kirkstall, Bramhope, Pudsey and Cookeridge, with highly conjectural dates and any other details that the caller could remember. All these could conceivably be checked against police records. He was not convinced that, if the couple somehow or other lost their baby in a way that made them unwilling to contact the police, they would have stayed on in Leeds, simply moving to another squat.

149

Stephen was beginning to get restless, and the other two positively bored, when something closer to gold was struck.

'Sorry it's taken me so long to get through,' said another elderly female voice, very down-to-earth sounding, 'but I've tried twice before and you were engaged, and I'm minding the grandchildren –'

'Yes – you are? –'

'Edwina Bartlett. I was brought up in Millais Terrace, and I was still at home in 1969. I think that's the street you're after. There was a pair of hippies with a baby took over the house two down from us – it would be number 14.'

'That's very helpful. Have you any more information?'

'Not much. It was a rather larger house than the rest in that street, and it had been up for sale for quite a while because the neighbourhood wasn't in its favour. They were there for some months, and then suddenly they were gone – overnight, it was, but that's usual, isn't it? I suppose that's what squatters generally do, disappear into the night.'

'You didn't talk to them, get to know them?'

'Not on your life! Me mam would have been down on me like a ton of bricks. How old are you, Mr Harper?'

'Coming up to forty.'

'I can give you ten years or so. I can tell you, children and adolescents were not encouraged to talk to hippy squatters in 1969. In fact, me mam was the holy terror of Millais Terrace.'

'You've not followed in her footsteps?'

A fruity laugh came down the line.

'Not on your life. Nor my daughters either. When I was eighteen I got pregnant, and me mam and I didn't

150

exchange so much as a word for more than twenty years.'

That, at any rate, was concrete information, and pointed the way to further investigation. The children, however, were unimpressed. Their restlessness was becoming distracting, and they signalled their boredom by saying things like 'You haven't got *much*', or 'I don't see what use *that* is'. It was nearly half past nine, and Matt was just putting together his papers when the phone rang again.

'Mr Harper? I'm glad I've caught you. I'm not on the phone, you see, and I delayed ringing till I was on the way to the Club.'

'I'm still here, Mr —'

'Welland. Bill Welland. I used to live in Millais Terrace.'

'Ah – Millais Terrace!'

'Has someone got in first?' He sounded downcast.

'Someone's just been on, mentioning it. A Mrs Bartlett.'

'Would that be Edwina? Edwina Smithy as was – lived just up the road from us. Her mother could have taught Mrs Thatcher a thing or two about intimidation. We lived – the wife and I, that is – at number 16, just next door to the hippy couple you're interested in.'

'Ah, really!' said Matt encouragingly. 'Mrs Bartlett said she'd never been allowed to talk to them.'

'Well, she wouldn't have been. It wasn't just her battle-axe of a mother: working-class folk didn't take kindly to that kind of thing back in the sixties. Squatters did no work, and sponged off those who did, that was the general feeling. But we talked to them, the wife and I. Went in there now and then, even smoked pot with them. Still do that, if I get a chance.'

'Then you can tell me who they were.'

'Aye, I can. Dougie and Sandra they were called. I've been straining my brain to remember the surname, but for the life of me I can't. It'll come back. If you'll give me a number to ring of an evening I'll call you when it does.'

'Thank you. Its Leeds 2574945.'

'Right you are. Of course we never kept in touch because they were gone overnight. But we got on well. We loved little Bella – we were newly wed, and hadn't had any of our own, then, though Milly – my late wife – was desperate to have them. So little Bella was a star in our eyes, and we were fond of Sandra too, though she was two sandwiches short of a picnic.'

'Really? This is news.'

There was a humming and hawing at the other end as Bill Welland dithered as to how best to put it.

'Not *quite* all there – know what I mean? A bit simple. Had no thoughts of her own. If Dougie said they were against marriage, she said they were against marriage. If Dougie said the world was made of blue cheese, it was Gorgonzola for her too. But she was sweet with it, a lovely mother, and she'd do anything for you if it was in her capacity. If it was something beyond her she'd just say no, she couldn't, and that would be the end of it. She knew she wasn't quite like other people.'

'Do I get the impression you were not quite so fond of Dougie?'

Again, there was a pause as he thought how best to put it.

'Uncertain about him. Didn't quite know where he was coming from. He was bright enough, had the gift of the gab, and if he talked about what he – they – believed in, it made sense. But I wouldn't have sworn

152

he was straight, or sincere, whatever you like to call it. Was he just taking advantage of Sandra's simplicity? He wasn't the type women would flock around, so we thought sometimes she was just a convenient lay for him. And not just a lay, because she gave him blind devotion, which must have been nice. On the other hand, she can't have been much of a stimulus for an intelligent bloke. No, about Dougie I'd have to say I didn't *know*. I just wondered whether he maybe knew perfectly well what he was after, and what that was was the best for number one.'

'Look, I wonder if I could have your telephone number –'

'Don't have one – not since the wife died. Had it cut off. I prefer to see the face of who I'm talking to, see if I'm boring the pants off them.'

'Of course, you said. Address then?'

When he had taken down the address, in Pudsey, and told him he might drop round if anything else occurred to him that might be of help, Matt rang off and turned to the children.

'I think we can wind things up now.' There was a general and ungrateful sigh of relief. 'And *don't* say that wasn't anything very much, because it was the names I wanted of the hippy family, so it was spot on, and the reason I made the broadcast.'

Isabella, throughout the last five minutes, had been looking much more impressed.

'What were the names?' she asked.

'The pair were called Dougie and Sandra, and the baby was Bella.'

As it came out he suddenly wished he'd omitted the baby. A pained and then a dreamy expression came into Isabella's face.

'Bella! And that could be the little baby in the attic! And then I come and live in the same house. Almost like a reincarnation . . . Isn't it wonderful that you can find that out just by appealing for information on television . . . Bella!'

Matt's heart sank. It was not quite clear whether the experience was driving Isabella in the direction of becoming a clairvoyant or something-or-other in television. He hoped the former, because he had no desire to found yet another BBC dynasty. But either way it seemed as though Isabella's days as a fledgling master chef or society caterer were numbered. That was an awful pity, Matt thought. Chefs and caterers were at least useful.

Rory Pemberton was showing signs of cracking. It was the second session of interviews, and he'd now been at Millgarth nearly eight hours. He was not looking good. When the session was interrupted by a lengthy bout of coughs and sneezes from Pemberton, WPC Younger whispered to Charlie: 'It's almost as if he was still drunk.' And that was spot on. He certainly had not gained any supply of alcohol – the mere smell of him told them that: stale whisky and nicotine, as before. But he exhibited increased disorientation as the second session wore on, and Charlie was unsure whether the coughs and sneezes were genuine or a ploy to gain some semblance of self-control. When the man finally straightened up and nodded to him to continue, Charlie said: 'Do you wish to reconsider your decision not to have a lawyer present?'

Pemberton shook his head arrogantly.

'Why should I have one? I've done nothing illegal. But I'm getting on to him the moment you let me go.'

'Right,' said Charlie, suddenly changing his tone to brutal directness. 'Let's stop faffing around, shall we? Thirty-one years ago you and the other children in Houghton Avenue were a little group playing together, in and out of each other's houses. At some point the attention of all of you was caught by a family of squatters living just off the Raynville Road.'

'I don't know what you're talking about.'

'A young couple, with a baby.'

'How would I know?'

'That's the baby in the attic of Elderholm, isn't it?'

'I don't know anything about any baby in an attic.'

'Oh yes you do. At some point you and the others decided to take the baby and kill it, didn't you?'

The bloodshot eyes were staring now, wild with memory and fear, but he just spluttered 'No!'

'Was it some other plot that went wrong, then? Some sort of kidnap, perhaps?'

'Talk sense! What could we have done with a kidnapped baby? Who would pay ransom? The hippy couple? Don't make me laugh!'

'Then what does that leave? Did you all get the idea that a baby born to hippy parents was better off dead?'

'No!'

'Better . . . off . . . dead?'

'No, of course we didn't! We were just children!'

'Then how did the baby die?'

The man's face screwed up in anguish, and he burst into sobbing, throwing himself across the interview desk towards them. The shoulders heaved, the sobs kept breaking into something like howls, and he seemed to be blubbering out a word that Charlie, before he turned the tape off, tried hard to catch. Afterwards he and

WPC Younger agreed that what the word sounded like was 'Bella'.

'We had to let him go,' said Charlie, late that night, as he lay in bed with Felicity, having only just got home.

'Why?'

'We had nothing on him. Later, in the third session, he spun us a story about a plan to kidnap the baby being talked about among the children, and he'd thought it a joke at the time, but when he heard recently about the bones in the attic . . . and so on and so on. It was pure flim-flam, but we've got nothing to go on to prove anything else, or to prove that he was involved.'

'Have you talked to Matt about the television appeal?'

'No, I'll ring him tomorrow . . . Matt thinks there's someone in the background, some dim figure –'

'Manipulating the children, prodding them into doing things?'

'Something like that. Perhaps even someone that most of the children never saw, never talked to.'

'"As I was going up the stair/ I met a man who wasn't there./ He wasn't there again today./ I wish, I wish he'd go away."'

The rhyme amused Charlie immensely.

'Hey, that's rather good. Well, if Matt is right, what we really should be going after is the man who wasn't there. And if he was a lot older than the children, it's quite likely he's dead, and not there nowadays in that sense.' He grimaced. 'I can see why the big bosses upstairs don't want to waste police time or money on this.'

An expression of pain crossed Felicity's face.

'And yet when I think of those little bones –'

'You think of Carola. Do you think I don't?' And turning to her he began to make a sort of exhausted love.

About the same time, Rory Pemberton got out of the taxi that had brought him home from Leeds. For once he did not haggle about the charge, but he did give the driver the exact fare, and he did demand a receipt for tax purposes. Some things are ingrained, and proof against exhaustion and disorientation. Once inside the house he went straight to the whisky bottle and poured himself a hefty slug, adding a whiff of soda. But instead of downing it, as he normally would have done, he drank it slowly, pouring himself another small one afterwards, and drinking it equally slowly. Then he went thoughtfully up to bed. Some instinct of self-preservation told him that heavy drinking could serve him very ill in the days and weeks ahead.

When he woke in the early hours he lay on the bed as light began to glimmer through his curtains and thought of his involvement with the hippies and little Bella. None of the things that came back into his mind gave rise to anything but disgust and self-loathing.

# CHAPTER 13

# Fallout

Television has a terrible power. Perhaps, Matt thought to himself, that is why countries like America and Italy keep it relentlessly and one hundred per cent trivial. That way it stirs up nothing more dangerous than the desire to be exhibitionist and the desire to watch exhibitionists. Matt should have known that the fallout from the *Look North* interview would not confine itself to the phone-in afterwards, but he had put such knowledge to the back of his mind, so he was surprised in the next few days by the persistent stream of phone calls and letters, many of them, as before, totally irrelevant, but most of the rest at least adding some tiny chip to the mosaic in his mind about the children and the houses.

There were letters from people who had lived in the Houghton Avenue houses, but not at the time he was interested in. One reminisced at length and said the houses 'had a good feel' to them; another did the same, but thought 'there was something sinister' about the old stone residences. Several phone calls mentioned the hippy pair in number 14, Millais Terrace, but it was only Bill Welland, his memory returning, who phoned in with a surname.

'How could I forget?' he said to Matt, when he phoned him at home around nine, he himself being as usual on his way to his Club. 'It was Woof. Pronounced to rhyme with "roof", maybe to make it sound less doggy. Though if you're called Dougie Woof, it's going to sound doggy anyway. It was *his* surname. I don't think I ever heard hers, but if you called her Sandra Woof she didn't object, in spite of being against marriage. It's not a common name, is it, so that might help, if you're going to be looking for him.'

It was out-of-the-way, but still there were four in the Leeds telephone directory. None of them was a D., and when Matt rang them none had a Douglas in their immediate or extended family. One of them, though, was quite chatty.

'It's not a common name,' he said, he himself being Frederick Woof of Morley, 'and you might strike lucky if you cast your net a bit wider than Leeds. It's a corruption of "Woolf". The books say a lot of Woolfs were European immigrants, often Jews. I did some family research once, and I rather hoped I might find some relationship with Virginia Woolf, or her husband rather, but I never did. All the Woofs I found were irredeemably English.'

Matt perked up his ears.

'Have you still got the work you did on your family?' he asked.

'Probably. Up in the attic, I expect. Want me to rummage around in it and see if I can find a Douglas?'

'I'd be very grateful if you would,' said Matt, giving him his phone number. Frederick promised to be in touch, but said it might take time.

The most interesting of the letters came the day after the broadcast. That in itself was intriguing. Someone

159

had gone out to a central Post Office with a late-night collection. The postmark was Nottingham. Though the address had the usual anonymity of a computer effort, Matt thought he had seen that particular printer before. When he tore the letter open, he was sure.

*Dear Matt,*

*I hope you don't mind me calling you that. It seems the most natural way to talk to you. I wrote to you before, if you remember.*

*I saw you tonight on* Look North. *I've been watching it, wondering whether you'd be on, because of course I know you work there at Radio Leeds. I may be on the wrong track, but I thought you looked happy, underneath the worry about the dead baby. That pleased me.*

*But there was something about the way you talked – not* what *you said, but the tone – that made me think you'd got the idea that the children in Houghton Avenue had got together and planned to murder that little child. That pained me. Did we really strike you as a gang of teenage murderers? They exist these days, as I know all too well from my job. Am I naive in thinking such a group would be very rare back in 1969? And is that really how we struck you? Do you remember us as seething with vicious impulses?*

*And even if you had never known us, doesn't it strike you that this is a pretty unlikely scenario?*

*We were a group, we played together, but like most groups we were a mass of conflicting personalities, impulses, tastes. Perhaps that is the reason – or one of the reasons – why most of us have had very little to do with each other as adults.*

*Some of us are dead. I think none of us really knew what we were doing. I don't know how much you have*

*found out, and can't guess how much you are likely to*
*find out, but I do know that nothing you learn is likely*
*to increase anyone's happiness, soothe anyone's grief or*
*unease. In fact, I truly believe your investigations will*
*do nothing useful at all.*

*I hope you will consider this, though I am not*
*optimistic about its making any difference. I expect you,*
*like all of us, are haunted by the thought of that pathetic,*
*unprotected little baby.*

*Sincerely.*

Again there was no signature. This time there was
nothing to mark it out as coming from Peter Basnett,
yet Matt felt sure that it did. He took the letter round
to Charlie Peace at Millgarth next morning on his way
to work.

'What do you make of it,' he asked. 'Is he anxious
for us to find him?'

Charlie read it through carefully, then pursed his lips
sceptically.

'Let's say I wouldn't bank on him living in Nottingham.'

'Why not?'

Charlie's mind went to a recent case of what the
British are really good at: serial murder. It was a case
on everybody's minds, not just those of policemen.

'Take Harold Shipman. He's already murdered from
15 to 180-odd women. Then for the first time he decides
to forge a will leaving an entire estate of an elderly
widow he intended to kill to himself – quite a big estate,
not a piddling little amount. Never any financial motive
before. He types the will on a decrepit old manual typewriter that he keeps in his home. As any fool knows,
matching a typescript with a manual typewriter is the

161

easiest thing in the world. And where would be the first place that you'd look for the typewriter that typed a will leaving everything to one person? Added to which, the daughter of the woman supposedly making the will, soon to be murdered, is a solicitor. That was Harold Shipman's equivalent of the letters murderers sometimes write to the police or newspapers. What does it add up to?'

'He wanted to be stopped.'

'Maybe.' Charlie's expression showed his scepticism. 'But did he want to be stopped because he was sickened by what he was doing? I prefer another explanation. He'd murdered elderly women so often that it had lost its thrill. Now he'd moved on, and he wanted the thrill not of killing but of having it *known*. Of being the most successful mass-murderer in British history. Being a secret killer wasn't enough any longer. He wanted his cleverness trumpeted.'

'Eat your heart out, Fred West and Yorkshire Ripper?'

'Exactly. Now do you see either of these impulses in the letter that you received? The desire to be caught, or the desire to be known as a murderer? Quite the contrary, I'd have said.'

'What do you see?'

'Muddle, most of all. A muddled mind. A man who's got himself into a moral dilemma – he's been in it for decades, remember – and who is pulled all ways, part excusing, part protesting grief and guilt. He's so mixed up about himself, his life and prospects, the morality of what he's done, that he's desperate to say something about it, even to justify some aspects of what he did all those years ago, and particularly to you, so young, an outsider, yet on the fringes of what happened, almost involved.'

'Still, it's interesting, what he says about the children.'

'Very. If it's true. If it's not just part of a process of self-justification.'

It was characteristic, not of Charlie, who was spot-on at least as often as most policemen, but of the unusualness of the case that he was quite wrong in at least one of his guesses – the home location of the letter-writer. How far he was right in his other comments would be a matter of opinion even after the case was closed.

Oddly enough, some confirmation of the letter's account of the children came two evenings later. Isabella and her brothers had found a family of friends through talking to them at the bus stop, and they were down the hill in Armley Ridge Road, cementing a new alliance. It was soon after seven when the doorbell rang, and Matt opened it to find an elderly woman, grey giving way to white, standing nervously on the doorstep.

'Mr Harper?'

'That's right.'

'My name's Carpenter.' Matt's lack of recognition showed in his face. 'We used to live, many years ago, in The Willows, two doors down.'

'Ah!' Matt stood aside. 'Please come in. The children are all out, so we can talk.'

'Oh, you have children. That's nice. But upsetting for them, to find what you found.'

'Yes. Though more for me, really. The children were shocked at first, but they came to terms with it quite quickly. Perhaps children do.' A shade passed over the woman's face, and Matt said quickly: 'I'm sorry. That was insensitive. You are Caroline's mother, aren't you?'

163

'Yes. But perhaps I came on a fool's errand. You seem to know already what I've come to tell you.'

'I don't *know* anything,' said Matt, painfully aware of the truth of that. 'But I think your daughter may have been mentally disturbed by things that happened many years ago.'

He gestured Mrs Carpenter to a seat, and she sank into it gratefully, glad to take the weight off her feet. She accepted Matt's offer of a sherry, talking nervously as she sipped it.

'I've got a sister in Armley, so Desmond and I could get away without too many questions from Caroline. I saw you on television two nights since, when luckily she was out of the room, so I could switch it off before she came back. She heard you on the radio some weeks back, and it – well, it gave her one of her bad spells. Please understand: I'm not blaming you. All sorts of things can give her bad weeks. But you see she's got a job now – nothing splendid, just a dinner lady at a primary school, but she's so pleased and proud to have it, and to be bringing home money that –'

'I understand,' said Matt.

'They know about the problem, the people at the school, and they're very sympathetic, and as a rule it's only perhaps once or twice a year that she gets troubled – that's the word we use among ourselves – and has to take a week or so off. They've got someone who's glad to cover.'

'And all this began when?'

Mrs Carpenter shook her head, doubtfully.

'Well, not in 1969, but looking back we can see the seeds of it then. At the time we just thought it was a phase that would pass. Caroline, you understand, was always a quiet child. She has a brother, but he's seven years older, so they were never playmates. She was middling at school, enjoyed singing in the choir, went to Sunday School. You could see when she was playing with the others in these houses that she was always the quiet one, the one they took for granted.'

'Did that worry you?'

'Not overmuch, not then. Nothing wrong with a quiet child. My feeling at the time was that she was quiet because she thought about things a lot. Wondered whether it was right to do things or not. Even if we told her to do something there'd always be a little pause before she'd do it. Oh, I don't want to make her out to be a little saint,' she said hurriedly, perhaps imagining scepticism in Matt's face. 'I expect she could be naughty, though I don't remember any example, not of any importance. She certainly could dig her heels in about things, though . . .'

'And then?'

'That time you talk about, the summer of 1969, she went quiet – even quieter. It was difficult to get a word out of her. She didn't want to mix, she spent more and more time in her room – just sitting, so far as I could see – and it made me sick with worry. But, well, I put it down to – you know – adolescence.' A blush spread over her face, telling Matt something about the household Caroline had grown up in, its difficulties in talking over potentially embarrassing subjects. 'Anyway,' she went on hurriedly, 'it was two or three years later that the real crisis came: in the run-up to her O levels. She wasn't a brilliant student, like I say, but we might have expected her to do solidly well. But her school work had suffered, and there was a lot of pressure on her and . . . well, we thought that was it. I think now it was just the last straw: that *on top of* what had gone before.'

'What happened?'

She looked down into her lap. All the really serious things, Matt thought, went undiscussed in the Carpenter household.

'Oh, I don't want to go into too much detail. It seems like disloyalty to Caroline. She just went off her head – babbling nonsense, crying, refusing to leave her room, then suddenly going out at night, going missing, being found wandering miles away.' She paused, reluctant to reveal to him the next thing, but in the end making up her mind she had to: 'Sometimes when she was found she'd say she was looking for the baby.'

There was silence in the room for a time.

'I see,' said Matt. 'Did you understand then what she was talking about?'

'Never. And she never said anything in her better times. No, it was not until . . . Well, it's not your fault, and it's better to know, isn't it? At the time we began to think that the talk about a baby was some hidden pain and distress disturbing her, that not having one was a sort of symbol to her of her inability to lead a normal life.'

'And there was never any question of marriage and children, I suppose.'

'No, there wasn't. For about twelve or fifteen years things were bad, really bad. One good day, one bad day, one good week, one bad week. We tried mental institutions, we tried different psychiatrists, it felt as if we'd tried everything. The pattern for all that time remained pretty much the same, until gradually, very gradually, the good times began to get longer, her grip on reality stronger. Oh, the bad times were still there, and during them she would often disappear, making us mad with worry.'

166

'I think that on one occasion she came here.'

'Yes, I'm not surprised. We had moved to Barnsley, you see, when my husband had got promotion in his job. That was two or three years after the bad times started, when Caroline was eighteen or so. I'd never associated her illness with these houses, but perhaps I should have done . . .'

'And now she's improved so much she can even take on a job.'

'Yes.' She smiled up at him. 'We thank God for that, and we're so proud of her. She loves being with the school-children, she loves just having to get up in the morning, take the bus, have a routine. So – you'll have guessed I have something to ask you.'

'I'll do anything I possibly can.'

'I wouldn't want to hinder you in trying to find out what happened to this poor little baby. That would be wicked. But I *know*, as surely as I know this is my right hand –' she held it up '– that Caroline can't have been involved, not really involved, beyond perhaps *knowing* what happened, and for some reason blocking it out, or feeling she has to keep quiet about it.'

'That sounds to me like what must have happened.'

'Obviously I'm asking you not to trouble Caroline.'

'I can promise you that straight away.'

'I'm also asking if you would let me know if you're going to be on television or radio. When she heard that radio interview she had one of her worst setbacks in years. I need not to be on tenterhooks the whole time as to whether it might happen again.'

'Of course. I'll willingly let you know. Give me your telephone number –'

Mrs Carpenter was already scrabbling in her hand-bag, and she handed him a scrap of lined paper on which she had already written her address and number. But she was looking for something else too, and finally she handed him a small colour photograph.

'That's Caroline, about three years ago. One of the good times, of course. I always thought she was quietly pretty. She would have made such a good mother.'

The face looked out at him shyly. Behind the figure was a promenade and a pier. Presumably the face said something different to her mother, but to Matt it said: 'You want to think I'm having a good time, and I'll try to convince you of that.' But behind the smile, in the eyes, in the set of the mouth, there was a timorous dread, a sense of disaster around the corner. He registered that the 'fairish hair going grey' that Mrs Goldblatt had used when describing the strange woman in the back lane perfectly described the hair of the woman in the snapshot.

'Yes, she is pretty,' he said, handing it back. 'Will you promise me one thing? Will you tell me anything that she says that might help me to find out the truth about what happened?'

'I promise, but she won't. I know that,' said her mother with conviction. 'She has blotted it from her mind. Even during her – her bad periods, she never lets anything slip, beyond the talk of a baby. She's rather cunning at those times – looks at us as if we're expecting her to say something about what's troubling her, but she's not going to.'

'I wasn't just thinking about the baby's death,' said Matt, 'but about the whole situation among the children living in these houses at that time, or anything she might say about any one of the children she played with.'

'I see. Well, if she does say anything, certainly I'll

pass it on. But you see the children who lived here are all part of what I now realize is the problem: the death of the baby. I can't recall that she has mentioned any of their names in years, so I don't expect she'll start mentioning any of them now.'

'Unless hearing the broadcast has stirred up memories.'

Mrs Carpenter got up at that.

'Yes, but we can't select the memories, can we?' She paused at the door of the living room. 'If she remembers the children round her that she used to play with, she'll remember the baby. I don't want that. Those children should all be in their early-forties now. But I can't forget that two of them are dead.'

'Two of them?' Matt's face showed his surprise. 'I knew about Eddie Armitage.'

'Poor Eddie. The nicest lad you could meet. And Colin Mather, the boy who came every summer to stay with his grandparents. He injected himself with an overdose of heroin when he was twenty-one. I heard about it as soon as it happened, because, though we'd moved, I was still friendly with the Mathers. The inquest said accidental death, but there's accidents and accidents, as I'm sure you know, being in news and broadcasting and that. I love my daughter, Mr Harper. I'll do anything to protect her. There's no way I'm going to bring up those names, or try to get her to talk about them.'

When she was gone, Matt thought about what she had said. Two children dead from ten children who'd made up the two five-a-side teams was probably above average, but not wildly so, remembering the dangers, pressures and epidemics such as AIDS that had been the lot of young people since the sixties. Still, he could

169

well understand Mrs Carpenter's fears that pressuring her daughter could lead to a third.

He wondered about his own unwillingness to press the matter. He thought that if he'd been a police officer he would have felt obliged to take things further, ask Caroline about her obsession with a baby. He on the other hand had immediately felt that his concern about the baby's death was not worth any threat to a living woman's mental stability. He was investigating out of curiosity, and for personal reasons. No one was vigorously investigating the baby's death as a crime.

Yet that, surely, was what it was.

## CHAPTER 14

# 'Resta Immobile'

The next day, disaster struck. Matt's remarks to Jason Morley-Coombs about the punishment taken by a professional footballer's body had been heartfelt, because some of the injuries he had sustained had a nasty habit of putting in a reappearance. The next day an old sporting injury did just that, and Matt went into the by now well-practised routine from previous visitations: he rang Radio Leeds to say he'd be off for two or three days, but could be ferried there and back if there was something that imperatively called for him. Then, disliking staying in bed, he had the children move an easy chair in his study close to the phone and settled into it, still in his pyjamas because dressing was more trouble than it was worth, and surrounded by newspapers, books, notepads and pens. He went carefully over his notes from his first finding of the bones and found himself in one respect more puzzled than he was when he started.

The main phone call of the day, rather to his surprise, was one from Harry Sugden.

'They told me you were laid up at Radio Leeds. I'm in a house waiting for t'paint to dry, but the bloke says it's OK to ring you. No news to speak of, but I just wanted to tell you that I've driven round the old streets I used to live in a couple o' times, trying to pick on t'house where Lily Marsden used to go visiting. Not much luck there. I've noted down six or seven places where 'appen it could be, but t'truth is, I could've noted six or seven more. There were never one place where the bells rang and said: "It was'ere." Sorry about that.'

'You've done your best,' said Matt. 'Perhaps if you slipped the addresses into the post I could do some following-up. Unfortunately I heard yesterday that your other spy, Colin Mather, died quite young.'

'Aye, 'appen I did hear about that, years ago. We were never close.'

'There's been something niggling in the back of my mind, Harry. Do you remember the day I first came up here to Houghton Avenue and scored that goal?'

'Oh aye. Couldn't forget that.'

'One of the girls – I'm pretty sure it was Marjie – went off to dancing class, and I played the rest of the game in her place.'

'Aye.'

'But whenever I came up to play later Marjie played too, but I still had a place in the team. So there must have been someone playing in that first game who never played later. I've counted up: there were eight Houghton Avenue children, plus you, plus me – two five-a-side teams. Who made up the tenth before I came along?'

Harry Sugden could almost be heard thinking.

'Oh aye! Of course!' he said at last. 'That would'a been Ben Worsnip. He allus went away wi'his family to Blackpool in the middle o' August, but he liked a game o' football, did Ben ... Now you mention it, 'e used to come along wi' Colin an' me, spying on Lily Marsden. He started the idea she were showing her all to some dirty old man. Allus had a mucky mind, did Ben Worsnip.'

'Any idea if he's still in the area?'

''E wor three year sin'. Sold me a package of life insurance – a good 'un too. Good terms because we were old mates. 'E wor wi' Commercial an' General then. 'Appen you could ring them and contact him that way. You could drive around wi' him an' see if you have better luck than I did.'

'That's an idea. Does he still have a mucky mind?'

'Oh no. Happily married man wi' bairns – takes it out of a man. No time for that sort o' thing. But he's still football mad. Keep him sweet an' on the ball by telling him some tale o' playing against Gary Lineker.'

'I never did, even in the Cup. And in general he was always out of my league.'

'Well, make up a few whoppers for Ben Worsnip.'

Matt thought long and hard, sitting there in his swivel armchair, and occasionally wincing with pain, about how best to approach Ben Worsnip. He had no mental picture of the boy he had been – and why should he have one? He had probably only been there for that one first game.

In the event, the approach couldn't have been easier. He rang the head office of Commercial and General, was told Mr Worsnip was now working there, and was put straight through to him.

'Mr Worsnip? Your name was given me by Harry Sugden.'

'Harry?' said the voice at the other end, which had put aside its Yorkshireness in a way Harry had never felt the need to. 'Well, it's a while since we did business. Is it some type of special insurance you're after?'

'No, no – or not immediately anyway. My name is Matthew Harper, and I work for Radio Leeds. It's a very old matter I'm hoping you can help me with – the time when you and Harry used to come up and play football with the children in Houghton Avenue.'

'Ah –' Matt could almost hear the brain ticking over. 'I haven't seen you on the telly, but the wife has mentioned you. The wife was a childhood sweetheart like, and came from the Raynville Road area, so she was interested.'

Matt had jolly visions of adolescent fumblings in the field by the Kirkstall Power Station or in the thickets of Gotts Park Golf Course.

'I don't know what she's told you –' he began.

'No, wait,' said Ben Worsnip, who knew what he wanted, and seemed trained to get it. 'I want to get this clear in my head. You're Matt Harper who played for Bradford City a while back?'

'Yes.'

'Now, are you also the little boy called Matt who came up and played with us one summer, starting with a brilliant goal that I saw and going on to a few more that I heard about when I got back from bloody Blackpool?'

Matthew knew there could be no point in denying it.

'Yes. We're trying to play down my involvement at the time for the moment. How did you latch on to it?'

'I think it's been in the back of my mind since the wife mentioned the case, and the name of the person who wanted information about the people in the Houghton Avenue houses. Then again, I could have

174

seen you reading the news, and your face could have rung a bell. If I could read how the human mind works I wouldn't be peddling insurance. Now, how can I help you?'

'Like you said I think you were playing five-a-side that first game, when I came up to watch you all and showed off by joining in and putting in a goal. Then I think you must have gone away on holiday with your parents.'

'Yes, that's what I've worked out too. Blackpool in August was regular and non-negotiable. I certainly don't recall playing again with you after that first game. The word was that you went from strength to strength.'

'That's true, though I say it myself. I was brilliant all summer. That was my peak season, when I was seven.'

'Don't put yourself down. I've seen you play for Bradford City, and you were always good. Not brilliant, but good.'

'Thanks very much. Now, though you went off to Blackpool or wherever –'

'Blackpool. Like I say, non-negotiable. My family must have been out of their minds.'

'Still, I believe you were already, with Harry and Colin Mather, keeping an eye on Lily Marsden.'

'Lily Marsden!' said the voice, with delighted recognition. 'There's a name I haven't heard in years.'

'Why were you so interested in her?'

'Because we thought she was taking her clothes off for some dirty old man,' he said promptly and without embarrassment. 'If it wasn't something much worse.'

'Right,' said Matt. 'That's what I'd gathered. And this was because she was making mysterious calls at a house in the Raynville Road area.'

'Aye, that's right. We saw her go there once, all

secretive and surreptitious, and then we kept a watch on and off and found out she made frequent visits. Colin saw more of her than we did, and he said she had a money supply from somewhere.'

'Did you ever find out who she was visiting?'

'Not while I was around.'

'Why didn't you just go up to a neighbour and ask who lived in that house?'

'Too straightforward, I suppose,' said Ben, after a moment's thought. 'Kids don't think like that. We were Emil and the Detectives or maybe the Famous Five. And we were most likely afraid we'd be sent away with a flea in our ears – probably would have been too. Why would kids want to know something like that?'

'So you never heard later?'

'No, I'm sure I didn't. I expect when we came back from Beastly Blackpool all my usual mates were back from holiday too, so I didn't have much to do with the children from the top.'

'Now, the sixty-four thousand dollar question: do you think you could identify now the house Lily was visiting?'

There was silence.

'I could try, Mr Harper. Maybe we could drive around all those little streets slowly. Something might come back.'

Matt repressed the remark that Ben could drive round those little streets on his own. He knew perfectly well the man was trading his knowledge for insider football chat.

'That would be fine,' he said. 'I'm laid up at the moment with a recurrence of an old injury. Doesn't usually last more than two or three days. What about early Saturday evening?'

'Couldn't suit me better.'

And so it was fixed up. Matt relaxed, slept pleasantly, and cosseted his painful foot and ankle. The children cooked him a meal (though Isabella announced that cooking was 'boring') and waited on him when they remembered. Their new friends from down the hill and the Quinton boy from along the lane called on them in the evening, and the house resounded with a terrible din that Matt rather liked. It reminded him of football crowds. He whiled away time, without consciously deciding to, by entertaining in his mind his impressions and memories of the Houghton Avenue children. Peter Basnett, lively but responsible – a carer in the older sense, who had been driven for a time into moroseness after the baby's death, but who, to judge by his letters, had come through that now. Marjorie, who must have been one of the leaders in the hiding of the body, also a carer, who had fled her memories by making an early move out of the area. Pathetic Caroline, whose memories drove her further – into madness, on to the margins of society. Rory Pemberton, the non-belonger, the never-accepted, who embraced drink as his only friend. Colin Mather, apparently confident and decisive, whose parents' endeavours to educate him into the dangers of drugs had, as so often, precisely the opposite effect to the intended one. Most pathetic of all, Eddie Armitage, who never came to terms with the baby's death, perhaps because he never really knew who he was. Then there was Sophie Basnett, his opposite: pretty, sexy, effective in getting what she wanted – he'd never heard talk of her being scarred.

And then the ambiguous figure of Lily Marsden – the willing outsider, the promoter of unease, the propagandist of unacceptable notions, that she sowed among them like poison weeds. Was his predominant impression of her one of hardness, or unhappiness?

On the third day the foot showed cheering signs of improvement. Matt phoned Radio Leeds and told them he would definitely be in the next day. In mid-afternoon he took the two hefty sticks he had used on previous recurrences of the injury and took himself out of the back door. Slowly he made it to the back gate, then began an exploratory walk along the back lane. He found Hester Goldblatt in her garden, and received meekly a mini-lecture from her on new varieties of roses. He had no intention of planting roses in his garden, having a vague notion they were a major cause of premature ageing. Plants that flourished with minimal care and attention were his aim. Probably he'd land up with a garden of bay trees.

Moving away he heard a door opening further down the lane. Then he heard a voice he thought he recognized.

'It was really good of you to see me like this, on your dad's day off.'

Similar but different. Was that because last time it had been drunk?

'No problem, Rory old sport.' Guess immediately confirmed. The second voice was that of Jason Morley-Coombs, and it immediately was lowered, but not so far that Matt could not distinguish the words in their assumed upper-class twang. 'As I say, Dad's advice would be the same as mine: go on playing it with a straight bat as far as the police are concerned. But when it comes to the push, you've no reason to go on shielding that one person, particularly as she's nothing to you.'

'No . . . I wish I knew who was behind it all.'

'Does it matter? Probably no one who means anything to you either.'

'Probably not . . . I'm wondering whether Peter Pennymore knows . . .'

'I wouldn't think of contacting him if I were you. The less you know, the less the police can get out of you.'

'Right . . . Right . . .'

Rory Pemberton sounded irresolute, but also sounded as if he had nothing more to offer on the subject, so Matt turned and hobbled back to his gate. Standing just inside his back garden he watched as the man came out of Dell View's gate and strode to his car. The confident steps seemed assumed, a pose, but Matt noticed that they were at least steady, and not the walk of a drunken man.

That evening Matt had a sick visit from Charlie Peace, with Felicity and Carola. The baby made Stephen's day, and even Isabella, who said 'Babies! Yuck!' when she saw them coming up the front path was, after half an hour, glancing with surreptitious fascination at Carola's perfectly ordinary baby motions. Charlie and Matt took advantage of the general absorption in her to swap a few words on developments.

'Peter Pennymore? So you're assuming that's Peter Basnett?'

'Don't come the cautious detective with me,' said Matt sharply. 'I'm not assuming anything. But he's obviously someone who's very much in the know about the baby business.'

'Do you want me to get on to it?'

'Maybe, eventually. But we've got all the telephone directories for the region *Look North* covers at work. Leave it with me for the moment. I've got a duty

Saturday tomorrow, but if anything emerges from my drive around the Raynville Road streets tomorrow night, I might need your help on that.'

The drive the next evening threatened to be a trip down Memory Lane in the wrong sense. Ben Worsnip had no sooner got Matt into his car than he began banging on about goals and confrontations and yellow cards and everything he remembered about Bradford City ten years previous (which wasn't all that accurate, because naturally he had been a Leeds United supporter). Matt tactfully put a stop to it by suggesting that they concentrate on the matter in hand until they'd been round the streets in the hope of a house, or one or two houses, ringing bells in Ben Worsnip's brain. After that they'd find a pub, settle down over a pint, and talk football. Ben was delighted, but even then it took some time before his brain began to wean itself off the excitement of being sat in a car with a real footballer. With gentle encouragement from Matt, however, he slowly recovered his mental processes back to the old days and the other excitement of salacious childish gossip. Gradually the lure of the past began to get a grip.

'That's my old home. Nothing much, but it was quite a happy one. My mother's in sheltered accommodation now. I know it wasn't in my street that Lily Marsden went visiting, but I'm just trying to get my bearings . . . That was Harry Sugden's house. I was back and forth between Lansdowne Avenue and Grenville Grove where we lived for most of my teenage years. And now this is where Edwina Smithy lived – with her horrible mum.'

'I've talked to her.'

'Have you? What did she know about it?'

180

'Keep driving. You might remember yourself.'

'Let's see: we're in Millais Terrace. Ah, this big house. Squatters. A drippy pair with – oh yes, a baby. It's not? – '

'Keep your mind on the matter in hand.'

'Grenville Street. I don't have any memories of this one, but that's perhaps because none of my mates lived here.'

'My Auntie Hettie did, at number 12. Did you know her?'

'I don't think I had the pleasure . . . Lansdowne Rise. Hmmm. Don't think it was here.' He drove slowly on. Matt, though, kept his eye on the mirror, and he saw the door of number 8 open, and the figure of Lily Fitch emerge from the front door, coated and handbagged, and clip-clop down the street assertively in their wake. He was glad when they turned off into Raynville Road. She aroused in him feelings that were partly irritation and partly – maybe a hangover from his childhood – fear, unease, distaste.

'Now we're getting closer to the canal,' said Ben. 'The houses here were a bit posher than ours were, thirty years ago . . . Leighton Terrace . . .'

He pulled the car up. Matt saw a two-sided street of Victorian two-storey houses, most of them with attic conversions. Possibly these days the attic rooms were let to students from the nearby Leeds Metropolitan University – the old Polytechnic in new (and lucratively confusing to foreigners) guise. Matt could see that the rooms would be higher and larger than in the Victorian house six streets away where his auntie had lived. In the sixties the social gradations would have been of greater importance than they were today.

'Let's get out,' said Ben.

They got out, Matt still walking rather gingerly. Ben immediately made for the higher corner, away from the Raynville Road. He looked around him with a growing excitement.

'I'd bet my bottom dollar we used to stand here, waiting and watching. In sight of the school, see, but that didn't bother us because it was summer holidays. We stood on *this* side, because the house was on the other side . . . *That one!*'

He pointed to a house halfway down that section of Leighton Terrace. Matt walked slowly down to it.

The house seemed to have little to mark it off from its neighbours, beyond the number 8 on the front door. It was a heavy old door, probably the original one. There was a little bay to its right, with dormer windows, and before the front door was a solitary substantial step. Matt looked round enquiringly at Ben Worsnip.

'You're sure?'

'Absolutely.'

'What makes you so sure?'

Ben pointed upwards. On the lintel above the door there was an old stone flower container, a long oblong one the length of the lintel itself. It was now profuse only in prickly weeds and dandelions.

'It had geraniums then. It was the only house that had flowers over the door. I'm as sure as I can be that it's here that Lily used to come.'

He looked at Matt expectantly, like a puppy that has retrieved a stick and expects a reward. So they got into the car, drove to Matt's Auntie's old pub The Unicorn, and sat for an hour or more discussing Lineker and Robson and John Barnes, and how the kind of football played in that millennium year differed from the kind played ten years before, and was light years away from

182

the sort that had been in vogue when England won the World Cup in 1966. Matt had to restrain himself from expressing the view that British footballers earned a ridiculous amount of money for playing pretty poor football. It would sound like sour grapes.

Next day Matt rang Charlie from work and gave him the address: 8 Leighton Terrace. Within twenty minutes Charlie rang back with the information: in 1969 the house had been owned by Mr Cuthbert Farson.

# CHAPTER 15

# Guardian Angels

When Charlie told Matt the name of the owner of 8 Leighton Terrace he said too that he was off to Halifax on a routine police matter but was hoping to squeeze in something that connected with the dead baby. If he got anything of interest he'd try to drop in on the way back, or if not call him later in the evening.

Between bulletins and his own radio show Matt settled down with Television North's collection of telephone directories. He tried first the reasonably local ones – Bradford, Halifax, Huddersfield, Harrogate. Then he went a bit further afield: Doncaster, Sheffield, York. Then he tried Nottingham. He'd assumed that Charlie Peace was right when he guessed that the second anonymous letter being posted in Nottingham did not mean that the sender lived there. But Charlie was wrong – at least potentially so. There was a P. Pennymore, and an address: The Cottage, Hurst Green, Belling Joyce. He looked it up in his AA map and found it was a village south of Nottingham. He got his colleague Phil Bletchley to ring the number, telling him to use his bloody imagination if it was answered, but though Matt sat close to hear the voice, the rings went on and on.

He was pondering after the mid-afternoon bulletin what to do next, whether he wanted to take off as soon as he had a spare day and see if this was indeed Peter Basnett, when he had a call from Reception that Charlie Peace was there to see him. He went down and fetched him, and sat him in an easy chair opposite his desk.

'I mustn't get comfortable,' said Charlie. 'This is all borrowed time. I remembered the other day what you told me about the Armitages worshipping at the Methodist Church in Bramley Town Street, then moving away. The Methodists aren't exactly flourishing these days – I know that because my mum is a Methodist, among other religions. I thought it might be worthwhile ringing around all the obvious towns in the area with a Methodist presence. I struck lucky in Halifax. The family worshipped in Southowram for years, getting smaller and smaller.'

'The congregation, you mean?'

'No, the family. There was a son, and he committed suicide many years ago, so I knew it was the same lot. Now there's just the mother, and she's in a hospice with cancer. When I got this routine matter at Police Headquarters in Halifax I got it out of the way quickly and used the time afterwards to go along to this hospice, which was on the road to Hebden Bridge, and speak to her.'

'Brilliant!' said Matt, rather too cheerfully. 'Was she *compos mentis*?'

'Oh yes. But in a lot of pain. She was just lying there, trying to cope. The sister said the effects of the last pain-killer were wearing off.'

'Poor old thing,' said Matt, rather more appropriately.

'Yes. But she talked. She'd lost everybody close to her – been alone for quite a while, and really I don't think it was distressing for her, talking about her son. I think she thought of herself as about to join him.'

'That's what religion does for you.'

'Yes. Nice if you can believe it. Anyway she talked, like your Mrs Carpenter, about the changes that came over the children that summer . . .'

'I think we were the first to realize it,' said May Armitage, gazing up at the strong but sympathetic black face. 'Eddie was such an *open* boy. He never quite *found* himself, even before that summer. Like he was somehow unfinished, a pot that was still on the wheel. Of course he was only a child, but he was more unsure of himself than most children. So we were watching him, waiting for him to find out who he was, what he wanted to make of his life. When he changed we saw it at once.'

'Did you try to talk to him about it?' Charlie asked.

'Of course!' said May Armitage, with a slight access of force in her weak voice. 'Over and over. He said he wasn't feeling well, but the doctor couldn't find anything the matter. He didn't want to go around with the other children any more – in fact the group seemed to have broken up. Eventually we moved, thinking that might help. There was always a fish and chip shop up for sale somewhere. First we went to the other side of Bramley, then to Halifax. We thought a change of company would do him good, but Eddie was never a child who made friends easily.'

'So it made things worse rather than better?'

'It did. Even before the move he'd got really troubled – you know, in his mind. He'd had to go away for a time. It nearly broke us. But it wasn't just us, you know. By the time we moved other parents were noticing changes in their children. A lot of them moved too. I don't know that it did any good.'

'I know the Carpenters had trouble with Caroline for many years,' said Charlie.

'Did they? Oh, poor people.'

'I suppose it affected his school work?'

'Of course. Eddie was never brilliant, but he did *have* a brain. The school said he had potential. That was all lost. His whole life fell apart. Of course we could have used him in the chippie, but we thought it would be better if he cut himself loose from us. He went to work for Morrison's supermarket, and we hoped he might put in for trainee manager. That was just us not facing up to things, I think. He swept the floors and stacked the shelves and rounded up trolleys in the car park and that was it. He had no thought of aiming higher.'

'He never had a girlfriend?'

'Oh, nothing like that. No friend of any kind. Never went with the other lads to films or football or anything. He had no life . . .' She grimaced with pain, and Charlie felt it was not her cancer alone that caused it. 'You'll want to know about – *you know*.' Charlie nodded. 'I came home on a Saturday afternoon after we closed, and there he was hanging from the stair-rail. He'd been dead for several hours. Please can we not talk any more, not about *that*.'

Charlie waited a minute until she was calmer, then leant over her.

'He sounds a lovely boy, Eddie. That's the impression we've got. I'd have thought he'd have left you a message.'

She looked into his eyes.

'There was a note on an old school pad in his bedroom. It said: "Mum, if there's ever any trouble, tell them it was an accident." The police didn't think it had anything to do with his suicide, so it never came up at the inquest.'

Charlie nodded, squeezed her hand, and left.

'It had to do with his suicide,' said Matt decidedly. 'And still more to do with the baby's death.'

'Sure,' said Charlie. 'The police knew nothing about that then, remember.'

'I'm not criticizing them. I expect they thought it was a pathetic attempt by a mentally-unbalanced young man to hide the fact of his suicide. But that phrase "if there's ever any trouble" is a give-away that he's not talking about his suicide. He's practically looking ahead to what's actually happened: the discovery of the baby's remains.'

'Looks like it,' agreed Charlie. 'But then, what weight can we place on the second part?'

'Not much,' said Matt reluctantly. 'He's certainly not saying outright it *was* an accident.'

'Why cover up an accident anyway?'

'Oh, I think we could make a guess at that,' said Matt, who had thought about the situation a lot more than Charlie; had it with him day and night. 'Because they'd taken the baby, or one of them had, or some of them in collusion had. Once that happened the baby's death was serious, however it died.'

'Fair enough,' admitted Charlie, thinking it through. 'And that is probably why they seem to have taken some kind of collective vow of silence after the death – or maybe just some mutual support scheme which makes them clam up, or only talk about people who are dead and whom they can't harm.'

'Yes.' Matt thought for a while. 'Either all the children

were involved in the taking of the child – let's call her Bella, even though we're not absolutely certain – or they were all somehow participants in the death.'

'Not actively,' said Charlie. 'That's impossible.'

'No, but by collusion, or just witnessing. Or perhaps this mutual support scheme as you call it is just to hide the fact that one of their number *was* responsible.'

'One such as Eddie Armitage,' suggested Charlie.

'Yes. That seems much more likely than if it was Lily Fitch,' said Matt. 'Except for one thing. No two.'

'What's that?'

'Eddie seems the last sort of boy to take the initiative. Uncertain, unformed, a born follower. And it's continued long after his death. It seems to me most likely that the main participant is still alive.'

He sat for some time in a brown study. Charlie stirred, preparing to go.

'Just ring Peter Pennymore,' Matt said, noticing his movements. 'It won't take a minute. Please. A colleague tried earlier, but there was no reply.' He handed Charlie a slip from his pad with the number on. 'He'll recognize my voice from radio and television.'

Charlie took the slip, held the telephone as near to Matt's ear as he could then dialled.

'Two three five seven six oh seven,' said a male voice.

'Who's that? I wanted to speak to Esmeralda,' said Charlie, nothing if not inventive.

'I'm afraid you've got the wrong number,' said the voice.

'It's him,' said Matt, as Charlie put the phone down. 'That was Peter Basnett.'

There was never any doubt in Matt's mind that he had to go and talk to Peter. The question was when. He felt he had to put the Farsons on hold until he'd done so. They weren't going to take off anywhere. They weren't even suspicious that their name was in the frame – if it was the father he was beyond it, if it was the son Matt felt he had given him no cause to be jumpy. What, if he was right, could anyone be charged with? Sowing seeds of ideas in adolescent minds was hardly a crime.

He had a rare weekday off the next week, but he felt insufficiently prepared both factually and emotionally. The next day entirely free was on Saturday week, and he pencilled this in. He wondered whether he could drive the children over to Nottingham and leave them at a football match while he went on to Belling Joyce and tried his luck. The football season was in its very last gasp, and when he rang City Ground he was told there was a friendly against a team from Estonia. No likelihood of crowd violence there. No likelihood of much of a crowd, except last-ditch addicts. Ideal. It would be Lewis who would protest at the plan, not Isabella: how football was changing! Like most parents he considered in his mind various plans for bribing Lewis into agreement.

He was feeling tender about the children at that time, after the sad little night talk with Isabella. He felt that he had in some way taken them for granted – not neglected them, but failed to realize that their trust in him was still fragile, had to be protected and nourished. They had needed to have things made explicit and definite to them, and like most English people he had preferred to leave the emotional things unspoken and – because the words had not been spoken – fuzzy round the edges.

His tenderness for them, his sense of leaving things undone, was increased by a phone call from Aileen.

'Are you alone?' she asked.

'Yes, they're in bed and asleep. I listened ten minutes ago.'

'Matt, I'm in my last week or ten days here. I'm in Durban briefly at the moment, and if I can't book a direct flight home I'll get one from Johannesburg. It's Monday today – it should be in the first half of next week.'

'Hooray! Hallelujah!' said Matt, his voice swelling with delight. 'I don't see why the children had to be asleep before you told me that. I've a good mind to wake them up now.'

'No don't, Matt. The morning will do.'

'So Tom is really better?'

'Tom is . . . better. Still needs nursing, but it won't be by me. I'm just putting his affairs in order here, insofar as I can, then I'll go back to the farm for a few days, arrange for the care he needs, then pack up and tell him I'm off the moment I see the Land Rover coming up the track to get me.'

Matt considered, his heart heavy.

'Tell me. I think I'm guessing.'

'Yes. It's starting up again.'

'He hasn't –'

'No. Don't go all macho. He hasn't, but the signs are all there, and God knows I should recognize them by now: it's *starting*, but it hasn't happened. Of course the moment he started to regain strength and stop feeling sorry for himself he wanted me back in his bed.'

'I hope you told him where to stick his bed.'

'In no uncertain terms. He only wanted me because I was *there*, like Everest. Of course he used all the "You're still my wife" arguments, which made me think a lot. And he can't take being refused. He's like a small

191

child. And after the refusal had festered for a few days, the signs started showing themselves.'

'Like?'

'Like plates being thrown when the meals weren't to his taste, my wrists being taken and twisted when he thought I was getting cocky and he wanted to punish me for it. He hasn't entirely lost his strength, but he wasn't any match for me . . . And do you know the oddest thing?'

'No, what?'

'He kept pestering me to bring the children out on a visit. My God, that's the last thing, the very last thing, I would do – start that up again. I haven't forgiven myself, and I don't think I ever will, for letting it go on as long as it did. It was more psychological than physical, I suppose that's my only excuse, so I saw the results rather than anything actually happening, or scars afterwards.'

'The children were afraid you'd take them back to live with him, Isabella anyway.'

'Yes I feared that's what she must be thinking. She's the only one who really remembers. The thought of them living with him sends goose-pimples up my spine. If he lived in England the most I'd want him to have is the customary afternoon at the zoo with them. And then I'd probably set a private detective to tail them.'

'I'm at your service any time, though I'm still very much at the apprentice stage. So you're just doing a bit of business stuff for him, then you'll book a flight, go back for a day or two to see about nursing arrangements –'

'Yes. I've nearly got that worked out anyway.'

'And then you'll be home!'

'Home. The new home.'

'I feel like taking off my clothes and dancing round the garden.'

'Don't. A partner in jail on an indecent exposure charge is not my idea of the ideal homecoming. What gives in the baby business?'

'I'm on to Peter Basnett, and I'm organizing a trip to see him. But I'll fill you in on that when you come. I can't think of anything else now but your coming home. So you want me to let them know at the Education Department you'll be back at your desk soon?'

'Yes, I suppose so. But I'll need a full week of rest and recovery. And I don't mean just from the flight. And come summer I'll need two or three weeks of *real* holiday, all of us together, in somewhere *nice*. Not exciting, or stimulating, but relaxing and *nice*.'

'As always you present me with a challenge. Where can you find somewhere nice in school holiday time? Everywhere's overrun with kids.'

'You love children, Matt.'

'*Ours*. I suppose you'd rule out Australia or New Zealand?'

'Another long flight would kill me.'

'What about the bottom of Italy, on the Adriatic side? At least most of the children will be locals.'

'And if ours don't have anyone much to hang around with, they and I can get to know each other again. Sounds promising.'

When the call was over Matt didn't take his clothes off and dance around the garden (he thought the Goldblatts could take it in their stride, but the Cazalets would be dialling 999 at the merest glimpse), but he did do a triumphal caper, something obviously inspired by memories of football victory celebrations, around the front room. Then he went upstairs, opened the door to

Isabella's bedroom, and in the light from the landing watched her for a moment as she slept. Then he went across to her, sat down on the bed, and gently shook her shoulder.

'What's wrong? What's the matter?'

The girl's assumption went to his heart.

'Nothing's the matter. I've just been talking to your mother.'

'Yes?'

'And she'll be home next week.'

'Next week!' Isabella's face creased into an enormous smile. Then it faded a little. 'For good?'

'Yes. For good.'

And then she threw her arms around his neck, and for minutes it seemed she lay with her head on his shoulders, crying happily.

'So Daddy won't be with her then?'

'No. I don't think you'll be seeing Daddy in the near future.'

Half an hour later, as he piled dirty pots and pans in the dishwasher, he paused and went into the hall. There were voices from upstairs. Isabella was telling her brothers. Children usually know the right thing to do where they themselves are concerned, Matt thought. It was a sign, too, that terror at what might happen had spread from Isabella to the younger ones. Matt wondered how he would have coped at Stephen's age.

He had already got the children's agreement to going on their own to the Nottingham Forest friendly that coming Saturday. Lewis's consent had been purchased at the price of a meal afterwards at the pizza restaurant of his choice. Lewis was a connoisseur of pizza chains, able to weigh up the merits of a Margherita here against a Quattro Stagioni there. Matt wondered what his reaction would be to a real Italian pizza should they get to the Mezzogiorno in the summer holidays. Ecstasy or rejection? He felt a bit guilty at dangling the dazzling choice in front of him because he had memories of Nottingham from his footballing days, and eateries of any description had been notably sparse on the ground. Still, anything could happen in ten years. Leeds itself had been transformed in the same decade, and now made token appearances in the class nosheries sections of the Sunday colour supplements.

To make the point that his life was complete without football (or any other game or form of physical activity, come to that) Lewis brought along on the trip his copy of *Harry Potter and the Goblet of Fire* to read for the fifth time during the match. Isabella knew enough about the Nottingham Forest team, an esoteric subject, to lecture Stephen on who they should be watching out for. Matt dropped them off outside City Ground without too much compunction: the crowd was good-humoured if foul-languaged, and Isabella displayed her usual competence and apparent confidence, which Matt still trusted in when it came to practical situations, though it might fail her in emotional ones. Then he made, without any major mishaps, for the A52, stayed with it as it veered round, then left it to drive eastwards for Belling Joyce.

He slowed down as he approached it. It was a pleasant, unremarkable large village, near enough to Nottingham to attract commuters, but not sufficiently picture-postcard to send house prices rocketing. The Green was its central point, and two pubs, a corner shop and a post-office-cum-newsagent's reinforced that position. The road on either side of the Green stretched wide, and Matt simply stopped the car, locked it because villagers are not what they once were, and began to walk around it in search of The Cottage. The houses were of many kinds and periods, but modern ones were few, and the feel was of an agricultural past long before the Common Market, for a time, transformed rural life into a prosperous and forward-looking one. It seemed a pleasant, friendly, open place – escapist perhaps, but it was hard to see it as a prison for those too poor to own a car.

It took Matt five minutes before he came to The Cottage: a warm red-brick affair, with peeling paintwork, and the air of love and care being more evident in the garden (small and neat at the front, but apparently with a lot more land behind) than on the outside of the house. Matt swallowed: would there be anyone at home? How would he be received? He paused only for a moment, then walked through the gate and rang the bell on the front door. Footsteps – male footsteps surely? – then the door opened and a figure stood in front of him that could only be Peter Basnett. Matt smiled tentatively, then a second later found himself locked in a warm embrace which went on and on.

'Matt! It's good to see you. I feel I'd have known you even if we'd only passed in the street and even if I hadn't seen you on television.'

'I feel the same.'

'Come on in. There's tea brewing. There usually is in this house.'

And Matt was drawn straight into an inviting living room, and had the oddest feeling of coming home. Peter was still looking at him.

'I've often asked myself what I'd do if I saw you – when I saw you, maybe I should say, because I knew you wouldn't give up. And I knew I'd do what I've just done, because I couldn't help myself. Sit down, and I'll fetch the tea things.'

He bustled off into the kitchen, leaving an impression of a slim, energetic man, busy, committed, but with a face – was Matt using prior knowledge, he wondered? – that put on a public front to conceal pain. And, Matt conjectured further, behind that busy, practical façade there was a divided man, whose instincts and moral codes pulled him in various and irreconcilable ways. But perhaps he was reading too much into the bustle which somehow seemed excessive, and a cover for uncertainty. Perhaps he was just relying on Charlie's judgment that this was a muddled man.

'By Golly, you bring back some memories!' said Peter Basnett, as he once was, sitting down. 'The tiny cockney wizard with the ball! It was a pleasure to watch you – an excitement. I bet other people have been telling you that.'

'One or two,' said Matt. He thought Peter was on the point of asking who he had talked to, but if so he bit back the question and went on in the same mode.

'You were somehow so – fresh. I nearly used the word innocent, but you weren't that. You were pretty knowing, really – a street kid. But – it's difficult to explain – you knew it all, had taken it in, in such a childlike way that you didn't seem beyond your years. One wanted to protect you somehow.'

'That's the role I remember you in: my protector,' said Matt, truthfully.

'Perhaps if we'd learnt from you a little too . . . But that's –' Peter faded into silence.

'I have very few memories of that time,' said Matt. 'One or two have come back since – since the find in

197

the attic, but not all that much to the purpose. Of course I've talked to people where I can.'

'Yes, I was going to ask –'

'I know you were. Rory Pemberton I've talked to, and Harry Sugden, Ben Worsnip.'

'They weren't really members of the gang, Harry and Ben.'

'I know. They were from down the hill, like I was. But sometimes the outsider sees most. And Lily Fitch, of course, Lily Marsden as she was then – I've talked to her. And Mrs Carpenter came to see me, and the detective on the case with Yorkshire Police has talked to Mrs Armitage.'

Peter sat for a moment silent, considering the list.

'The Armitages, they were the saddest thing,' he said eventually.

'I know. She's dying.'

Peter nodded.

'Lily married while Sophie and I were living in Houghton Avenue.'

'Yes. There's a son I believe.'

'Oh yes. She was pregnant when she married.'

'There seems to be a complete breach between them.'

'The husband and her?'

'Yes, but I meant between her and the son.'

'The story of Lily's life.'

'You mentioned Sophie. I've never had any lead on her.'

'Wild, really wild, for a bit. Then suddenly she settled down. She's a housewife in Truro now, parent governor at her kids' school, that kind of thing. She's into being a pillar of the community with an understanding side that can sympathize with teenage rebellion. She was, I suppose, the least affected of all of us.'

'And you the most?'

'Oh, I don't know. There was poor Eddie. And Rory is a complete dipsomaniac, as I suppose you've found out.'

'Making tentative steps in the direction of the waggon, I think. You felt the need to change your name, get yourself a new identity, didn't you?' Peter spread his hands wide.

'It was one of the things I tried. Just took my mother's name. I was never close to my father. It was in the seventies, during the feminist revolution. It seemed the thing to do. Solidarity and all that . . . Of course I was trying to escape. Yes. If only it was that easy!'

'You keep in touch. All the gang as you call them.'

'Yes. Minimally. We tell each other if we move, or the telephone number changes. We pass on any information. It's not fail-safe. I never quite know if I get through to Rory Pemberton. It's always been difficult to find a time when he could take it in.'

'I can imagine. This movement towards the waggon – it's as if he is trying to get a grip, but perhaps only because he senses he *has* to, rather than because he wants to.'

'Poor Rory. He never fitted in anywhere, not even into his own family. His parents were repellent, simply on the make. I think we half-realized that at the time. Looking back, I get the feeling he and Lily never had a chance.'

'*Why* do you keep in touch?' Matt asked, looking at him straight. Peter held his look, but with difficulty.

'That was what we decided . . . *then*.'

'Why? Why protect the people responsible?'

'They were part of the gang. And in a way we all felt responsible. But also – there was someone else – still

199

alive, so far as I know. At least none of us has ever heard to the contrary.'

Matt nodded. 'I've guessed a bit about that person.' Suddenly he asked, because he so much wanted to know: 'What happened to Marjie?'

'Marjie?' Peter looked at his watch. 'She should be here soon.'

'Here? But why? You didn't know I was coming.'

'She's at a WI annual get-together. We live together. Have done for five years.' He saw that Matt was moved by this, and said quickly: 'Oh, it's not something terribly romantic. Both of us have tried romance. It works for us still less than it does for most. We're just two bruised people who are better off together than hurting anyone else. And of course we always liked one another. We tell people here that Marjie's husband is a Catholic, which is true, and that she shies away from divorcing him, which isn't.'

'My partner's a Catholic, with a husband,' said Matt. 'Even more problematic. So what does Marjie do?'

'She's a journalist. Works on the *Nottingham Echo*.'

'And you?'

'I'm attached to the Home Office, with responsibility for Children's Homes in the North – and I occasionally have to look at fostering arrangements too if big problems or controversies have arisen. Children, you see – the workings of conscience. I travel around, making spot checks and unannounced visits. What I told you in my letter was basically true.'

'I'm sure.'

'What I didn't tell you was that, once I'd heard you on Radio Leeds, on my car radio, I always turned to it if I was within range, and, knowing you worked there, I've always watched *Look North* if I could, and some-

200

times have seen you doing local bulletins during the day.'

'Why? Did you *want* me to turn up, asking questions?'

'Half of me, Matt. Half of me. Ah – here's Marjie.'

The door, which had opened a crack, was thrown open when the newcomer heard voices, and a substantial woman burst in.

'Matt! I saw the car with a Leeds number plate parked by the Green, and I wondered – no, I knew!' They threw arms around each other as if they'd been lifelong friends, then Marjie held him at arms' length. 'Well, I'll say this for you: you've grown up bonny!'

'You too, Marjie.'

'Fat and frumpish, and nobody cares less about it than myself. If you can't let yourself go when fifty beckons, when can you? Ah, tea – is there still some in the pot?' She poured herself a cup and grabbed a handful of biscuits. 'Lunch was a Women's Institute quiche which suggested the Institute is losing its grip on the housewifely arts. Have they been taken over by Professional Women, I asked myself? If so it's been done by stealth, because I've heard no whisper of it.'

The grown-up Marjie was plump, forthright and funny, and if she was bruised as Peter said, she hid it better than he did. She was so evidently and undisguisedly pleased to see Matt that her enthusiastic manner warmed his heart.

'You know, I must have seen you doing the daytime bulletins in the past without realizing who you were. Once we'd identified you Peter did call me in one time, but too late – I just caught a glimpse. But I do follow the local stuff on *Look North*. I have to as a journalist, which we both are in different ways.'

'I'm a sports journalist if anything. Otherwise I just do talk shows – interviews with local notables and would-be notables, and read things put in front of me.'

'Local radio seems all talk these days. The music used to be crap, but the talk is crap too. Present company excepted.'

'Not excepted. But I'm pretty good on football.'

'So you damned well should be. Well, you don't want to be exchanging polite nothings with us, do you?'

'Actually that's exactly what I would like to be exchanging for as long as you like. Trouble is, I have three children at a football match who have to be picked up afterwards.'

'Yours?'

'Partner's. As near mine as I can make them.'

'That's nice . . . We have talked about this, Peter and I. So we're prepared.' She looked in Peter's direction. He turned to look straight at Matt.

'We realized there was a strong possibility of your turning up. We disagreed a bit about whether to contact you directly. Marjie wanted to, but I thought we should stick to the line we'd agreed all those years ago. As it was, our contacts with you probably fell between two stools – either saying too much or too little.'

'They were diagnosed by an expert as the product of someone in a muddle.'

'Between the two of us, we were,' said Marjie.

'But knowing you might turn up, we've thrown around the question of what we could tell you. We feel that we owe you an account of how the baby died. And that's something that doesn't incriminate anyone, not seriously at any rate.'

Matt just nodded, not wanting to commit himself at that stage to being satisfied with what they were willing to tell him, or to accept the spin they put on it. Even if they were reluctant, the agreement with the rest of the gang would force them to do that.

'It's quite simply told,' said Peter, and his voice took on the rote-telling sound of someone who's been over before what he is prepared to tell. 'It was the day after you left to go home, like I said in the letter. We'd been kicking the ball around on the Catholic School playing field as usual. We were lacking you and Lily and Harry Sugden, so we didn't have the men for a proper game. Then we all wandered along to my house, to Dell View, and there, on the stone-flagged bit in the front, was Lily Marsden. With a baby in a pushchair.'

'Why at yours?'

'She knew our mother was away, Sophie's and mine, visiting her brother in Barnsley. And next door, the Pembertons, were both out at work. Lily's mother must have been in – probably subjecting herself to some new beauty treatment. She was obsessed with her looks, mad about preventing wrinkles or sagging cheeks, and spent hours pulling out grey hairs. She was a horror, and always making disparaging remarks about Lily's lack of attractions. So there she was, standing outside our front door with a pushchair and a baby in a pair of cotton shorts and nothing much else.'

'And Rory Pemberton too?'

'Oh no. Rory had been playing with us. But I saw a look pass between them. He knew she was planning to do something like this.'

'Fulfilling what she'd already been talking about quite a lot?'

Peter looked down, and there was a second's pause. That was something that he might have tried to gloss over.

203

'Yes. You remember that?'

'I remember talk about people not being allowed to breed.'

'If it were only that. That was only the beginning . . . I don't think we can say much more about that.'

'She was being fed notions.'

'Yes. And some of the others in the gang went along with her . . . Anyway, we were gobsmacked for a bit, just saying things like "But you can't" and "That's kid-napping", and so on. She'd done exactly what she always said she'd do, and we couldn't believe our eyes. She said she'd met up with the male hippy, the one we called Dippy, on Armley Park. I expect in fact she'd followed him from home, or the squat rather. He'd got a puppy with him, and he and the little girl, Bella, were playing with it. So she stood around for a bit, and before long it ran off. Dippy wasn't sure what to do, and Lily said she'd mind the baby while he went to catch it. Once he'd run off in search she just wheeled the pushchair back home.'

'But what was she planning to do with Bella?' asked Matt. 'I can hardly believe what she'd been talking about was anything but talk.'

'She was planning to take her down to "my friend".'

'Who you didn't know the identity of.'

Peter hesitated, and Marjie chipped in with 'Not then.'

'So Marjie started saying we should go to the police, or ring them, and Lily started crying, and saying "You can't. I'll be arrested." And we dithered . . . fatally . . . until at last Marjie said "I'm going to ring them anyway".'

'If only we'd just gone, as a gang, a group, and taken the poor little mite from her,' said Marjie, anguish in her voice.

204

'But we weren't a gang, weren't united,' said Peter. 'There were those who were on her side: Rory Pemberton for a start, and Colin Mather too. What happened next has been in all my nightmares since – probably in all our nightmares. Marjie started off in the direction of her house –'

'Sandringham.'

'Yes. But she'd only gone a few steps when Lily grabbed the baby from the pushchair and started off towards the road. I took a step towards her to stop her, but the nearest to her was Eddie. He had been horrified by all this talk that was going on, talk about people not breeding, the future of the race, and crap like that. Eddie'd had a baby sister who died. He rushed forward and began tussling with her to get the baby from her. Rory Pemberton ran over to drag him off her. That's when it happened.'

Peter looked at Matt. Matt felt he was being willed to supply the words Peter left unsaid, words he didn't want to supply. He remained silent. Peter had to go on.

'The fight only lasted a second or two. Bella fell on to the balustrade, on her head. She'd been crying, and suddenly the cries stopped. We just stood there, gaping. When we went to pick her up, she was dead. But we'd all known that anyway.'

'I don't suppose we need to go into our feelings,' said Marjie. 'After a time, after all the recriminations, and there were plenty of those, we had to decide what to do. Lily wanted to take the body down to her friend's, but that seemed horrible to us: like a cat bringing a dead rat home as a sign of its hunting prowess. We said we'd be on the phone to the police the moment she started down the gill. Somehow that transferred the onus of what to do on to us. Lily began to get terrified we were going to "dob her in", as she kept calling it. We couldn't hide from the police the fact that she had taken the baby, and she knew it. And yet after a time we began to think that the last people hippy squatters would go to would be the police. We began to think that though we couldn't deal with the squatters, maybe Lily's "friend" could. We sent her off to try to fix that, and we'd somehow or other conceal the body.'

'And you decided to put it in the attic of the house you were looking after for Mrs Beeston,' I said to Marjie. She looked down into her lap.

'It seemed the best thing. It seems fantastic now, but remember we were just children. We thought of throwing the body into the canal, but that was too horrible, and we thought it would be dragged if the disappearance became official. I had the key, and I went in every day to give an appearance of its being lived in, and I aired it periodically, so if there was a smell open windows wouldn't cause any comment among the neighbours.'

'It was mad,' said Peter.

'Yes, it was mad. But we knew Mrs Beeston, who was arthritic, would never go up there, couldn't if she'd wanted to. So after a bit it seemed the sensible thing to do.'

'We took the body up there,' said Peter, 'just Marjie and me and Eddie, and we laid it out at the far end, behind the little raised walls, and we thought even if anyone went up to the attic, no one would go to that bit. We thought something more was needed, so Eddie said a prayer. He was the only church-goer.'

'Then we stood around awkwardly for a moment,' said Marjie. 'Not knowing what to do, feeling we couldn't just leave the poor little body. Suddenly Eddie sort of exploded in tears and – oh, *cries* they were, like a wild beast. He stumbled down the ladder, ran out of the house and to his own home, and really he was never the same again. He'd never associate with us, feeling terrible guilt I suppose.' She stopped, and there was a few seconds' silence, as if for the dead baby. Peter took up the story.

'And in fact the whole gang broke up, quite quickly. We just didn't want to be with each other, didn't want the sort of feelings and recollections the others brought back to us. I suppose what we wanted was to avoid guilt by association.'

'I see.' Matt sat for a long time, then looked at his watch. 'I have to go. I can't leave the children waiting around after a football match ... One thing bothers me.'

'Yes.'

'The parents. The hippies. I'm taking it they disappeared that night. I know from their neighbour that's what happened at some point. How was that managed?'

'We don't know in detail,' said Peter. 'But Lily said her friend had managed it. When we talked it over we thought there must have been talk of a "tragic accident", of not wanting the children's lives ruined by a piece of carelessness, and perhaps of money changing hands. But that was one problem we couldn't have handled ourselves. We were just glad someone had done it for us.'

Somehow the parting could not be the same as the reunion. The joy had gone, the worm had entered the rose, and the worm's name was suspicion: Peter and Marjie were uncertain how far their version of events had been accepted, and they were right to be so.

'We'll meet up again when all this is over,' said Matt,

wanting to make it clear this was not the end. 'Then we can be more . . . more as we were.'

'Maybe,' said Marjie. 'A little more as we were.' She knew, and Peter knew, that their lives had changed for ever on that day in late August 1969.

They embraced again and Matt went back to the car. He was thoughtful on the way back to Nottingham, but then the problems of dealing with a departing football crowd took his mind off other things. The children, when he picked them up, were so exuberant, even Lewis, that he had no chance to retreat into pensiveness, and the mood remained rowdy over four massive platefuls of pizza – Lewis nicely balanced quantity and quality in his choice of pizza chain.

It was only at night, when they had finally sunk exhausted into bed, that Matt sat in his favourite chair, with a can of beer, and went through the day's new information. And when he did, he became still more certain than before that something, maybe *the* vital thing, had been left out.

# CHAPTER 16

# Families

'And did you believe them?' Charlie asked, when Matt rang him late that night. Charlie's voice, though not unfriendly, had bed tones in it, and Matt felt rather guilty.

'I believed them as a working hypothesis,' he replied. 'It will do to be going on with . . . On the purely human level I felt myself rather often being looked at – quick glances, you know? – to see if I was accepting the tale.'

'Hmm. That's not necessarily conclusive,' Charlie said, being judicious if not actually judicial. 'They may have been conditioned since that day to a belief that their story would *not* be accepted. They couldn't account for the baby-snatch without bringing Lily's "friend" into it, and his belief that some people should not be allowed to breed. That being on the table, a death that's pure accident starts to seem distinctly unlikely.'

'But not impossible. None of those children had baby brothers or sisters, so none of them had any training in how to treat them. They seem to have fought over it as if it were a doll. But you're right, and I'll believe the story they told me until I have reason to do otherwise. These are two seriously nice people, and if they're lying or holding something back it's to protect someone else, not themselves.'

'So the next step – the last step, maybe – is to contact the Farsons, I suppose?'

'Has to be. I'm expecting Aileen back in the next few days, so I'll leave it till after then. In any case, I doubt there'll be any point in talking to the father . . . You know, I should have latched on to him much earlier – we both should.'

'Oh? Why?'

'Here's someone who moves from a modest house to a much larger and a rather more prestigious place when he's approaching retirement age. People don't do that. Wife or husband dead, children leaving home, you start looking for a place that will be *less* trouble, usually a bungalow, something much cheaper to maintain and run. That's what Mrs Beeston did. It should have been what Farson did, but instead he went in the opposite direction.'

'Point taken,' Charlie agreed. 'But if we're suggesting that he bought the house to make sure no one else discovered what was in the attic, then that creates another problem, doesn't it?'

'Yes, it does. Why didn't he dispose of it while he lived there?'

'Was he physically capable of getting up there?'

'I think so. The Goldblatts talked of him working in the garden right up to the time he started losing the plot and doing it in his pyjamas. And if he couldn't get up there, what was the reason for buying the house?'

'To make sure no one else did in his lifetime,' said Charlie.

'That's a point.'

'But you need to think this through before you go

and see the younger Farson. You mustn't think you can go on a sort of fishing trip using half-baked allegations as bait. Better than that would be a simple, open-minded talk aimed at getting information, painting in the whole picture.'

'Thanks, grandmother,' said Matt genially. 'You know, one day I hope you have a really serious case involving football and footballers – not the current bunch of yobs misbehaving at nightclubs, but something really baffling.'

'Oh? Why?'

'Then you can call me in as consultant, and I can be as condescending to you as you are on this case to me.'

'Well! And I thought I was just being helpful.'

Thinking things through over the next few days was hardly on the agenda. Matt and the children were getting increasingly excited about Aileen's return, and on Tuesday evening they had the call they'd been waiting for: she was in Johannesburg, and would be boarding a plane for Manchester in three and a half hours' time. Elderholm went ballistic with delight, and when Matt tried to calm the children down and form them into a sort of pioneer corps to put the house in some kind of order, their resistance was total.

'Mummy's not going to care one little bit if the house looks a tip,' said Isabella, and Matt had to admit that she was right. He busied himself doing all the obvious things to make the place look fairly tidy, more for something to be doing than for any other reason, and the children went into the garden and managed to pick a great bunch of Mr Farson's perennials, accepting contributions from Mrs Goldblatt's more kempt and couth garden to make a monster display in the only large glass vase they could find. Matt silently agreed it did more for the house than his clean-up.

That night they all took Beckham on his late walk again, and this time they were all convinced they saw a fox's brush whisking away round the hedge beside the Presbytery.

Next morning Matt rang the two schools in Pudsey the children attended, and said their mother was coming home after three months' absence and he was taking them to meet her. When one school demurred he said they'd been very unsettled by her absence, he not being their father, and he felt it important they actually met her on her homecoming – 'so that the process of bonding can begin again' he actually said, feeling a terrible phoney. The school caved in immediately. They had more than enough problem children from broken relationships, and they felt obliged to be supportive where it seemed necessary.

They all packed into the car, including Beckham, who loved long journeys and controlled his urinary weakness remarkably well on them. Matt had always thought airports were hell on earth, and though many people said Manchester was several cuts above Heathrow or Gatwick, to Matt it was a pretty standard sort of hell-hole. Still, they were able to take Beckham into the Arrivals area, registered that Aileen's plane was only half an hour delayed, and settled down to junk food and coffee. They were by the passageway leading out of Customs at least half an hour before Aileen could reasonably have been expected to get through, surveying the streams of passengers as they emerged. Stephen even demanded of one lot whether they were off the Johannesburg plane, and had they seen his mother. His siblings pretended they weren't with him.

And then there she was. Wheeling a single suitcase, as she had when she left, and with an old airline bag slung over her shoulder, she marched out into freedom looking so pleased, and tired, and excited, and desirable that Matt could hardly bear to let the children go first and jump up and kiss her, scream their ecstasy at seeing her again, take her case, push Beckham's whiskery nose in her face, and generally forget all about Matt.

'Time's up!' he announced commandingly, and folded Aileen into his arms in a long, long kiss and embrace that almost had him whimpering with pleasure and relief. And certainly when he held her at arms' length to get a good look at her, her cheeks were blotchy, though she also looked wonderfully happy.

'Celebratory drink, or home?' he asked.

'Home. I've had enough of those damned little bottles,' Aileen said.

So it was back to the car, with Beckham in the luggage area this time, his old place, and a return to the motorway, through the gloom of Saddleworth moors, the spiritual backdrop to mass murder, then over the border into Yorkshire, with lots of singing, innumerable questions and all too many bad jokes treasured up from the playground, then finally the horror of the Armley gyratory and home.

It occurred to Matt as he got them all inside, that not one of their questions had been about their father.

He'd prepared a meal before they left, of lamb chops and fresh peas, and it could be ready in half an hour at the touch of a few switches. At nine o'clock Stephen fell asleep on the sofa, and by half past the older children were unashamedly wilting too. When he and Aileen were alone Matt poured two glasses of wine, looked at her, and said:

213

'You do like the house?'

'Love it. Matt?'

'Yes?'

'Do you want to get married? Somehow?'

'Don't give a damn. We are married.'

'I love you so much.'

And then it was back together, the first time in what seemed an age, and endless pleasure and sleepiness. Matt had cunningly arranged two days free by swaps with colleagues, and when the children had been got off to school next day it was back to bed, more love-making, and then lots of talk. Most of it was about the children, but one little bit was about the dead baby. When Matt had brought Aileen up to date, she said:

'I can tell from your voice that you're not entirely satisfied. You want to believe what they told you, because you like them so much, but there's something – I don't know – something that doesn't gel, isn't there?'

'Yes. But I can't pin down precisely what it is.'

Aileen lay there considering.

'I'm not sure I can pin it down, but I see what you mean. I can understand all the stuff about poor Eddie Armitage. Feeling that he was responsible for the baby's death was enough to send a boy already pretty unsure of himself over the edge . . . Is it the conspiracy to protect Lily Marsden that doesn't gel?'

'Not in itself, I don't think. Peter was always by nature a protector. I used to feel that. If there was any chance of Lily being taken to court on a serious charge – at the least, kidnapping Bella – then I think both he and Marjie would persuade the others to gang up to protect her.'

'Then is it his reluctance to give a name to her friend, even though it seems he and Marjie know it now?'

'No, it's not that. You couldn't accuse the friend without accusing Lily too, even if the influence he had would lessen her guilt – a strong personality twisting an under-aged and unhappy girl. You might just accuse Lily and keep the friend out of it, but you couldn't do the reverse.'

'I suppose not . . . It beats me. A collection of adults who don't particularly like each other, who have had little or nothing to do with each other for thirty years, *except* this conspiracy to keep shtoom about the baby.'

'But that *is* a very important matter. Have you or I had anything remotely as important in our lives, let alone our *young* lives? It was potentially a murder or a manslaughter charge. I can see that, once the conspiracy was entered into, it was vital to keep it up.'

'There's only one thing to do.'

'What's that?'

'Go and talk to the younger Mr Farson.'

'He's all of sixty. But you're right. That's where the answers are. I've just got to get my mind around the right way to approach him, Charlie says.'

It was a week later – the happiest week of his life, Matt thought – that his car pulled up outside Carl Farson's gate. He had been given the address in the correspondence over the purchase of Elderholm, but it had meant nothing to him. It was, he now saw, a house for people who didn't bother about their house. It was one of a collection of boxes, probably built in the last five years, varying slightly in size, offering the buyer a choice between a triangular arch or a flat slab over the front door, but otherwise a machine to live in, in the most soulless and dispiriting meaning of that phrase. Only the vicinity of Farnley Park gave the estate even the faintest semblance of desirability. The ridiculous thing was, these houses had probably not been cheap.

It was half past six. Carl Farson, the estate agent had told him, was manager of one of the branches of Freshfare, the supermarket chain. If he was on the evening roster Matt was out of luck, but there was a light on at the end of the hallway and when he rang he heard footsteps almost at once.

'Oh – it's Mr Harper, isn't it?'

'Matt, please. Are you busy?'

'No, not at all. Just finished my meal – one of our own convenience foods, I'm afraid, with a convenience pudding to follow. I never learnt to cook while I was married, and I've never bothered to learn since we split up. Come on through.'

Not interested in his home, not interested in his food. Matt wondered idly what button you would have to press to get from him commitment, involvement, enthusiasm. What sort of buff was he? Snooker, darts, the Masons, table-tapping, steam locomotives? He came into a room where a bit of minor untidiness was the only relief from the prevailing anonymity. The television was showing *Look North*, and Carl Farson reached to switch it off.

'You're not on tonight, then?'

'I usually only do fill-ins,' said Matt. 'Though there's talk of something a bit more challenging.'

'I've not seen anything recently about this baby business,' said Farson, looking him in the eyes.

'No. There's been nothing that could be broadcast. Really we could only tell the full story if we had a trial and a conviction, and I don't think that's on the cards. But it's about that that I've come.'

'I thought it might be. But I think you'll be wasting your time. I know so little about those houses –'

'I realize that. Just to fill you in on that: we think

216

that the baby was taken from her father in Armley Park, taken back to Houghton Avenue, there was some kind of struggle over her between two of the children who lived in those houses, in the course of which she fell on to the stone balustrade at the front of Dell View and was killed instantly.'

'I see . . . You've done good work.'

'The thing I'm interested in is why the child took the baby in the first place. It was just one of the group who did the snatch. It seems she had come under some very strong external influence. Let's not beat about the bush: let's say a malign influence.'

Carl Farson's face was a mask of thought. By his side in the armchair his hands started clutching and unclutching themselves. He saw Matt noticing them, and stopped.

'And?'

'During the day, this particular child visited a house off the Raynville Road on a regular basis. It was a matter of comment – smutty speculation – among the other children. The house was 8 Leighton Terrace.'

'Yes.' Something like a sigh escaped him. 'I suppose that would be the reason you've come.'

'Were you still living there at the time?' Matt asked.

He shook his head emphatically.

'No. I married when I was twenty-five. We were still pretty much in the love-bird stage in 1969, with a new baby. Sad . . .'

'And your father is, I suppose, beyond questioning now?'

'Oh yes, mostly. Even on his best days you couldn't get anything out of him about what happened in 1969. You might as well say 1469 or 69BC. In any case, at that time, as I think I told you, my father was still working.'

217

Matt creased his brow.

'I think you did. But I don't see your point.'

'My father did not work as a night watchman or a night manager in a hotel. Apart from weekends he was never there during the day.'

'And you were married –' A dim shaft of light shone in Matt's brain. 'Someone mentioned a daughter.'

'My sister Nesta.' He shifted uneasily in his chair. 'She died last year, so I can tell you about her. Even so, it's not easy.'

'If she was the person who had this child under her influence, then I'd guess she wasn't an easy person,' Matt said gently.

'She wasn't. It's funny, I always felt slightly scared of her, even though she was a year younger than me. Later on I tried to tell myself that it was jealousy, not fear: she got on, made something of herself, in a small way made a name. But it wasn't that. Almost from the first it was uneasiness. She never wanted to inspire love in people – not in our dad, not even in our mam, who died when I was about fifteen. She preferred to arouse uneasiness, shading off into fear. You never knew where you were with Nesta. And she came out with things that nobody else could ever have found words for: things about yourself, things about our background, how it held her back, locked her in . . . She was bitter, she specialized in saying nasty things that you suspected might be true, but were better left unsaid. There was no doubt she was bright. With other bright kids you might say "bright as a button", but she wasn't bright like that. She was sharp as a knife.'

Matt suspected that this was the key that had to be turned to unlock Carl Farson's mind, the thing that had obsessed him, rankled with him, and had done all his childhood and throughout his adult life. His sister was a phenomenon he had wrestled with, tried to get to the bottom of. And probably failed.

'I can see she was rather an unnerving family member to have,' he said.

'*She was terrifying at times*,' Farson said abruptly. Then he swallowed. 'Anyway, she got a place at a teachers' college. She could have gone to university, but she said we couldn't afford it. I think Father could have managed it, and there were grants then, but I think she wanted the shorter course and the independence it would give her earlier. She did psychology and P.E., and came top of her year. I remember reading her references from College once, and was surprised at a certain lack of enthusiasm that seeped through, as though they were holding something back. But it didn't stop her getting a good job as games mistress at a good private school near Harrogate.'

'And was there trouble there?'

'Not in the way I think you mean. Not that I knew of. She'd been there teaching for two years when she had a bad accident in the gym: she fell from a climbing rope, or rather it wasn't properly secured and she fell with it and injured her spine very badly. She was in a wheelchair for the rest of her life.'

'I think I'm beginning to understand,' said Matt, getting a sense of a fiery, awkward, contradictory spirit horribly imprisoned.

'She got good compensation – good for that time, when they didn't hand out small fortunes at the drop of a hat. It was handled by Morley-Coombs in Armley, and he was brilliant. There was no doubt it was part of the caretaker's job to set up and maintain the gym equipment, not my sister's. But there she was, back in a home she hated, spending day after day in the front room, watching people pass by, listening to the radio, doing the crossword in the paper. "Being banged up" she called it.'

'I can't imagine the girl you have described really being content with that. There must have been escape routes.'

'There were, of a kind. She enrolled for an Open University course the moment it started up. The major component was philosophy. She did incredibly well, got special help, and eventually – but this was several years after the year you're interested in – got a job with them. They put her in a special flat in Milton Keynes, with all the aids to independence you could think of, and she learnt easily to do most things for herself. Yes, she made her escape.'

'But that left her emotional life unsatisfied.'

Carl Farson considered this.

'I think maybe her emotional life was always going to be a problem, accident or no accident. There was talk when she was on the staff at Milton Keynes about an unhealthy influence on students, but it never came to anything, because of course they were all adults, and presumed to be capable of taking care of themselves. More serious, when this "political correctness" idea came in, there were complaints that she was peddling obnoxious ideas in her lectures and seminars. They had some kind of enquiry or official hearing into those complaints.'

'I suppose this was notions of racial purity, was it? Eugenics I think they used to call it.'

'That and other things. Denying the Holocaust, what she called the paralysis of democracy, sterilization of the unfit.'

'They all seem to point in a certain direction.'

'Yes. But Nesta argued that she threw around other arguments of a quite different political colour, but they didn't arouse the same ire in the "political correctness" people. And Nesta was clever – she probably did. In any case her answer was that it was her business to test students' responses to ideas, to float apparently outrageous theories in front of them, to stimulate their reactions and test their philosophical judgments. Students needed to know, she said, why notions that were perfectly acceptable in one generation could become intellectually beyond the pale to the next. I'm sorry if I'm not explaining this very well. I'm rather out of my depth.'

'Far from it. I think you must have heard her talking about it, didn't you?'

'Only now and then. But when she did, I certainly remembered it. Nesta had a hold on me, you might say. She wasn't a frequent visitor back home, as you might guess. Her physical condition made visits difficult unless she was fetched, but in the early days Dad could drive down and get her, or I could. It didn't happen often. She wasn't really interested. But by the way, if she did come up to Leeds, you could be sure she'd go and visit Lily Fitch, as she had become.'

'I see. So we can be open about who we're talking about.'

'Oh yes. She was the favourite among the disciples. "Acolytes" Nesta used to call them. I had to go and look the word up. The acolytes started back in the late sixties, the time you're interested in. They were all children: early teens or a bit later. First it was doing errands for her, for small sums of money – things from the butcher's or grocer's, magazines from the newsagent's. Then maybe it was into town for library books. And

221

soon she had them in her coils. Don't ask me how, don't ask me what they did together: I think there was a sexual dimension, but I've no evidence of it. And if there was, it wasn't the really important aspect. That was filling their minds with her ideas: taking a sort of mental control, and then using it to its fullest extent. I suppose Nesta would be called a control freak these days.'

'I think she would,' Matt said. 'Were you never with them when they were together, her and Lily? So that you could get an idea what the relationship depended on?'

'Never – only if I happened to be visiting, opening the door and showing Lily through to her, that kind of thing . . . I did once listen.'

'Outside the door?'

'Window, actually. One summer much later on, in Elderholm. Those houses, though they're terraces, are very private, shielded – as of course you'd know. In any case Nesta could hardly run out and catch me at it, and Lily was just a visitor. Still, I felt pretty scared, I can tell you, just like when I was a boy.'

He faded into silence. Matt waited, but then had to prompt him.

'When was this?'

'Late seventies, I'd say. When she was back on one of her rare visits from Milton Keynes, and Lily was a mother, with a child just starting school . . . They were talking about the things you've mentioned, and it was almost as if Nesta was giving her a sort of refresher course. She always had a lot of the teacher in her – or preacher you might say, preacher of a particularly twisted kind. I heard her say: "In the long term sterilization is probably the answer. In the short term, it has

222

to be human extermination." My blood ran cold. It brought back all those terrible pictures of Auschwitz and Buchenwald . . .'

'Was there anything else?'

Carl Farson shook his head, regretfully.

'Lots. Too much to want to remember. The sort of thing I've just mentioned she might have hinted at to Dad and me: playing with us, teasing us, apparently just wanting to shock. She *did* shock, but that kind of thing seemed so remote by the 1970s, so much a part of the terrible past, that it seemed to have nothing to do with our everyday lives. But I heard her say to Lily: "The governing impulse of all creatures is to control. You see that in animals, you see it in humans: in the schoolroom, in the workplace, the family. I control this family, poor little victory though *that* is. The impulse to control takes many forms. Its ultimate expression is what people call murder: the assertion of authority by the cancelling out of another existence – one that threatens or offends. Because it's the ultimate expression of the most basic impulse, it is also the ulti-mate thrill, and the ultimate satisfaction."'

Matt and Farson both sat for a moment lost in thought.

'Yet she never did anything about the body,' at last Matt said.

'Nesta wasn't in a position to *do* anything herself.'

'But she could get Lily to do it, on one of her visits.'

'Not easy, with Dad retired by then and usually pot-tering around the house or the garden. How do you justify having sent your visitor up to a virtually empty attic if he was to find her coming down the stepladder. Not easy to think of an excuse.'

223

'True. Yet I suppose it was Nesta who persuaded your father to buy the house.'

'Oh yes. She put up half the money herself, from the money she got as compensation for her terrible injury. If she'd still been alive she'd have got the whole house when Dad dies and I'd have the rest – the cash. Oh, she nagged him into it: he'd no wish to have four bedrooms, a large dining room, that kind of thing, particularly at his age. She said it was a better house for a disabled person – no steps at the back, and she could take over the ground floor for herself, apart from the kitchen, and leave the upstairs to Dad. Dad wasn't at all keen, but what Nesta wanted, Nesta got. She had, as she said, control over the family. And the house was no sooner bought than she was offered the job in Milton Keynes – lectureship as it was then. It was genuinely out of the blue, I'm quite sure about that, but once she got over the surprise she was over the moon. Accepted like a shot and never looked back. In the event, having just moved, Dad enjoyed the garden, perhaps enjoyed being on his own, and didn't care a bean about the house. He didn't even bother to furnish some of it, and never did any redecoration. He was a typical retired person: only happy when he was pottering about weeding and mowing and tying things up.'

'I begin to understand about the body,' said Matt. 'She didn't need to do anything about it. She was safe for the rest of her life.'

'Yes . . . And there's another thing,' her brother said. 'I think it appealed to her sense of danger. She was an active woman, imprisoned in a damaged body. She desperately needed excitement – the sort of thing that other people get from sex, affairs, travel, driving fast – whatever. Her excitement was up there in the attic.'

'A rather safe kind of excitement,' commented Matt. 'In her lifetime the house couldn't be sold.'

'Perhaps – I don't know – perhaps she wanted it known, after her death.'

Matt remembered Charlie's remark about Harold Shipman: in the end serial killing was not enough. He needed to be acknowledged as one of the world's most successful mass murderers.

There seemed to be nothing more to be said, so Matt got up, and extended his hand to Carl Farson.

'I'm grateful to you,' he said. 'It can't have been easy.'

'Oh, I don't know. Nesta is dead. No great bravery called for. What I would have done if she had still been alive I don't know.'

'Referred me to her, I suppose,' said Matt. 'She doesn't sound the sort of person to welcome anyone acting as her spokesman.'

'No, she wasn't . . . Do you know what she was when she died?'

'What she was?'

'Her title in the Open University. It was Professor of Moral Philosophy. Makes you think, doesn't it? Makes you hope she didn't influence a whole generation of students who took her courses. God help us if she did!'

Later that evening, after a half hour's talk on the phone with Matt, Charlie Peace sat down over a late night coffee and said to Felicity:

'Looks as if Matt has identified the influence behind those Houghton Avenue children.'

And he told her about Nesta Farson, her life and ideas, and the sense he got of her single-minded perverseness.

'Odd,' said Felicity when he had finished. 'It *is* all a bit like *Dombey and Son*.'

'Why *Dombey*?'

'It turned out to be a daughter after all. And the man who wasn't there turned out to be a woman.'

'Anyway, that seems to wrap up the case. She's dead, there's no way we can prove any intention to kill or harm at this late stage, so Lily Fitch is in the clear. All neatly wrapped up, though Matt will be upset, and I'm not happy.'

'The little bones crying out for justice?'

'Something like that. I don't have your turn of phrase, but it's something I feel in my bones, my blood. Put unromantically, it's unfinished business.'

## CHAPTER 17

# Aftermath

But there were still one or two pieces missing from the jigsaw.

The high-ups in the West Yorkshire police reacted to Charlie's report in the way he expected them to: there was no possibility of securing a conviction, no reason to think a major crime had been committed, so no further action would be taken. Charlie, bringing the news to Matt, said that there was no way he could quarrel with that decision: there was no conclusive evidence that the bones were those of little Bella, and no certainty about how the child had met its death. End of story.

Matt, having mulled over the decision for a few days, decided to ring Peter Basnett and Marjie Humbleton with the news. He knew there was more to be got from that quarter, and hoped this might be the means of getting it. In the event it was Marjie who was in.

'Basically the case is shelved, and that means permanently,' he said, after the initial salutations and courtesies. 'There's really no chance at this date of getting new evidence of the sort that would persuade the Crown Prosecution Service that it was worth bringing a case – you probably know they take some persuading,

227

even in cases that don't have this difficulty about the length of time since the offence and so on. So that's it, really . . .'

'You're disappointed?' Marjie asked.

'Yes, I suppose I am.'

'I'm not. Oh, not for any tenderness towards Lily – it's more than twenty-five years since I've seen her, and she may be a quite different person to the one I knew, but somehow I don't think any new Lily is likely to be my type. It's just that it's such a long time ago, everyone has gone on – scarred, sometimes irreparably, but . . . Oh dear: I'm afraid in essence I feel what we made, through our decision, is such a *mess* that a trial would leave it still more of one, not less of one.'

'At any rate Lily is now in the clear over it. Does that make it any easier for you?'

There was silence at the other end.

'I'm not sure I get your meaning.'

'I got a strong impression that you and Peter were holding back on something when we talked at Belling Joyce. If Lily is now in no danger of prosecution, I'm just wondering if that alters matters for you.'

Silence again.

'Perhaps . . . The thing we held back on could probably never have been part of any case, but . . . oh, it's the thing that shocked us most, made us do what we did when the child died. And perhaps it explains – even better than what we told you – what happened to poor Eddie Armitage.'

'Tell me. I promise it will go no farther.'

This time the silence was to get her words into their best order.

'We told you about the scuffle, when Eddie tried to grab the baby. We – Peter and I – were several feet

228

away, and that's all it was to us: a scuffle. But when the poor little girl lay dead on the stone floor of the balustrade and we'd all run up to stand beside and over it, Eddie turned on Lily, panting and sobbing: ''You threw her down,'' he said, crying, sobbing. ''You'd got her back from me and you *threw* her down. I could see your face. It was horrible. You were smiling. You're evil!'' '

'Oh God,' said Matt. 'I see why you held it back.'

'So then we knew, you see, what we'd spawned, as a group. Not that we'd initiated it or nurtured it, but that we'd let it grow up among us. Eddie looked around at all of us. Rory Pemberton said ''You're making it up,'' but nobody believed him. Rory had been close to the scuffle, but he hadn't tried to intervene. He'd been the one who was most sympathetic to Lily's ideas, or the ideas that had been fed to her. I don't know if you can understand this, but it was the fact that we knew Lily was guilty that made us determined to cover the whole thing up.'

'I see,' said Matt, 'or think I dimly do. I suppose if you'd thought she was innocent you might have trusted to the justice system.'

'Yes – we might. But knowing she was guilty, not just of kidnapping but of killing the poor little thing meant we couldn't. It was partly that we had to protect her, little though we liked her, but partly too that we had to protect ourselves. We felt that we were all involved. Peter and I were the obvious ones to do something, but we just shrugged it off: we'd heard the talk, we'd rubbished it and ridiculed it, but we'd done nothing. Not gone to her parents, not gone to our own. And some of us – Rory, Colin – were a bit more involved, more sympathetic. And so we made the pact, and so

229

we kept it, until now. I don't say we were wise, I don't say we would have done it if we'd been a bit older, I certainly don't say it was better that we did it, but that's *why* we concealed the evidence.'

Matt was still digesting this when Marjie spoke again.

'We did it. We were probably wrong, and the consequences – just the ones we know about – were terrible. But – that awful phrase! – we meant well.'

'I suppose so,' said Matt carefully. 'But I still have the impression of a lot of lives that went wrong, just because of that decision.'

'Not because of the decision,' said Marjie, with steel in her voice. 'Our lives went wrong the moment we saw that little body lying on the stone . . . Matt?'

'Yes?'

'I think we should keep hold of our memories of the good times. Just the memories. Goodbye Matt.'

And before he could say anything he heard the click of the phone being put down at the other end. But if he'd been quicker, what could he have said? His bones told him that Marjie was right. Among the other, more important things that that frail, tiny body had destroyed was any possible relationship between the three of them. The burden of their concealments spoiled any possibility of their coming together in any sort of unshadowed way. He honoured both Peter and Marjie, but he felt he had heard the last of them, and he didn't protest.

By pure coincidence Matt met up with Lily Fitch again only a few days after his talk with Marjie. He had been interviewing a resident of an old people's home about Bramley in the old days before Town Street had been vandalized by the local council. On his way home he popped into the Bramley Shopping Centre to pick up some steak for a cosy meal for two with Aileen – the children being off to the swimming pool with friends. It was as he was heading for the meat section that he saw Lily coming towards him, pushing a trolly laden with sliced bread and assorted bottles.

She saw him a second later. She was by then only a few feet away. A cunning little smile spread over her narrow lips, and Matt could have sworn she was going to ask some pert question about the dead baby or comment on the lack of progress in the investigation. But the habit of a lifetime reasserted itself, and she passed him still smiling, but silent. Immensely self-satisfied, but silent.

Matt slowed down, grabbed some steak, and tried to plot her progress. He saw her pass between stacks, and from a distance he could swear the smile was still on her face. When he saw her piling her trolleyload on to the checkout counter it was still there.

He had obviously made Lily Fitch's day.

It was several weeks after this that Matt received a communication that surprised him because he had forgotten entirely his conversation with the genealogically-inclined Mr Woof of Morley. Mr Woof himself, it was clear, had let the matter slip from his mind for a long time until, chancing to have business in his attic, he had remembered Matt's interest in his research among the various twigs and branches of the Woofs. He had retrieved his plastic bag of notebooks and got Matt's address from the pad by the telephone.

*'Anyway,'* he wrote, after profuse apologies, *'in all my papers there's only one Douglas Woof, so if he's not your man then I'm afraid you're up against a blank wall. He is the son of people who I think may have been*

*distant cousins of my parents – their birthdates are both*
*in the 1920s, so it's perfectly possible that one or both*
*of them is still alive: Richard and Gladys Woof, of Gran-*
*tham. They had two children, one of them a son, Doug-*
*las, and he was born in 1945. Good luck in your search.'*

Work next day was distinctly interesting. The possibility
that he might be promoted to share the presenters' job
on *Look North* had firmed up and become a matter of
general discussion. He found the prospect enticing, both
for the chance to make changes to a stale and over-coy
format, but also of course from the money point of
view. Not least of his causes for satisfaction was that
the moment the possibility of his promotion spread
round the BBC North complex, Liza Pomfret began spit-
ting blood. She had never forgiven him for being interviewed on developments in the case on *Look North*
rather than her own show. Her list of the unforgiven
was longer than Pooh Bah's list of victims. He heard
her on the phone during the day using all her wiles
(mostly bullying and abuse) to get a transfer back to
London and the big time. It made sense. It was the
only place she did feel at home in, and it was full of
like-minded people she could make unhappy.

Her holiday programme had been shown, including
a clip of the young reporter in the door of the helicopter,
carrying on the shot to within a fraction of a second
before the chopper decapitated him. O Brave New
World, that has such gritty television journalism in it!

But he found time, in among his pleasanter preoccu-
pations, to look in the Lincolnshire telephone directories, where he found a Woof, G. living in Grantham.
Going into surrounding towns he lighted on a Woof,
D. in a Nottingham directory, resident in Retford. That

night he decided to approach Dougie, if that were he, indirectly. He had always been an indirect footballer, relying on cunning quite as much as speed and accuracy. He felt he should know a little more before he set up any sort of meeting. So the next day at work he dialled the Grantham number, 01476 963 5744.

'963 5744,' said an elderly voice. Didn't bother with the area code, Matt thought, because almost all her callers were local.

'Hello, is that Mrs Woof?'

'It is. Who's calling?'

'My name is Freddie Morton,' said Matt, thinking to limit the number of lies that could later be laid to his account. 'Excuse me ringing you out of the blue, but I have a feeling I used to know your son –'

'Oh?' An element of reserve entered her voice.

'Could you tell me, if I'm not being intrusive, whether you are the mother of Dougie Woof?'

'He never likes being called Dougie these days,' said the voice with a touch of sharpness. 'It's always Douglas.'

'Most people called him Dougie at school, I seem to remember,' said Matt, chancing his arm. The voice unfroze a little. Knowing Dougie at school, Matt guessed, was more acceptable than knowing him in the years immediately after school.

'Oh, you knew him at school? Yes, they did, but I never liked it, and it doesn't do now. If you're an accountant you can't do with a name that sounds rather comic, can you?'

'No, of course you can't. So Doug – Douglas is an accountant, is he? I seem to remember he was always good with figures.'

'Oh, he *was*,' said the voice, pride entering into it for

233

the first time. 'Mathematics was always his very best subject – a top mark in his O level. He could have gone to university but –'

'Oh, I chose not to go to university myself,' said Matt, with some truth. At the age of sixteen his world had been the world of football, and he had left education behind.

'I suppose at that age,' said the voice vaguely, 'and at that *time*, when the world seemed to go mad, it's forgivable to go a little wild, do odd things . . . Anyway, that's all in the past. Douglas is very well settled now, has got a lovely house in Retford, lovely family, and is doing so well in his job. Independent you know, and lots of clients. What was it you wanted him for?'

'Oh, it was about another schoolfriend I think he may have kept in touch with.'

They chattered on for a minute or two, and then rang off. Matt was so confident he had now identified his man that he almost forgot to ask for his telephone number. It was the number he had already, and he felt sure that he had got him. All that remained was to consider how to approach the father of the dead Bella.

He devoted a great deal of thought to that, and decided that the only way that had any chance of getting anything personal out of him was face to face. That being so he had to abandon the old schoolfellow lie and come up with something that couldn't be contradicted by their respective appearances – all of fifteen or sixteen years between them, he calculated. He consulted the Nottingham directory again, saw that Douglas Woof had a business as well as a home address, and rang it.

'My name is Harper,' he told a secretarial voice at the other end, 'and I work for Radio Leeds and on *Look North*.'

234

'Oh, how interesting!'

'The thing is, it seems I'm about to get a good promotion, quite a lot more money, and just possibly a shift to the Nottingham area, and it seemed to me that I ought to get myself an accountant.'

'I'm sure Mr Woof would like to talk to you about that. Will you hold the line while I get him for you?'

The fatal lure of television. But the upshot was a long talk with a very respectable-sounding Douglas Woof. Matt explained his prospects in mendacious detail, explained that he'd got Woof's name, highly recommended, from a man he'd got talking to in a pub, and the conversation continued with Matt telling him quite a lot of true things (football, chat programmes on radio, football commentaries on both media) as well as quite a lot of lies. The upshot was an enthusiastic invitation to come over to Retford ('spy out the territory, eh, old man?') for a business dinner together.

'Quite a good little Italian place in the centre. They give me a table in a little alcove when they know I'm with a client, so everything will be perfectly confidential,' said Douglas, in his reassuring voice. 'Nothing will go beyond those four walls.'

Three walls if it's an alcove, thought Matt pedantically. Still, a bit of privacy was best if the conversation went as he hoped. The dinner was fixed for the following Tuesday, which turned out to be the first real downpour of rain for some time. Matt found the Tavola Toscana without difficulty, asked for Mr Woof, and was shown across to a little box with a table and window in it and shook hands with a man with a fair, well-tended moustache, a less well-controlled paunch, and a convincingly trustworthy manner. He was less tall than

235

Matt remembered, well below him in height, but then his memories were those of a seven-year-old of someone in his early twenties. Someone different, somehow 'other', and therefore rather frightening.

'Good to meet you,' said Douglas Woof heartily, giving his fair moustache a loving stroke or two. 'A drink to start with? Then we can get the menu read and get down to a chat.'

The strictly business matters, mainly fictitious on Matt's part, lasted through the soup and antipasti, and it was Woof himself who nudged the talk in the direction of the personal.

'You're very wise, you know, getting your finances properly looked after, though of course it's not my place to say so. You've no idea how many silly things people do with their own money. It's not just themselves they should think about, but their widows and children, should the worst come to the worst.' Another stroke of the moustache. 'Are you a family man yourself?'

'Partner and her three. I regard them as my own.'

'Still at school?'

'Oh, very much so,' said Matt, bringing out a snapshot.

'Lovely-looking kids,' said Douglas, with the sort of sincerity that suggested he would have said 'rotten-looking kids' if he had really thought so. He too fished in his pocket and brought out a picture of his own, all around the swing in a back garden, all three of them of primary school age.

'You started late,' commented Matt. Douglas nodded as if it was a matter of pride. 'No bad thing,' Matt continued. 'We're contemplating one of our own. I was married before, very briefly and when I was much too young. Thank heaven it was childless.'

Douglas Woof seemed about to say something, but they were interrupted by the arrival of the vitello milanese and the grilled prawns they had ordered.

'Sorry, you were about to say something, weren't you?' resumed Matt as he took up his knife and fork. 'Did you have another, earlier family? Don't tell me if you'd rather not. I know it can be painful if you lose touch. It's something a lot of people call in about on our phone-ins.'

Douglas thought for a moment, then said:

'I wouldn't tell this to everyone – not your respectable local businessman, for example. But you having been in the sporting world, and now in television – well, you're a man of the world.' He leant forward as if about to divulge a budget secret: 'I went through a really wild phase in the sixties.'

Matt raised his eyebrows and suppressed a grin.

'No! I'd not have guessed that. But I do just remember that time. A lot of people went through a wild phase then. Some didn't live to come out of it. What form did your wild phase take?'

'Oh, the lot. Flowers in my hair, ghastly smock-thing, a nice little chick and a baby – you name it, we did it, including squatting and marijuana. Still indulge now and then, in the privacy of my own home. No harm in it so far as I'm concerned, but I wouldn't want the children to find out. Thank God I never went on to anything dangerous, though.'

'Well, well,' said Matt, putting on a wondering look. 'And I suppose you and the chick broke up and you lost contact with the child?'

Douglas shook his head. He was quite enjoying the confessional.

'Not quite. She was a lovely girl, by the way, but she

237

went a bit far – swallowed all the prevailing notions, going a bit over the top.'

'And you never did?'

'Not like *that*. Don't get me wrong – she was a real sweetie, and she thought the world of me – we did of each other, of course, but I don't think it could have lasted, she was just too . . . other-worldly. And then our little Bella died, and that was the beginning of the end for us. Within a year I was back in the real world and studying accountancy. Funny old business, life.'

From hippy to bar room (or in this case Italian restaurant) philosopher in thirty glorious years.

'There's a lot of sadness around,' contributed Matt. 'Nothing more devastating than a child's death. What was it? Meningitis?'

'No, it was an accident. Child was looking after it – perfectly responsible teenage girl I'd thought – and the next thing we knew poor little Bella had been dropped – landed on her head on a stone balustrade and that was that.'

'How terrible! And you weren't there at the time?'

'No – I was chasing a little puppy we'd got for Bella. Never caught the poor little thing. This was in Leeds, your neck of the woods. That was where we were squatting. Anyway when I got back the girl and the pushchair had disappeared. I was worried but not frantic. It was a park we were in, and something could have happened to make her uneasy. I went to the houses where I knew the girl lived, but they were silent as the grave, and I didn't know which she lived in, nor even her name. But she knew where we lived – squatted – so I went back, expecting to find her there, or that she'd come and bring Bella back soon.'

'And she came, but not with Bella?'

'No, but with someone else. When I got home I found Sandra – that was my girl's name – half stoned when I got there. I rolled myself a joint, but then I thought I'd better not smoke it in case I needed to go to the police and get them to look for Bella. In theory I despised the police, of course, but – you know –'

'I know. They have their uses.'

'Of course, of course. I'm talking about then,' Woof said very insistently. 'No one is more supportive of the police than I am today. And I suppose there was a little of the later me lurking in the hippy one, waiting to get out. And then there was a knock at the door, and when I went to open it there was this woman in a wheelchair, being pushed by the girl who was looking after Bella. "Where's Bella?" I shouted, and the woman asked if they could come in.'

'Who was the woman, then?' asked Matt, feigning ignorance. 'The girl's mother?'

'No. No relation. Friend, she said. She was trying to be nice, sorrowful, understanding, but somehow . . . There was an intensity, a terrible caged energy that – well, I'll be frank: that *frightened* me. They came in. Sandra was far gone – and the woman looked askance at *that* I can tell you. Anyway, they sat down, and then the story came out: the accident, how it wasn't Lily's – that was her name – fault, just not being used to small children. And then there came a new thing: how the publicity over it could ruin Lily's life, how sensitive she was, how devastated by what had happened. And then there came an offer of money.'

The real Matt suddenly took over.

'Surely you must have smelt a rat?'

Douglas bridled a little.

'Oh, I did! "Hang on," I said to myself, "what's going

on here?" If this was an accident, how come I'm being offered money to hush it up? And the first thing I thought was that this woman wanted a baby, and she was offering us money for ours. For all I know now that could be the case, but somehow –'

'She just wasn't the maternal type, by the sound of it.'

'Not in the least. But the maternal isn't one type, is it? She'd be all right as the tigress guarding her cubs. It occurred to me we hadn't much to offer Bella, except love: a life of drifting and of benign neglect when we were high. And though Sandra was a good mother in her way, it was a sort of inadequate way. But I have to admit that as they went on talking, trying to argue me round, I became convinced that Bella was dead.'

'Why?'

'The dominance, the fearsomeness of the woman, the sullen smouldering of the girl who was supposed to be so penitent. But it was mainly the older one: somehow she had death written in her face. And I wondered whether I could go to the police now, when my stupidity in letting this girl barely into her teens take care of Bella had resulted in her death. And then they started mentioning sums of money. I gulped at first. And then I thought: "If you've killed our Bella, you're going to pay for it!"'

'How much was it eventually?'

'It started at five hundred pounds. Of course I wasn't going to go along with the first offer. Eventually it was a thousand pounds. That was a lot of money in those days.' Something in Matt's expression alerted Woof to the fact that he was making a bad impression, and he added: 'I'm not proud of myself.'

Matt shrugged.

'Who am I to pass judgment?'

'Anyway, the deal was that we'd be out of the house and out of Leeds by nightfall. They handed the money over in cash – would you believe it, they'd been to the bank in Town Street and got it out before coming to talk to me? The exact sum. She was a smart cookie, that woman: she knew how much it might cost, and if I'd tried to go higher she'd have stuck at what she had in cash. I packed up the few things we had in the squat, roused Sandra to some species of awareness, and got her on to a bus going to the station. We went to my parents in Grantham. They were pretty straight-laced, but I reckoned telling my mother of the baby's death would bring her round a bit.'

'And did it?'

'In the short term. In the longer it couldn't work out. Sandra was devastated by the loss of the baby, never really understood it. How could she? I didn't understand it myself. She took off after a few weeks, and the last I heard she was with a new bloke. Hope he was better for her than I was. I wouldn't know now whether she's alive or dead.'

'And you became an accountant?'

'I suppose that's the long and short of it. That was the end of hippidom for me anyway. Within a year I was at college, and working for my certificate. I didn't marry for years – felt I'd done all that. But when I did I got a cracker. Maureen's a wonderful mum to the kids, and she makes sure she has a bit of herself left over for me.'

I bet she does, thought Matt. I bet she has to. He was conceiving a dislike for this man: his complacency, his self-importance, his casualness with other people's fates. He had sold justice for his baby for one thousand

241

pounds, and not because he didn't believe in human justice, but to lay his hands on the loot. Matt was willing to bet that his parents financed his studies, and also that they were never given a hint of the existence of Nesta Farson's blood money.

'Well, that's my sad little story,' said Dougie, wiping Marsala gravy off his chin. 'Tell me about this promotion that's in the offing. Nice little hike in salary you said.'

Matt was already drafting in his mind a letter explaining that his promotion did not after all involve moving away from Leeds, and that he was forced to look for an accountant closer to home – a letter he actually sent three weeks later. For the rest of the meal he talked about the BBC in its regional manifestation, the techniques and dangers of radio phone-ins, and the off-pitch life of a professional footballer. He believed in paying for what he had eaten.

As the summer wore on Aileen went back to work, and the school holidays started. In August Matt's promotion to a linkman's job on *Look North* was confirmed, Aileen discovered she was pregnant again, and the police released the body of the little girl found in Elderholm. Charlie said, apologetically, that there was no one to release it to, and he wondered whether Matt would take responsibility. Matt said he didn't need to be apologetic, and didn't need to ask. That night he talked over with Aileen what to do.

In the end they decided on a simple cremation service conducted by the local Church of England vicar, with prayers and lessons. There was no publicity, nothing on *Look North* or in the *West Yorkshire Chronicle*. It got round among the people in the stone houses in Houghton Avenue, many of whom had secretly enjoyed the publicity surrounding the body. Several of them (but not the Cazalets) said they would come to the funeral service, and Aileen asked them to sandwiches and coffee afterwards. Isabella refused to have anything to do with the catering, being now well into her investigative journalist phase, but all three children went to the funeral, and even brought some of their more ghoulish friends. It was a beautiful day, and in the afternoon neighbours, children and others, including Carl Farson and Charlie, Felicity and Carola were quietly happy inside Elderholm and out in its front garden, now coming out of its wilderness phase.

Almost everyone at one time or another asked Matt what had come out about the dead baby, and Matt found himself saying:

'It turned out to be a tragic accident. The children who lived here at the time unwisely tried to cover it up. The police have now closed the case.'

Charlie, who knew Matt well by then, heard him say this more than once, and observed his face.

'It hurts, doesn't it?' he said to him quietly, the two of them standing away from the throng under the laburnam. 'Rankles.'

'Yes, it does,' said Matt without hesitation. He had been thinking a lot about the death in the days leading up to the funeral. 'The little bones crying out for vengeance, like we once said. The little bones are still crying.'

'It doesn't help that Lily Fitch is a pretty unhappy person?'

'Lots of people are pretty unhappy, through no particular fault of their own. Lily Fitch deserves worse than that in her life.'

'Being a policeman, you give up expecting justice in this world,' said Charlie.

'Maybe . . . Has it ever occurred to you,' asked Matt, looking at Charlie closely, 'that Lily Marsden's nearest and dearest have a habit of vanishing off the face of the earth?'

Charlie frowned.

'No, it hasn't.'

'Her parents die in a car accident.'

'I know.'

'Immediately afterwards she marries, and the bloke is a car mechanic.'

'I don't think you told me that.'

'They have a son. Then first the husband then the son take off out of Lily's life.'

'Perhaps she's the sort no one wants to live with.'

'Maybe. And maybe she's someone who studied in a school for murder at the feet of a passionate and committed teacher with refresher courses thrown in. In fact, there's no maybe about that: we know she did.'

Charlie's eyes glinted for a moment. Then he pondered.

'It's a thought,' he said at last.

'Yes, it's a thought.'

'A pretty thin one, though. Not a scrap of evidence. For a start there're no bodies.'

'You could try the attic.'

Charlie stayed decidedly pensive for the rest of the party.

244